"A thoroughly engag
developing and growin   ı
Hunter's Blood, reachi   x
via drug dealers, doc
crash (really gut-churning) and the antics of the two   e
rogues. A thrilling and engrossing story."

Michael Jecks – *Best-selling author of Templar Series,
Vintener Trilogy, Bloody Mary Series, Scavenger Series*

"Another great addition to the Edinburgh Crime
Mysteries featuring the irrepressible DI Hunter Wilson,
who is faced with some challenging personal issues.
A must-read for crime fans."

Stuart Gibbons – *retired Murder Squad DCI & best-selling
author of The Crimewriters' Casebook and Being a Detective*

"Another gripping novel in the thrilling Edinburgh
Crime series by Val Penny who weaves an exciting
story of power, politics and revenge."

Erin Kelly – *Best-selling author of psychological thrillers
including Broadchurch, The Poison Tree and He Said/She said*

"Hunter is a terrific character, always a pleasure to read
about, and here he leads another fascinating cast of old
friends and new acquaintances in this, his latest adventure.
It's fast paced and intriguing, full of twists and turns, and
leaves you continually wanting to turn the pages to find out
what happens. A great read, thoroughly recommended."

Simon Hall – *Best-selling author of the TV Detective Series
and University of Cambridge lecturer, Cambridge Judge
Business School*

Hunter's Blood

The Edinburgh Crime Mysteries #4

Val Penny

Also available:

Hunter's Chase
Hunter's Revenge
Hunter's Force

www.darkstroke.com

Discover us online:
www.darkstroke.com

Join us on instagram:
www.instagram.com/darkstrokebooks/

Include **#darkstroke** in a photo of yourself
holding his book on Instagram and
something nice will happen.

To my dear friends Lisa and Bill who put up with me and gave me time and space in their lovely home to write this book.

Love you guys so much.

About the Author

Val Penny is an American author living in SW Scotland. She has two adult daughters of whom she is justly proud and lives with her husband and two cats. She has a Law degree from Edinburgh University and an MSc from Napier University. She has had many jobs including hairdresser, waitress, lawyer, banker, azalea farmer and lecturer. However, she has not yet achieved either of her childhood dreams of being a ballerina or owning a candy store. Until those dreams come true, she has turned her hand to writing poetry, short stories and novels. Her crime novels, Hunter's Chase, Hunter's Revenge, Hunter's Force and Hunter's Blood are set in Edinburgh, Scotland. The fifth book in the series, Hunter's Secret, follows shortly.

Acknowledgements

While writing a novel is sometimes a solitary occupation, the completed novel is produced through the combined talents of several people.

My most sincere thanks go to the amazing team at darkstroke. Particularly my editor Laurence Patterson whose courtesy, patience and valuable suggestions improved the rough draft of this book immeasurably. Thanks also go to Steph Patterson and Jo Fenton for their help and encouragement.

Thanks must go to Anna McDonald who inspired me by hurting her cheek at Singing for Fun and to Kate Dapre for her time and suggestions about the early draft. Staff Nurse Michelle Wilson from Crosshouse Hospital, Ayrshire, gave me open handed advice on medical procedures. Any errors are mine. To Liz Hurst, Patricia M Osborne and Allison Symes and all those at Swanwick Writers' Summer School my thanks for their help and support. Of course, Swanwick's own Andy Roberts won a competition to have a character named after him in this book. I hope you are pleased with the results, Andy.

I remain, as always, eternally grateful to Dave, Lizzie, Vicky and Jo for their belief in me and unswerving support.

More than that, I thank each and every one of my readers. Without you, I would not write.

Hunter's Blood

The Edinburgh Crime Mysteries #4

Chapter One

"Fucking shit! Did you see that? How fast was it going? It could have taken my nose off!" DI Hunter Wilson roared as a red van raced past them in the outside lane.

"Your nose isn't *that* big, darling," Meera Sharma smiled.

"Huh, thanks. I think. Where are the traffic cops when you need them? And really, how fast was that van going?"

"Some are in a real hurry to meet their maker."

"I just get so angry. They don't even think about who else they could take with them if they crash and that was a business vehicle. I'll bet the owner wouldn't like their employees to be racing around like that."

"Probably not," Meera sighed.

Hunter was driving back from a leisurely lunch at The Steading at Hillend on the outskirts of Edinburgh, with the petite pathologist, Meera Sharma. He always enjoyed their time together. She was easy company, and they got on very well indeed. The Steading was a good place to eat after they had been for a long walk in The Pentland Hills. Maybe this time he would be lucky in love.

Meera changed the subject. "That was delicious, thank you. We should spend more time like this. There is no better exercise than walking you know."

"Oh, I can think of at least one form of exercise I prefer," Hunter grinned.

She turned and grinned back at him.

"You're very cheeky, you know that, don't you?"

"That's why you love me," he glanced away from the road

to smile at her.

Meera looked into Hunter's intense grey eyes and smiled at his traditional short haircut. He would look even better if his hair were just a *little* longer, but he complained that he looked like the cartoon character 'Oor Wullie' when it grew even just a little. She sighed inwardly. Hunter was one of the good guys. Maybe this time her parents would accept her partner of choice.

"Of course, we should make more time to go walking together," Hunter replied with a sheepish grin. "But you well know how likely that is with *our* schedules, doctor. In fact, I forgot to tell you, I've got to go back to the station this evening. There are a couple of things still I need to finish."

"Of course there are, Detective Inspector. There *always* are. But a girl can dream, can't she?" Meera smiled at him.

Hunter felt warm inside. He might have thought it was the sticky toffee pudding, but Meera's smile always made him feel like this.

***

"For goodness sake, can we just gather ourselves together and get this bloody show on the road? It's like herding cats trying to get you four organised!" Tim Myerscough said. The tall, blond detective constable helped his friend, DC Bear Zewedu, fit the back packs for both his friend and his girlfriend, Mel, into the back of his large BMW.

"Do you both really need all this stuff? We're only going for the weekend," Tim asked.

"Good job you've got a big beast of a car, Timmy boy," Bear smiled.

His dark eyes and short, curly, black hair contrasted strongly with Tim's colouring.

"It's cool this afternoon, isn't it?" Bear said.

"Cool enough for both of us to wear Aran sweaters," Tim smiled. "Great minds think alike."

The men had been close friends since their days at Merchiston Castle School, one of the most prestigious schools in Edinburgh. Tim closed the rear door of the car and drew down his Oakley sunglasses to protect his bright blue eyes from the low autumn sun.

"Really, Tim? Shades?" Bear joked. "That sky looks like a sheet of grey steel to me. Okay, smeared here and there by those few dirty rags of cloud fluttering over the city, but hardly weather for sunglasses. It's November, man!"

"Even on a November day, I take care of my eyes, big man." Tim smiled. He always protected his eyes. "And how much luggage does anybody need for a weekend break? We're only going across to Simon Land's farm in North Lanarkshire."

"You won't need those shades for long, Tim, it gets dark so early now that the clocks have changed," Bear said.

"Never mind about my bloody shades. Get in the car and let's get going," Tim shook his head and grinned at his friend. "You girls okay in the back?"

"We're fine!" Mel said, slamming the door much harder than was necessary and, ignoring Tim's pained expression, began chatting with Ailsa and Gillian.

"Trust you to change the subject," Bear said to Tim as he clambered into the front passenger seat.

"Well, you know, we're only going to be a few miles from home. Even Gillian felt the need to bring the most enormous full suitcase and her guitar with its cover. Why does she need all that stuff? Did she think we were on *Britain's Got Talent*?"

"*She* may have a lot of stuff but she's not deaf, Tim," Gillian said. "Ailsa mentioned that Simon played the fiddle and we might have a sing-a-long – so of course I brought my guitar."

Tim shook his head and looked across at Bear. When had he become so big? He must be lifting weights at the gym again because his shoulders were broader than Tim remembered. Bear didn't used to take up this much space, surely?

"You been eating more cake, big man?" Tim asked.

"That's rich coming from you! Your chest must easily be fifty inches," Bear said.

"Forty-eight," said Gillian from the back seat.

"And with you two still keeping up the rugby training, I think your thighs are almost the size of my waist," Mel laughed from beside Gillian. "How did the two of you ever fold yourselves into Sophie's Fiat 500 to get to rugby practice?"

"Carefully," said Bear.

And that was the nub of the problem – not that Tim would admit it – but the lovely Lady Sophie Dalmore would be at the bonfire party this weekend, too. The lying, cheating, murdering beauty that was Sophie Dalmore. Tim knew his ex would be attending the party with her new boyfriend, Lord Lachlan 'Lucky' Buchanan.

"Good Lord! Did you see that van?" Bear shouted suddenly from the front passenger seat.

"Of course. But not for long. It was going at some bloody lick. When I'm driving it means I'm watching the road, big man," Tim Myerscough, replied sourly.

"No need to be like that."

"What the hell? If it hits anything, it'll take them right out," Mel exclaimed.

"I'd like to drive that car up their bloody backside. So damn dangerous," Gillian said.

"God, look! It's swerved violently. Shit! Oh fuck! It's rolled over and over. There! On the other side of the road. See, Tim?" Bear pointed.

"Thank God it's the other side of the road! They could've wiped us out."

"Stop sniping, you two. I hope everybody in the van was wearing seatbelts," Ailsa, said. "The people inside will be lucky to get out alive. They'll be all cuts and bruises, even if they were. Look what a mess they've made of the bushes and trees too."

"That van was going at a fair lick," Mel commented. "But I don't think the trees are the biggest problem: we'd better phone emergency services."

"Should we stop? After all, we have a doctor on board," Bear smiled back towards Ailsa.

"And cause another crash by making a crazy move or an

6

emergency stop? I don't think so, Bear," Tim said.

"I don't have any equipment. An ambulance will be better able to give any help that's needed," Ailsa said.

"I've got my phone here. I'll call the emergency services. They'll be quick, I'm sure, and, as Ailsa says, better equipped to help than we are," Gillian said.

"Good idea, pet," Tim said. "I think they'll need police as well as an ambulance."

Gillian nodded, taking out her mobile phone.

Tim smiled back at her through the rear-view mirror and watched as she dialed 999.

"And as this is meant to be one of my few weekends off, could you and Bear just stop bickering for a few hours?" Ailsa said, trying to change the subject.

"We're not bickering," Tim grumbled.

"You could have fooled me, bro. I'm really looking forward to Simon's bonfire party weekend. Just don't spoil it, Tim."

"Okay, but I'm sure he only invited us because you're back in town," Tim commented from the driver's seat of his comfortable car. "I always thought he had the hots for you."

"Ha ha, very funny," Ailsa said.

"And I could do without Lady Sophie bloody Dalmore being there," Tim grumbled.

"Oh, *that's* why you're in such a bad mood!" Bear said.

"I am not in a bad mood. I just prefer to avoid that woman."

"Really? You could have fooled me, Timmy boy," Bear grinned. "Don't worry, you have Gillian to protect you from the nasty lady, You will, won't you Gillian?"

Gillian pointed to her phone as she informed the call handler of her details and the place they had seen the van leave the road. When she finished the call, she replied. "Always! I'll take care of you and keep Sophie at bay. You'll be safe with me, Tim," she said.

***

"Wow! Did you see that van roll, Frankie?" Jamie Thomson asked his cousin as he drove them along the Edinburgh ring road.

They were on the way back from a visit to see Jamie's dad, Ian Thomson, who was, not for the first time, living in the big house that was HMP Edinburgh. Jamie's eyes missed nothing and, despite being into his early twenties, he still had a cheeky face that was framed by a mop of light brown hair and the newly grown designer stubble of which he was most proud. Even Frankie's girlfriend, Donna, said it looked good and she hardly ever complimented Jamie.

"Couldn't miss it, could I?" his younger cousin, Frankie said. "That bright red van swerving then hurtling around and around."

Frankie was taller than his cousin, so he sat slightly higher in their car. Although he was less confident than Jamie, Frankie would have been the more handsome of the two of them had it not been for the tell-tale scars from the acne that had marred his school days. Jamie never let that worry him. His positivity guided him easily through life.

"Glad I missed it! It must have been going way over the speed limit," Jamie joked.

"You can talk Jamie. You seem to think the speed limit is a suggestion, not a rule!" Frankie grinned. "Should I call the cops, let them know?"

"Yeh, do that. Get them to send an ambulance too. Whoever is in there will need help. But don't give them your name. You know what the cops are like."

"Should we stop?" Donna, asked. Her worried expression rested on Frankie's little red-haired twin daughters.

"Nah, wha' do we know?" Jamie said. "I don't know first aid."

"Anyway, we need to get home and give the twins their tea," Frankie said.

"True enough," she smiled down at the girls.

"Aye. I'll just call then," Frankie agreed. Then he withheld his number before dialling 999.

Chapter Two

Twenty minutes earlier

I looked at my watch and couldn't believe how late it was. I shouted to Bob, "If you want me to take you to work, we have to leave *right* now. Come on! I *must* get this van back to my boss by six tonight, you know that new owner Mr O'Grady is strict! Get a wiggle on, boy!"

I had hoped to have enough time to share my news with him, but I didn't want to rush it. I was excited but wasn't sure how he'd take it, if I'm honest, so I wanted the timing and time to be right. It would have to wait.

I had been sitting in the van for so long that I had time to touch up my make-up. Eventually I saw Bob coming out of the front door. He was still wrestling with his jacket and won the struggle, then turned around to lock the front door. I couldn't help smiling. He's twelve years older than me, but such a good man. I've always known I was lucky to have him in my life, but I'd noticed he had been a bit forgetful lately. Eventually he opened the car door and stuck his head in.

"Oh blast, Linda, I'm sorry. I've left me piece box on the kitchen table. I'll have to go back for the sandwiches. I can't work a whole nightshift without anything to eat. Hang on a minute, love," he said.

I was getting irritated. "For goodness sake, Bob. Get a move on. Please." I waited impatiently while Bob retrieved his sandwiches, an apple and a knife from the Formica surface of the old kitchen table. He normally had a mind like a razor, but he had been acting a bit strange lately. Maybe it was the long hours. "Come on, hurry up!" I said under my breath.

Bob bounced back into the passenger seat.

"What have you got there?" I asked, looking at the collection of things in his hands as he struggled with the seat belt.

"My box of sandwiches, an apple and a knife. Why?"

"I couldn't see what the knife was. That's my paring knife, isn't it? For goodness' sake, don't lose it. It's my best one. Anyway, put it in your sandwich box, now. You shouldn't have a sharp knife like that on you, you know," I grumbled at him. It was my most useful kitchen knife and I didn't want him leaving it in the staff room at work and losing it.

"Stop fussing, woman. I need it to cut the apple – these ones you got are very hard," he complained.

"They're apples, not plums, of course they're hard. Now fasten your seat belt properly and let's get a move on!" I frowned at him, but it was impossible to stay cross with Bob for long.

Bob pulled on the seat belt with an exaggerated motion and pulled a face at me. I couldn't help smiling. Even when I was cross with him, he made me laugh, and that was very irritating.

"What's that in the back?" he asked.

"I couldn't deliver one of my parcels. Mr O'Grady will be furious. It was a last-minute addition to my route, and he said it was most important, but there was nobody in. What could I do?"

"You'll just have to tell him, love." Bob said. "Are all the vans this bright red colour now?"

"Yes, they've changed the company colours since Mr O'Grady took us over."

"I liked the black better, it was smarter. But I don't suppose they'll lose them being this bright."

"I liked the black better too, but nobody asked me. The manager says red is the new black. The new owner, Mr O'Grady, wanted the vans to stand out. Can you believe it? Sometimes the vans go missing. Where they go, is a mystery to me, but Mr O'Grady is offering a bonus to anybody who finds one of his missing vans. Now, enough of all this nonsense, do you want a lift or not? I'll have to hurry."

"Of course I do, darlin'. But what the manager says is

nonsense. Only black is black, not this intense red colour. Anyway, let's go, love!"

I moved the van slowly out of our driveway. I wasn't really meant to bring the van home and I certainly wasn't meant to give anybody a ride, but it was the end of my day. The last delivery I'd had to make had been in our street and this way I knew it would save Bob getting two buses to start his night shift at the Western General Hospital. And nobody would ever know, would they? What was the harm?

I planned to drive round the ring road, stop at the hospital, let Bob out and go back to the depot at DayGo Deliveries and drop off the van. The night staff at my work would fill up the van, ready for tomorrow morning's delivery run. Neat.

I drove to the end of our road and looked right and left, before easing onto the main street. I found the darkness at this time of year difficult to drive in. The clocks had turned back for winter and, all of a sudden, the streets were dark an hour earlier than I was used to. I was careful as I slipped the van into the flow of traffic and drove on towards the ring road.

The trees were losing their leaves quickly. I quite like the changing colours of autumn, but most of the leaves were gone now. Before too long, this year's Christmas celebrations would be upon us. There were a few decorated Christmas trees up in windows already and the ones in the shops had been up for weeks. Bob and I had decided to go to my Mum for Christmas Day and to his sister for the big Boxing Day Party that was so important to Bob's family.

My offer to make the Christmas pudding for my Mum had been snapped up, but Bob's sister had only asked us to bring biscuits and cheese. I wasn't sure she trusted me and Bob to bring anything more difficult to make. I always felt that I was seen as a wee lassie, not an adult to be trusted or taken seriously. Bob's sister was that bit older even than him. I had never been sure his family approved of me or really viewed me as a proper grown-up at all. I suppose I'm not that much older than his daughter, though, but it was exasperating. They would have to accept me as an adult when they learned my news, wouldn't they?

I had spoken to Bob about going up to the little cheesemonger's on Morningside Road, to choose a fancy selection for the party. Bob didn't seem to care, he only ate cheddar, but I wanted to show that I had put a bit of thought into our contribution, even if it was a simple one.

I'd been thinking about types of cheese we could get. I like brie. We could choose things to go with it too.I asked Bob, "Should we get some grapes and pickles to put with the cheese?"

"What? What cheese? I've got ham in me sandwiches tonight," Bob scowled.

"No, you numpty! At Christmas, going to your sister?"

"Linda, that's weeks away!" He replied. "I don't plan to worry about it until we do our big, holiday shop next month. And that'll be *after* we've been paid!"

I looked at him and nodded. Then I noticed he still had my knife in his hand. "Will you please put that away, Bob?" I asked. "You really are being very irritating. Even more than usual tonight."

"Thanks, and I don't think so," he said. "I will when I get out, but I can't see what I'm doing in here. It's too dark," he complained. "Anyway, I'm not sure it's me that's the problem, you've been tetchy for days. Is there something I should know? Have I done something really wrong?"

I felt like telling him, and that would shut him up! I wanted to shout that he was a right pain, and that this was the last time I would offer him a lift to work. All this bickering was too stressful. But I didn't, because I knew it wouldn't be the last time; I liked helping him when I could. I paused at the roundabout that took us onto the ring road. It was dark enough for each vehicle to need its lights. The big truck to the right of me had very bright lights and they completely dazzled me. I sat in the car until the truck moved and my vision returned to normal. I ignored the blare of the horn from the car behind.

"What's he tooting at? Daft bastard!" Bob shouted. "I'll show him what for if he does that to you again," Bob always came to my defense quickly. Even if it wasn't needed.

"Thanks, Bob," I said. I was grateful for his support but

didn't like it when he shouted.

"No problem, lass. I look out for you: it's what I do."

"Goodness look at the time! I better get a move on," I said. I revved the engine and turned up the pace. I like driving: especially driving fast.

"Watch it, lass," Bob said. "Don't go any faster than is safe, please."

"It's fine. Relax," I replied. "Who are you on with tonight?"

"I don't know, love. This is an overtime shift. I don't know who I'm on with. Still all the other porters are good lads, we get on well, have a laugh and get the job done."

"It's good you all get on, isn't it?"

"Aye and you'd be amazed at what we get up to! There's a new guy, Andy Roberts, did I tell you? Would you believe it, his gran's in Ward 52!? He's always skiving off to see her. But he's a nice lad. He even pops into see the old girl on his days off."

"Gosh, that must be really nice for the old lady, and it must make a big difference to all the patients if you porters can make them laugh. Especially if they are frightened or in pain," I said, more as a thought to myself than to him but I said it out loud.

"I never really thought about it, but I suppose it does. Of course, we try to stop or at least manage the patients' pain at the hospital," Bob said, smiling at me. "There's just one of the nurses that's a bit of an arse," he said. "Still, there's always one. You just going to get the bus home, or will your boss give you a lift?"

"Not sure. Either way, I'll manage."

"Fair enough."

"You know I always get home fine, some evenings it just takes longer than others."

"Aye, true," Bob said.

I glanced at the clock on the dashboard.

"Oh, bloody hell, look at the time! I hadn't realised we were *this* late," I said.

I sped up again. I was well over the speed limit now, but there were no police or cameras on this part of the road. I would need to go a lot faster in the old van if I was to have time to drop Bob off at the hospital and get back to the DayGo depot before it closed. I felt the van judder as its speed increased. The company should really have invested in some modern vans rather than just repainting the old ones, I thought, as I increased her speed further on the wide ring road around the City of Edinburgh.

"Oh Shit! what's that?" Bob shouted and pulled the steering wheel from my hands. The van jerked sharply to the left.

"Stop it Bob," I shouted angrily. "What the hell are you doing? Leave the bloody steering wheel alone!"

"A rabbit!" he screamed.

"Let go the bloody wheel, you fool!"

I jerked the steering wheel out of his hand but overcompensated sharply to the right. The car behind blared its horn. I wasn't surprised. I would have, too, if the idiot in front of me drove like that. I tried to look round, but didn't realise that there was no hard shoulder, the van veered out of control and off the road. It rolled over and over before landing upright amongst the trees.

My seatbelt pulled my shoulder. Both airbags went off at the same time with a bang. The sound pressure felt like it was bursting my eardrums. The silence after that was scary. I didn't know that, when airbags go off in your vehicle after a crash, the first thing they do is deflate, but they do. I suppose it makes sense, otherwise the airbags or passengers might become stuck in the van. What a lot of dust came out with the airbags, and it smelt funny and made me cough.

I turned off the engine. I suppose I must have been on automatic pilot because we were not going anywhere. Then I noticed the doors of the van had unlocked and I could tell the hazard lights were flashing into the dark autumn evening. Good. Someone would find us soon.

I thought about the crash and remembered that I saw the sharp paring knife fly in exaggerated slow motion. Random, rapid, horrifying movement. Past my feet as I was right side up. Then the car rolled, and I was hanging upside down, the knife sliced the bottom of my left ear. That stung! Right side up, the sharp little knife cut the material at the knee of my new jeans. Upside down, I saw Bob try to reach out with his hand and catch it. Right side up, he missed, and it flew past my head and sliced into the wrapping of the undelivered parcel. Lots of dust came out. It covered us. I licked it off my lips and it made my tongue feel funny. I knew immediately that it was cocaine because I tried it once when I was at college. I'd never do that again because I don't like being out of control.

The knife flew again to the front of the car and lodged firmly into the side of Bob's neck. His blood sprayed all over the inside of the van and splashed my face, covering the windscreen as if it was trying to make the inside as red as the outside. Too bright. I saw him clasp his wound. I tasted his blood. Warm. Metallic. Salty. His blood kept coming out on heavy, rhythmic spurts. An artery. The van rolled again.

"What the hell?!" I screamed. My head broke the door window and it showered me with glass. Shards cut my skin. Branches of a bush slapped me back into my seat and held me there tightly.

"Bob! Bob help me, I can't move! I'm stuck," I called. Bob looked at me but didn't say a word, just stared. His expression seemed to be one of surprise, then there was no expression at all.

I thought I heard his phone ring.

"Red is the new black," I muttered.

Everything went dark.

Chapter Three

"You will never believe it," the desk sergeant, shouted across the station reception.

"Probably not, but try me," Hunter said, walking across the room slowly. He had just finished donating blood at the NHS van that was parked in the station car park and, as Charlie Middleton was as well known for his practical jokes as for his cheeky wit, Hunter was not sure he wanted to cope with either. He was certainly as cautious as he was reluctant to be the butt of Charlie's humour.

"You know that central call handling system some genius put in place when we all became the one big happy family that is Police Scotland?"

"Yes Charlie," Hunter said in a weary voice.

"Well my boys were sent out to George Square, you know, University of Edinburgh territory, isn't it?"

"It is."

"Well, they get told there's some numpty flashing his dick at young women."

"Clever," Hunter said sarcastically.

"They get there and the only thing that greets them is Irish Mick, fresh out of HMP Edinburgh sitting on a bench singing Danny Boy. They know he's too drunk to stand never mind show off his wares and there's not a young woman in sight."

"What happened? Apart from Irish Mick ending up back in the slammer, I mean," Hunter asked.

"They contacted call handling, it was all kicking off in George Square, Glasgow – not here at all. The prick on the end of the phone forgot to get a postcode, so they just assumed it was here. I bloody ask you; the service is all going to hell in a hand cart. Good job it's not long till I retire."

"Well, that's two things we agree on, Charlie," Hunter

smiled.

"Piss off," Charlie grinned. "You'll miss me when I'm gone."

"Like toothache," Hunter quipped. "If you see DC Anderson, tell her I'm looking for her, will you?"

"No problem," Charlie smiled and got back to the paperwork on his desk.

Charlie was checking the form of the horses for tomorrow's racing. He hoped to get his choices made before the Friday evening influx of the feral and feeble-minded that experience told him would inhabit his cells before the night was out. Charlie took the view that almost half of those collared would be there to avoid a chilly night on the streets, and a similar number would be there because of the demon drink.

"Only three or four of those who darken our doors are truly criminal material, you know, Neil. The rest of them are just in out of the rain," Charlie said.

"What's that, Sarge?" PC Neil Larkin asked.

"I said, I could do with a cuppa," Charlie said.

"I'll make the tea," Neil sighed.

The door swung shut behind Neil. Then the phone rang and a bare-footed, elegant woman dressed in silk pyjamas entered the reception area. Not for the first time, Charlie wished he had turned his back on rank, and that he had made the drinks instead of getting Neil to do it.

"Police Scotland, how can I help?" Charlie said into the phone, determined to ignore the woman.

"Well, I seem to have left my slippers upstairs. Could you fetch them for me, there's a dear?" The woman smiled.

"Dear God," Charlie muttered. "No, not you, sir. What can I do for you?" He listened to the educated voice on the other end of the line. "You've lost what?" he asked gruffly.

"Nothing, Sarge, I brought you a biscuit," Neil replied opening the reception door with his rear.

"Just put it there," he said to Neil as he stood with the mugs of hot tea. "No, sir not you, yes of course I'm listening."

"Sorry, Sarge, I thought you were talking to me," Neil muttered.

"Just shut up, will you?" Charlie glared at Neil.

"No, not you, sir. Now what did you say has gone missing? An ostrich egg? Really, sir? Of course, part of a valuable collection, I'm sure," Charlie turned to Neil, covered the mouthpiece of the phone and said, "It is far too early for all this fucking nonsense. Posh bastards start drinking earlier and earlier and we get the thin end of their nonsense. Phone the police – my ostrich egg is missing – I bloody ask you." He took his hand away from the phone and said, "Yes, sir. I'm listening."

"Tea! Delicious. What a good idea," the elegant woman reached forward and helped herself to Charlie's drink. She took a sip and screwed up her face. "Oh, for goodness sake, you've put sugar in it, you know I haven't taken sugar for twenty years! And where are my slippers? Is this biscuit for me? Delicious."

Hunter walked back into reception.

"Sandra?"

Chapter Four

Charlie put down the phone with a sigh. "You know this crackpot? So far, she has asked me to bring her slippers down from upstairs and complained my tea is not to her taste. I'm not sure we're all here, if you know what I mean."

"Sandra, what are you doing walking around in bare feet at this time of year?" Hunter asked. "You must be freezing. Here, take this." He took off his jacket and placed it gently around the woman's skinny shoulders.

"Well, if I can't wander about in my own house as I wish, where can I, dear one?"

"Come through here and sit with me. How did you get here?"

"I came by taxi. Maybe you could go and pay him, Andrew. I seem to have forgotten my purse."

The woman felt the trousers of her pyjamas for pockets but found there were none. She glanced at Hunter in dismay.

"Of course, Auntie Sandra. You come and sit in this room here and we'll have a chat. I'll just go and pay your driver," Hunter said. He knew he looked a lot like his father, the reverend Andrew Wilson, retired, but Hunter was thirty years his junior. Sandra's confusion was doing nothing for his ego.

"Neil, could you get my aunt a cup of tea, milk no sugar, and perhaps a sandwich out of the machine? She seems hungry, judging by the way she devoured that biscuit." Hunter handed Neil a few coins to pay for the sandwich.

"Yes, sir," Neil said.

"Aye, and we already know how *Auntie Sandra* takes her tea, DI Wilson," Charlie growled.

"Good, then it'll be right for her," Hunter glared at Charlie before he headed out to pay the taxi driver.

"And who the hell is Andrew?" Charlie called after him.

***

"Kylie-Ann and Dannii-Ann are such lovely little girls, Frankie. I can't help loving your twins," Donna said. "And they are not fussy eaters at all."

"They wouldn't need to be, living in this house." Frankie smiled.

"That's true enough. Frankie is a rubbish cook," Jamie laughed. "It's just that I'm worse! It was good to see my pop today, wasn't it?" He went on. "He seems to have got back into the way of looking out for that copper's pop, Sir Peter Myerscough. I thought they'd have taken his 'Sir' off him by now, but nought seems to have come of that."

"Aye, yer pop was on good form. I just hope Uncle Ian doesn't get grief for minding the old buffoon. And did you hear that guy visiting Arjun Mansoor? Right strong Irish accent he had. I've never seen him before."

"I doubt Pop'll have too much of a problem, he's able to take care of himself… anyways, as long as the screws keep him and Arjun away from each other, he'll be okay. Last time they got together, Arjun looked like meat pulp, and Pop landed several broken ribs," Jamie said.

"All right for that old toff, isn't it? He gets sent to jail but folk still think he's better than me, being a 'Sir somebody'. And I still haven't been able to get hold of my dad," Donna sighed.

"I'm sorry, Donna. Maybe he's just busy," Frankie said

"Maybe. Shall I just make some scrambled eggs for the girls, Frankie?"

"Aye, love. That'd be good, wouldn't it, girls? You like a scrambled egg."

"I didn't like Pop's muttering about giving up the showroom. He says with my mam away there's no point in him keeping it."

"That's no fair," Frankie said. "You and me and Donna all work there, and it runs pretty well. We even made a profit last month."

"Well, that's what I said to him. Don't worry. It won't

happen. He's just down in the dumps about me mam taking off to Spain again. We'll talk him round. He's pissed off about being back inside too, and I don't blame him for that."

"He's lucky it's no for longer," Frankie said.

"I didnae think it would help to say that," Jamie said. He stood and stared at his cousin glumly. His father wasn't really given to rash threats and both boys knew that.

"Here we are, girls, let's get you sat down ready for scrambled egg and a wee drink of apple juice," Donna said. "Will you help Kylie-Ann if I help Dannii-Ann, Frankie?"

"Of course. Come on, wee one." Frankie smiled. "Is that you getting a text, Donna?" he asked.

Donna checked her phone. "That's odd, it's Dad's work saying he hasn't shown up tonight. It's really not fair, this is his fifth nightshift in a row, but he's solid my Dad. He'd never just not show up. There's lots of them at his work that play up with stress and that, but not him. I wonder what's wrong. I better give him a buzz and check he's okay."

Frankie watched Donna dial her dad's number.

She frowned as the phone rang out. "There's still no reply. I'll call again in a few minutes. He never doesn't answer when it's me. I think he still thinks I'm twelve and he has to look out for me! I was never so glad as when he got together with Linda and we could share the care he has to give." She smiled at Frankie as she redialled and absent-mindedly gave Dannii-Ann the rest of her apple juice.

"Any joy?" Frankie asked.

"No. It's really odd. It's just going to voicemail again. This has never happened before, but he has been acting a bit strange lately, quite forgetful. I think he's been working too many hours, the hospital is so short staffed sometimes."

"No wonder the staff are stressed. Maybe he is too if he's working that much. Leave him a message. He's probably just running late," Jamie said.

"Yeh. Suppose. So unlike my dad though."

Chapter Five

Simon was standing on the doorstep of the farmhouse watching as Tim's car drew up. The man looked every inch the rugby player and farmer as he stood an easy six feet tall with feet apart and hands firmly on his hips. Simon could not remember the last time Tim and Bear had been to the farm, but he knew that it was after Tim's mother died and before his father's disgrace. He thought about all that Tim had been through and about the unswerving support the man got from Bear. Simon's brother, Robin, had suffered so much more than Tim and he hoped Robin knew that he had his support.

Simon watched Tim and Bear jump out of the car. He saw they were still built like rugby players too and, at six feet four inches and six feet two inches tall respectively, they had always made better friends than enemies. He smiled at them as he considered the main difference between them: their colouring. Tim's blonde hair, sky blue eyes and pale skin contrasted starkly with his friend's dark skin, brown eyes and short, cropped, curly, black hair. All three men had been friendly since school days at Merchiston Castle and Simon knew these men were fiercely loyal to each other and their friends. Anybody they saw that needed help within their group had strong support from the big men, if they were willing to accept it. Robin had never been willing to accept help, until Derek and Lucky came on the scene.

Simon saw Tim look over at Lord Lucky Buchanan's Range Rover on the forecourt. "Lucky and Sophie are already here. I hope that she won't be a problem?"

"I won't make her one, Simon."

"Thank you, Tim." Simon nodded. "I saw your car coming up the driveway, so I thought I'd come out to greet you. Nice motor by the way. I take it your Mum's trust fund has come through." Simon grinned.

"Yes. A year or so ago."

"For him, but not yet for me." Ailsa smiled at Simon.

"Good to see you, Ailsa," Simon said. "I don't think I've seen you since you went down south to university."

"I've got a job back up in Edinburgh. It's good to be home."

"You didn't think to throw in the towel at the police, Tim?" Simon asked.

"He'll never do that! Tim works to make the world a better place. You and I work to pay the bills, Simon," Bear said.

"Said the former Ambassador's son," laughed Simon. "Well, all I can tell you is don't go into farming right now if you want to pay your bills."

"Really? Are things that bad?" Tim asked.

"Oh, it just helps to have a benefactor with other irons in the fire, you know? Now, come on in. It's good to see you all. But I don't think I know you," he said to Gillian.

"My girlfriend, Gillian Pearson," Tim said.

"You're punching above your weight, Timmy boy. Pleased to meet you, Gillian. Interesting hair," Simon smiled at the green flash in Gillian's fringe. "I see you've brought a guitar. Good thinking. We can get a sing-song going later. Let me show you all to your rooms and you can get settled in, then come down to the kitchen for coffee and cake."

"Has your Mum been baking?" Ailsa asked.

"A bit. Mum doesn't do as much baking now. Robin does a lot of the cooking."

"Your brother makes cakes? I'm in love!" Bear joked.

"Hey! I can bake cakes, big man," Mel laughed.

"You can, but you don't – you complain that I just eat them!"

"How is Robin, now?" Tim asked quietly.

Simon shrugged. "You never know with Robin. He brightened up a bit when Lucky arrived. Lucky has been a great help since my father died. But he makes me uneasy sometimes. You know he always seems to have his own interests behind anything he does."

***

The group put their bags in their rooms and came downstairs. Tim frowned slightly when he saw Lucky at the foot of the stairs.

"I thought I heard voices. How are you, Tim?" Lucky Buchanan shook Tim's hand. "Winston," he said to Bear, greeting the man by his given name. "Ah, Doctor Pearson, good to see you again." He smiled at Gillian and shook her hand.

"My goodness, so we have two doctors in the house. And my brother Robin's partner is a nurse. If we're going to have an accident, this is the time to do it!" Simon joked.

"I'm not that kind of doctor," Gillian blushed.

Simon smiled. "Lucky I took you at your word and put your driver in the room above the kitchen. It's nice and warm from the Aga in here this time of year. There is a shower room up there too, so your man has that part of the house to himself."

"You brought your driver, Cameron Wilson? You are a lazy sod, Lucky," Tim laughed.

"Thanks, Simon. I appreciate your hospitality," Lucky said, ignoring Tim.

"Least I can do after all you've done for us since Dad died," Simon said.

"No trouble. Always looking for new investments, and this one is very useful."

That comment brought a slight tension into the room. Simon did not know how to respond to Lucky's rather tactless comment. He was grateful when Bear broke the silence.

"I heard someone mention cake but I don't see any," Bear joked.

"Trust you to be thinking of your belly," Mel smiled and patted his tummy affectionately.

"Tell me, who's for tea and who's for coffee? And then I'll go and see where Robin has put his creations," Simon smiled.

"No need to come and find me, brother, here I am. And Mum has made some scones," Robin said. "There's tea and coffee already in the pots on the table. Grab a mug and help yourselves."

Robin came into the large farm kitchen from the scullery entrance carrying an enormous chocolate gateau in one hand and balancing a large plate of fruit cake slices on his lap as he wheeled himself into the room. His mother followed him rather diffidently. She carefully carried a large bowl of fruit scones in two hands. Simon smiled and nodded at her.

"Come along now, Mother, put the scones on the table," Robin said a little sharply. "That's why we made them."

"Such a lot of people," she said, looking around the room nervously.

Robin asked Simon to take the bowl from her and looked heavenward.

"Mrs Land, how lovely to see you again," Tim said. "It's very kind of you to agree to host us all for a party weekend and I am looking forward to these delicious scones. I remember them so well from when I was a kid."

"Yes, dear. You've grown," Mrs Land said as she looked up at the tall, handsome, man standing in front of her. "But you've broken your nose," she said.

"Your elder son did that trying to tackle me on the rugby field. He seemed to have forgotten that we were on the same side." Tim laughed.

"Oh dear, that must have hurt. You should take more care, Simon. You don't want to hurt your friends," she said softly.

"Sorry, Mum," Simon replied gently

"I got a lot more hurt than that. Don't I get any sympathy, Mother?" Robin asked sharply.

Tim blushed.

"Of course, dear. Sit down and rest," Mrs Land said.

"Like I have a choice!" Robin growled.

"Would you be kind enough to get the butter and jam for the scones out of the refrigerator, Mum?" Simon asked.

"Of course, dear. And then I think I'll take a little lie down. I'm quite tired."

"But you'll join us for dinner?" Tim asked

"Oh, are you staying? I haven't made anything."

"Yes, Mum, you have. Remember you made that big pot of

leek and potato soup while I made the cottage pie and the vegetable lasagne?" Robin sighed. He grinned a little too widely at his mother. Then, as if to help her remember, he nodded expectantly at her.

"My goodness, yes, everybody likes a cottage pie." Mrs Land smiled faintly and headed towards the stairs. "And will Derek be here for dinner?"

"Yes, Mum, he's on day shift, remember? Nurses work hard for their keep," Robin smiled.

"As if farmers don't!" Simon laughed.

Robin nodded at his brother. "You don't need to worry, Mum. Simon and I are here to look after everything just now," he said.

"We really need to find some nice young ladies for you two boys. It's all very well Derek taking care of me for now, and I know he's a good friend, but he can't stay forever, you know, boys?" Mrs Land said affectionately to her sons. "I like a nice wedding."

"I do too, but just now, I think I'll go and freshen up. May I come with you, Mrs Land?" Ailsa asked. Simon smiled at her warmly, grateful that his mother wouldn't be going upstairs alone. He always worried she might fall, but he didn't like to embarrass her by making a fuss. He nodded at Ailsa as she caught his eye.

"Of course, dear. And you are?"

"Ailsa Myerscough."

"Yes, your brother is so tall now but a very handsome fellow and such a polite boy."

"He can be, but sometimes he is quite cheeky," Ailsa winked at Tim.

"Don't mind that, dear. All boys are cheeky sometimes," Mrs Land said gently, patting Ailsa on the hand.

"They are indeed," Ailsa said with a smile. "Let me take your arm on the stairs, Mrs Land."

Chapter Six

I woke up with a start. My hair was matted with blood and it was hanging over the front of my eyes. I couldn't see because my hair formed a thick curtain over my face. It was so scary that I panicked. It was dark and I didn't know if this was because of my hair in front of my face or because it was still night-time, but I knew I was frightened. I was more frightened than I had ever been before and the thing I feared most in all the world was losing my sight. Now, had it happened? I remembered the crash - that fucking rabbit. Would it have been so terrible to run over it? I mean, I like rabbits but was it worth all this?

"Bob! Bob?" I shouted frantically. "Bob, I can't see!" I called out to him but there was no sound. The silence in the car was scary. I could hear traffic, but it was in the distance.

"Help!" I shouted.

Bob didn't stir.

"Oh God! I ache all over," I said. "Are you all right, Bob?" I was confused. Why wouldn't he answer me? He must still be unconscious.

I moved my left arm to wipe the hair out of my face. It felt horrible. Thick, sticky, knotted. My arm felt heavy because my muscles were so tense. My right arm was pinned to the side of my body by the broken steering wheel. It was sore. My leg was sore and my head hurt. Pain ran up my arm and into my neck; it wracked my body. Why wouldn't Bob speak to me? Was he sulking?

Why hadn't he just let me run over the bloody rabbit?

"Bob, are you in a huff? It was you that made me lose control, you know. Whatever possessed you to grab the steering wheel? It was only a rabbit. And now you know I'll be late getting the van back, and I bet you're already late for your shift. I hope the van isn't too badly damaged. I might get the sack. This new company owner has a thing about vans that go missing. I hope somebody comes to help us soon because I can't move. Can you?"

"Bob? Will you just speak to me! Bob?"

Then I remembered, Bob was dead and I screamed.

Chapter Seven

Hunter re-entered the station reception and saw Rachael walking towards him.

"Charlie says you were looking for me, boss," she said, flicking her hair behind her shoulder. Hunter couldn't help noticing that she dressed much more discreetly than she used to. He thought life with her partner, DS Jane Renwick, suited Rachael.

"Yes, but that's not important now. Something else has come up, so I'll catch you later."

"Anything I can help with?"

"Actually, maybe you can. My aunt is in the interview room. Will you come and speak to her with me?"

"Of course, but what on earth is she doing in our miserable, stuffy, interview room, boss? Has she been attacked?"

"I'll explain as we go. She's not herself at all. She escaped from hospital," Hunter muttered to Rachael as she followed him into the stuffy little room.

"Escaped, boss?"

"Aunt Sandra, may I introduce my colleague, Rachael Anderson? Rachael, this is my aunt, Sandra Button."

"Yes, dear, very nice. This sandwich could do with a little more salt. Oh goodness, you're pretty."

"I'm spoken for," Rachael smiled.

"So was my husband, it didn't make any difference, did it, Andrew?"

"That was a long time ago, Aunt Sandra. And I'm Hunter, Andrew's older son."

"Really? You look just like him. My feet are cold," she drew his jacket closer around herself.

Rachael noticed the woman's bare feet and wasn't at all surprised she was cold. Winter might not be here yet, but it wasn't too far away.

"Rachael, I have spare clothes in the bottom left-hand drawer of my desk. Could you get a pair of my socks and bring them down for Sandra?" Hunter said. He couldn't help feeling desperately sad as he gazed on his aunt; so vulnerable, so frail.

"Of course, boss," Rachael smiled. "I'll be right back, Mrs Button."

"Why did you bring me here, Hunter?" Sandra looked lost and confused.

"You came in a taxi, remember?"

"No. Have I paid the driver?"

"I paid him. What made you come here? Dad told me you were in hospital. Rachael's sister, Sarah, is a nurse at that hospital,"

"Oh, no, maybe she is one of my captors. You have no idea, Hunter, they were awful to me. Wicked. They beat me and tied me to the bed, they didn't feed me even though I shouted for help. I was left alone to die."

"At the Western General? I doubt that very much. It is one of the best teaching hospitals in the country."

"Have I ever lied to you?" She asked sternly.

"Not on purpose," Hunter smiled.

"I was one of the lucky ones. I got away and came here to the police and God sent me to you. You will save me, won't you? You will put them all in jail? That's what they deserve. Protect me from their wickedness!" She grabbed his hand and lowered her voice, glancing over her right shoulder before she spoke again. "You are my strong protector. You won't let them hurt me anymore, will you, Andrew? Save me!"

"Hunter," Hunter said absentmindedly. "Which ward were you in, Sandra?"

"The morgue. I'm sure they took me straight towards the morgue. I told them I wasn't dead, but they took me into a lift and to a room where they left me alone with only old, wrinkled half-ghosts for company. I saw the morgue with all the bodies. Cold, stiff, frozen bodies. Strangers. I was so afraid. Andy the porter came to get me. He's nice. Derek is nice, but some of them are horrible. Even the ice cream tasted horrible. Could I have a champagne sorbet to cleanse my pallet before dessert?" she asked, looking at the packaging that had contained her sandwich.

"Boss, here are the woollen socks from your drawer. I thought they would be warmer than your sports socks, I also found a wee pair of overshoes behind Charlie's desk to keep Sandra's feet off the floor. The floors in here are very cold."

"Thank you, Rachael."

"Let me help you get these on to keep your feet warmer, Aunt Sandra," Hunter said. Sandra didn't move, so he knelt down in front of his aunt and pulled the socks and overshoes into place. "Your feet are freezing." He touched her hand. "God! So are your hands."

"I do feel cold. Did I lose my slippers, dear?"

"I think you left them in the hospital."

"It's not a hospital, it's a hell-hole. Tortured me they did. Some of those nurses are wickedly cruel. You need to make them suffer for that. Arrest them! Lock them up! I think it much more likely that those beasts stole my slippers. They're very fancy ones, you know. Marks & Spencer's. Very nice."

"I think we'll get them back, honestly, without the need for torture or arrest. And personally, I think doctors and nurses are wonderful – I couldn't do their job."

"You might, get them back after all, you're a detective. You could find out what's wrong. Very highly trained and most observant, aren't you, dear?" his aunt smiled and patted him on the head.

Hunter stood up. "Rachael, before you leave could you phone the Western General Hospital and ask them which ward Mrs Sandra Button is in? And maybe you could get us another cup of tea and a biscuit or a piece of cake. Then I'll take Sandra back to the hospital."

"Don't worry, boss. I phoned Jane and told her I'd be late. We had nothing particular planned for tonight anyway."

"Yes, you did! You've been going on all week about your

meal at that new Thai restaurant. I'm so sorry Rachael."

"I've already phoned from upstairs and asked Janey to push back our reservation by an hour, just in case you needed me. It's just us. Not a big deal."

"Hunter, dear, I must find the lavatory. Do you know where it is in this establishment?"

"See?" Rachael smiled at Hunter. "Come with me, Mrs Button. I'll show you the way to the ladies' room, then perhaps I can get you a slice of cake or a biscuit from the machine to pass for a pudding."

"I'll make that call to the hospital. And thank you, Rachael. This is above and beyond," Hunter said.

"This way, Mrs Button," Rachael led Sandra, holding her elbow to steady her as they walked along.

Hunter was on his mobile to the hospital when Charlie came through from reception. He waited impatiently in the doorway of the interview room watching Hunter. Hunter was not saying much, just waiting for the phone to be answered. He waved Charlie out of the room.

"This is private, Charlie. Give me a minute," Hunter said.

"You're going to want to hear this," Charlie said, staring at Hunter and waiting impatiently. "You really need to know about this,"

"In a minute, Charlie. Bugger off!"

Hunter began speaking to the hospital about his aunt and watched Charlie's face go red. Hunter sometimes wondered about the man's blood pressure.

"Suit yourself. I'll leave you to come to me when you're ready." Charlie stormed off. "You'll be sorry," he muttered. He almost bumped into Rachael, who was walking very slowly with Hunter's aunt, as he marched back to behind the reception desk.

"Bloody Hunter Wilson," Charlie muttered.

On the way back to the interview room, Rachael stopped at the machine to get a tea and, after a brief discussion about what she would have, a piece of cake for Sandra.

"What's wrong with Charlie?" she asked Hunter.

"He's Charlie," Hunter said sourly.

Rachael nodded and put the plastic cup of tea and the soggy slice of fruit cake in its plastic wrapping on the table. "Have a seat, Mrs Button," she said. "The machine was fresh out of gin and tonic drizzle cake, so your aunt chose a slice of fruit cake," she smiled at Hunter.

"Wise choice, Auntie Sandra," Hunter said. "Thanks Rachael, you get away. I'll take Sandra back to her ward at the hospital when she's finished her tea and cake."

"If you're sure, boss? Which ward is it?"

"Fifty-two."

"That's my sister Sarah's ward. Do you want me to call her? Or even come with you? I know the way to the ward blindfolded."

"Don't bother, you have been such a great help, honestly. Off you go. But I really appreciate all you've done."

"If you're sure, boss. Goodbye, Mrs Button. It was really nice to meet you."

"Yes dear, and you. I'll see you tomorrow," Sandra said. Then suddenly Sandra gripped Rachael's arm. "And did they tie you up as well, dear? I heard you say that you were blindfolded. Stick with Andrew, he will keep you safe. He has a hot line to the Almighty, you know."

Hunter caught Rachael's eye and signalled for her to leave them.

Chapter Eight

"Come on then you city slickers! When you've quite finished the cake and scones, let's go and gather the wood for the biggest bonfire in the world!" Simon shouted.

He smiled as, with a whoop, the guests followed him out into the fields. They were bundled up in woollen hats, warm jackets, gloves and scarves, and well-kitted against the cold. Simon handed torches to Lucky, Ailsa, and Tim. He saw that Tim looked puzzled. "It may not be completely dark here, yet, but it will be amongst the trees."

"Of course, good thinking." Tim grinned and walked over to Gillian.

Simon watched as Tim breathed out hard and a breath ring left his mouth, floating for a moment before disappearing into the air. He heard Gillian laugh and saw her grab Tim's arm. Simon blushed as Tim held her close and kissed the green flash in her fringe. Then he watched them gaze into each other's eyes for a little longer than he thought they would. Tim always did wear his heart on his sleeve, Simon thought.

"Put her down and get a move on, Myerscough, you bloody slacker!" Simon shouted with a laugh.

"You'll be lucky!" Bear joked.

"Simon's calling us, pet. We better catch up," Tim said. Simon caught Tim's eye as he looked towards him, over Gillian's shoulder. Simon was striding out across the fields now arm in arm with Ailsa. He nodded at Tim and continued chatting animatedly with her.

Tim grinned and said, "I told you so. We've got Ailsa to thank for this weekend."

"I think it's going to be fun. Thank you, Ailsa," Gillian said and grabbed Tim's hand. "I think it would be good for Ailsa to have some romance in her life. Come on, I'll race you to her."

"Too easy," Tim laughed. He picked her up and held her over his shoulder and then ran to catch up with his sister.

Gillian squealed with laughter all the way across the field. "Put me down! Put me down you big oaf!"

Simon noticed that her tone of voice belied her words. Everybody heard Gillian's cries of delight. Nobody heard other screams that cut across the fields in the night.

Putting Gillian carefully back onto her feet. Tim smiled and gazed into her eyes then he kissed her tenderly. Her happy face looked straight up at him. Just then, Tim looked up and noticed Sophie staring at them. Did she have tears in her eyes? He turned back to Gillian and lifted her off the ground and held her in an effortless, strong embrace. He kissed her; a deep, long, passionate kiss. But it was Sophie he looked at across the dark field.

"My goodness, DC Myerscough, you completely took my breath away." "Do we really have to build a bonfire?" She looked up at him with a cheeky grin on her face.

"Not all night." Tim smiled at her. "Can you see Simon?"

"He's over there beside Ailsa."

"Of course he is! Where are we going to build this biggest bonfire in the world?"

"I thought we'd put it in the middle of the field over there. It's near enough to the trees for gathering wood, but far enough away not to damage them. It'll also be well away from the house and far enough from the caravans. And this field will be fallow next year too," Simon said.

"Who lives in the caravans?" Gillian asked.

"Travellers."

"Oh God! How awful," Sophie said, pulling a face.

"Not really. They're fine. We've got to know some of them. It's largely the same group every year."

"Horrible!" Sophie said. "Do they leave a dreadful mess and steal things?"

"Not at all, Sophie," Simon smiled.

"Is Sophie always such a snob?" Gillian whispered to Tim.

"No, sometimes she's worse," he said and kissed her ear.

"The leader of the group always knocks on the door of the farmhouse and asks if they can stay. Four or five caravans in the same field every year. It's always for the winter term at the local school. The kids go there, the women make jewellery and the men occasionally drive for one of the courier companies and they make wooden toys. They sell their crafts at Christmas markets and when they go, the field is pretty much left as they found it. No, some travellers may be a pain, but Jock Cowper runs his family like a tight ship. His brother-in-law, Jonny, is a bit of a wide boy, but they've generally been all right."

"Sounds like it. It's very unusual. You don't know how lucky you are," Mel said.

"Yes, as they come back each year it's fun seeing the children growing up," Simon commented.

"Mind you, some of them are little terrors, climbing trees and chasing sheep and turning up where you really don't want them," Robin said. "One of them did that to me today when Derek and I were making arrangements about something that was none of their business. They can cramp your style!"

"It's called being a kid, you grumpy sod. Now, enough standing around all of you! Let's get this bonfire built tonight or it won't be much of a party tomorrow," Simon laughed.

The group scattered to go and collect wood.

"You girls gather the kindling and Tim, Simon, Robin and I will collect the decent sized branches that will really burn," Bear joked.

"What about me?" Lucky asked.

"You do what you're good at and supervise, my Lord," Bear laughed, pretending to doff his cap.

"Thanks very much!" Lucky said, feigning indignation, as he followed them out towards the trees then kept on walking towards the caravans.

Tim watched Lucky walk away towards the caravans. What on earth was he doing while everybody else busy?

"Come on, boys, or we'll never get this bonfire built," Mel called out.

"Quite right, Mel," Simon said. Just then he saw a small, wiry, man marching over the field towards them, as Lucky was walking away.

"Jock. Good to see you, I was just telling my friends how your family is growing," Simon said.

"Aye, the bairns are growing fast," the man replied. "You havenae seen wee Nicky have you, Mr Land? She should have been back for her tea by now."

"No, I haven't seen any of the kids today, Jock. Have you Robin?"

"Not recently."

"Can we help look for her, Jock?" Simon asked.

"No, I don't mean to intrude. I'm just having a scout about for her. She's only five, but she knows better than to stay out when it's getting dark. Her mam gets right worried."

"And it gets dark so early at this time of year. Be sure that, if I do see the wee one, I'll mention that you're looking for her and she should get home as quickly as possible."

"Thank you. That's right good of you. You can tell her there's a smacking in it for her too," Jock smiled wryly.

"But I probably won't," Simon said with a grin.

"Maybe that's for the best, right enough, Mr Land. Thanks for keeping an eye out, and yourself, young Mr Robin," the man turned and wandered off to continue his search.

***

When the pretty people came out, Nicky watched them. She was shivering with the cold. She should have brought her jacket, but she didn't think. She'd left in a hurry and was frightened to go home now because Uncle Jonny would be cross. She'd seen him with that nasty man. She was surprised to see the pretty people with the nasty man. Also, she'd heard Pop saying she'd get a skelp. Although she was hungry, she didn't want that. So she decided she wouldn't go home just yet, but would come down from the tree and find somewhere to hide, out of the wind.

Chapter Nine

Hunter helped his aunt into the front passenger seat of his old Toyota. She was still wrapped in his jacket and wearing his socks and the overshoes Rachael had found for her. Still she shivered. He could hear her teeth chattering as she pulled the jacket tighter around her. Hunter shivered too. He knew he should have gone to his office to fetch his coat but, having sent Rachael home, he didn't want to leave Sandra on her own. Not even for a moment. So he put up with the cold east wind in his shirt sleeves, gritted his teeth and buckled the seat belt around his aunt before getting into the driver's side.

His door creaked loudly as he opened it. He knew that it would be sooner rather than later that he had to replace this car. He wasn't looking forward to that expense.

"So where are you taking me, young man?" Sandra asked.

"Back to the hospital, Auntie Sandra. The staff nurse was very worried about you and most apologetic that nobody had seen you leave. You shouldn't have left without telling anybody, Sandra. They are trying to help."

"That's what they tell you. But they keep me locked up and steal money out of my purse when I try to buy a newspaper or biscuits from the trolley and beat me black and blue when I complain. Look!" She showed Hunter the big bruise on the back of her hand and her wrists looked bruised too.

"I think that's where they have been trying to hold you so they can take blood," he said.

"What right do they have to do that? I never said I would donate blood, did I?"

"Probably not, but it is all for your own good, honestly. I donated blood earlier. It's a good thing to do," Hunter said softly.

"Some of them are nice, but some of them are so nasty and

38

hurt me, Hunter. Please help." Tears rolled down her cheek.

Hunter drove the rest of the short distance to the hospital in silence. He looked across at his aunt. She looked so miserable and vulnerable. It made him sad to see her like this. His aunt and uncle had never had their own children and had doted upon Hunter and his brother. Since his Uncle Ross's death, Hunter knew Sandra felt very alone and that she depended greatly on his parents for comfort and company. His father was her big brother, she his only sister, and they had always been close.

He stopped at the pedestrian walkway to let a young nurse cross the street when he saw Sandra fiddling with the car door and trying to get out. He swiftly applied the child locks and silently blessed Toyota for four door locking.

"Help! Help! I'm being kidnapped," Sandra shouted. But nobody outside the car could hear her and she wept.

***

"Where's bloody DI Hunter Wilson?" Charlie asked.

"I think I saw him leave for the evening, Sarge," Neil said.

"What the hell did he do that for? I needed to tell him about this," Charlie waved a piece of paper in Neil's face.

"What is it, Sarge?"

"Something that's going to have to wait until tomorrow but shouldn't, that's what this is, Neil. That's just what this is. I suppose DI Wilson left with that old nutter, his *Auntie Sandra*, did he? I ask you, that woman's barking mad. If it's hereditary, I don't fancy Hunter's chances, do you, Neil?"

"No, Sarge," Neil said unthinkingly.

"Don't tell me, DC Anderson has gone too?"

"Yes, she left before DI Wilson," Neil replied.

"Well, that's just fan-bloody-tastic, isn't it?"

"If you say so."

The phone rang and Neil had never answered a call more quickly, nor with more gratitude, than he did then. He watched Charlie get his newspaper out from under the desk and continue marking up tomorrow's runners.

***

Hunter drew up outside the Anne Ferguson Building at The Western General Hospital and jumped out of the car to help his aunt from the vehicle. He recognised the look of dread on her face. He had never liked hospitals either. The automatic doors swept open as they approached. The antiseptic smells assaulted his nostrils immediately. What kind of chemicals did they use in hospitals? It smelt like nowhere else on earth. He walked with Sandra along the long corridor to the elevators.

"Do I have to go back?" Sandra asked. She spoke softly, almost a whisper and, as she hunched over, Hunter thought how really small and scared she seemed beside him.

"Yes, Auntie Sandra, they will help you get better," Hunter said as he put his arm around her and guided her into the large, empty lift.

They stood silently, side by side until the doors opened at the top floor. The smell of antiseptic became increasingly strong as they walked towards the ward. Hunter pushed the door and was faced with a young student nurse, dressed in a smart, starched uniform. He felt Sandra's grip on his hand tighten as they walked past unsettling pieces of equipment discarded thoughtlessly to look like strange modern sculptures.

"That thing hurt me when they used it on me and nobody seemed to care – it's like an instrument of torture," she said softly, nodding at an articulated chrome instrument.

"Hospitals always give me the creeps."

"Then let's go now," Sandra urged, pulling his arm. "The doctors and nurses huddle in the corridors and doorways. It's too scary. I keep thinking they're all whispering about death. My death in fact."

"I doubt that. Come on Aunt Sandra," he put his hand behind her back and encouraged her to move forward towards the person behind the nurses' station. "Come on, you'll be fine. Staff Nurse Turnbull? We spoke on the phone. I'm DI Hunter Wilson returning my aunt, Sandra Button, to your care. I'm not impressed that she managed to leave the hospital alone and unnoticed. She is extremely vulnerable just now."

40

"Thank you for bringing Mrs Button back, DI Wilson," the Staff Nurse said. "Please accept my apologies, again, that none of us saw her leave. It is unforgivable, even though we are severely understaffed today."

"She was distressed and very confused when she came to the station, you know. My aunt kept confusing me for my father and claimed she was being restrained here and beaten."

"I assure you, nothing could be further from the truth. Your aunt is receiving the best of care. My guess is that she has urinary infection or the beginnings of dementia. Either can result in these kinds of delusions. We'll treat her with antibiotics to cure any infection and ask the therapist to see her in the morning."

"Shouldn't you check what the problem is first before starting treatment?" Hunter asked sourly.

"Of course. We took blood tests today to make sure, but the results are not back. Infections like this often cause delusions and anxiety. You may have seen the mark of the cannula on the back of her hand?"

"Yes, she showed me the bruises on her wrists too. Is Staff Nurse Sarah Anderson in this evening?"

"No, Sarah will be back in tomorrow. Day shift. I'm just glad Mrs Button came to you and that you were able to get her back to us safely," the staff nurse said solemnly.

"It was only by chance that she found me, to be honest. I think she asked the taxi driver to take her to the nearest police station. She told me she wanted me to lock you all up for abusing her," Hunter said. "For Sandra's safety and my sanity, I trust that she won't be allowed to leave the hospital alone again, until she is fully recuperated."

"Indeed it will not. It's a rare occurrence and will be investigated fully."

"Good. I'll inform my father, Sandra's brother, and I'll stop by to see her in the next day or two."

"I think I've met your father. You look much like him, but younger."

"Thank goodness for that. Hopefully my aunt's condition will have been diagnosed and her treatment will have worked by the time I come back. Right now, I must go. I have a darts match to win. I just hope I'm not too late."

***

"Clouseau!" Tom shouted as Hunter entered the Persevere Bar. "Your beer will be warm and flat, but that's the best you deserve for being late, again."

"You're probably right," Hunter shook Tom's hand and turned to pick up his pint. He took a sip of the beer and pulled a face. "Flat? I've seen livelier corpses," he chuckled. "How are we doing, anyway?" He looked over at Jim who stood at the ochy.

"We're getting hammered. No other word for it. This East Lothian team is unbeatable just now. It's not even a contest."

"Depressing, isn't it?". Hunter took another slurp.

"Anyway, you're up next. Show them some style, Clouseau."

"I'll do my best," Hunter said as he stepped up to the oche.

Chapter Ten

"Building that bonfire was a lot of fun, but it was quite hard work," Gillian smiled.

"Hard work? You wouldn't know hard work if it hit you in the face, Doctor Pearson," Bear joked. "There you were, wandering about carrying the occasional twig or a handful of dry grass, while Timmy and I were bent double under the weight of thick branches, and Lucky Little Lord Fauntleroy over there was shouting orders, shielding himself from the wind by using Sophie as a wind break!"

Tim laughed. "When he was there at all."

"I beg your pardon my man, without my expert supervision and direction, nothing would have been accomplished." Lucky laughed. "Want another beer, Bear?" He walked over to Simon's refrigerator as if he owned the place and opened the freezer section in error first, closing it quickly, and retrieved the beers from the fridge.

Tim noticed that Robin glanced at Lucky. Tim saw that Robin seemed anxious but said nothing. He saw Simon frown. He seemed confused.

"Silly question. When have you ever known Bear to refuse a beer?" Tim asked with a smile.

"Can I just ask everybody to help themselves to the food? There's soup and home-made bread. Then we have cottage pie or lasagna," Robin said.

"Or?" joked Tim. "Since when has this become a choosing household? I'll have some of everything, thanks!"

"No problem. Please, help yourselves everyone." Simon slapped Tim on the back. "Show them how it's done, Tim. Lucky, I'll go and fetch your driver to join us for some dinner. What's his name again?"

"Thanks, Simon. It's Cameron Wilson," Lucky said.

The group settled themselves around the large kitchen table. They were glad of the heat from the huge range that held the large pot of soup and dishes of food.

"This soup is delicious," Gillian said, warming her hands around the bowl.

"It is. Your mother hasn't lost her touch, Simon," Tim said.

"She has lost something, though," their host said, quietly. "Do you know everybody, Cameron?" Simon asked.

"I know who everybody is, except you, pretty lady." He smiled at Ailsa.

"Doctor Ailsa Myerscough, may I introduce Lucky's driver, Cameron," Simon said, with uncharacteristic pomp.

Tim raised his head to look at Simon. He thought it sounded as if their host wanted to emphasise to Cameron that Ailsa was out of his league. This was unlike Simon. He was usually extremely polite. Tim saw Cameron blush. He helped himself to cottage pie before taking a seat as far away from Simon and Ailsa as possible. Tim noticed that Ailsa frowned. She didn't seem to like the way Simon had spoken to Cameron.

"Ailsa," she said, reaching diagonally across the table to shake Cameron's hand. "And that's the nicest compliment I've received in ages, Cameron. Thank you," she said. "I believe your dad is my big brother's boss – we must get together and you can tell me all his secrets."

"Hey! Not if you know what's good for you, Cameron," Tim joined in the joke.

Cameron smiled. "I'm sure I can make something up," he said

Just then there was a call from the back door. "Hey! I hope you lot have left enough for a little one." A slim man with dark hair and glasses entered the kitchen. His marble grey eyes were flecked with gold. They swept the room and his smile was warm and inclusive.

"Derek, at last! You're so late, I was worried you had been held up. Let me introduce you." Robin moved his chair towards the other man who bent down and kissed him gently on the lips. "You're very hot," Robin said.

"Why, thank you," Derek said. "It's cold out there, and it's November, so I had the car heater on. I had a little matter to attend to towards the end of my shift. Some old bat needed extra medication to keep her quiet. Her nephew was a right pain."

"Yes, it may be cold outside, but you've just come from the car." Robin smiled and quickly made the introductions.

"Hi everyone. Actually, Robin, I went for a jog down to the caravan field and back just to clear the cobwebs room my brain." Derek winked at Lucky. "Now, I'm just going to get into my soup and lasagna eating joggies and I'll join you in a minute, people," Derek said. "Where's your Mum?" he asked Robin.

"She went up for a nap and hasn't come down yet."

"I'll help her up and bring her downstairs with me," Derek said. "The company will be good for her. She's been on her own too much since your Dad died. She needs to find a sense of purpose again. Maybe she'll take a little walk around about the nearby fields with me, after she's eaten. Fresh air and a change of scene is good for her too."

"A change of scene? It's too dark for her to see anything much, Derek!" Robin teased. "You are blethering tonight, man. I think you've been working too hard."

"That'll be it. Has your Mum had her medication?"

***

When Derek came back downstairs with Mrs Land by his side, he helped her to a small serving of cottage pie and ladled some soup into a bowl for himself.

"Your mother has a couple of nasty bruises, but she can't remember how she got them. Did you notice anything, Robin?" Derek asked.

"No, but we've been busy baking and cooking together. Maybe she bumped herself in the kitchen. Did you, Mother?"

"I don't know, dear. Don't be cross. It doesn't matter. Really."

"Nobody's cross, Mother," Simon said.

45

"Talking about injuries, we saw a van take a hell of a roll on the ring road as we were coming out here," Bear said to Derek. "The people in the van must have been hurt. Did they come to your hospital?"

"Well, I'm not in A&E. I work in the old folks' wards at the Western," Derek replied.

"I think it's our turn for emergencies right now, anyway," Ailsa said.

"Ailsa is an A&E doctor at the Edinburgh Royal Infirmary," Simon explained.

"Oh, really? Nice," Derek said and looked away from Ailsa. He turned his attention back to his soup.

"You're not working tomorrow night shift are you, Derek?" Robin asked.

"What? And miss the bonfire party? I don't think so! I switched a night for a day so I'll be there for all the fun and I can indulge in a glass or two of vino, as well," Derek said.

"Good thinking, batman," said Robin.

Derek said, "I'll be working with that battle-axe, Sarah Anderson. But anything for you, Robin."

Derek noticed Bear glance at Tim but neither of them said anything.

Tim just smiled. "Your jokes haven't improved any over the years, Robin."

"Neither has my running," Robin stated.

Derek shook his head at Robin. "That's true, but not fair, Robin," Derek said. The atmosphere in the room grew cold. Luckily the food was hot and filling. "This is great soup," the nurse chuckled as he tucked into his meal.

"So, what's the plan for tomorrow?" Tim said to Simon.

"You lazy lot can have a lazy start to the day while I see to the beasts, then we'll spend the afternoon getting ready for the bonfire party in the evening." Simon smiled. "I don't have any fireworks though, too dangerous for my blood! Where are you all off to?"

"I'm taking your Mum and Robin outside for some fresh air," Derek said.

In no time at all, Robin returned to the warmth of the

kitchen, his face and eyes glowing. "Too bloody cold out there for me. Derek and Mum don't seem to notice," he said, and rolled himself towards the fire, reaching out his hands to heat them up. Tim noticed Robin seemed much more cheerful than when he left.

"How did you enjoy your walk, Mrs Land?" Tim asked.

"I liked my walk with Derek. It was all dark and spooky and funny. I could hear the crying and howling and noises."

Tim was glad to see Mrs Land looking so much more lively and cheerful than when she went out. Clearly the fresh air had agreed with the woman.

"I'm glad you enjoyed it. The wind was noisy, wasn't it? It sounded strange, didn't it?" Derek said, excitedly. "Shall I help you to bed now, Mrs Land? We'll get your medication too."

"Thanks, Derek. You're so good with her." Robin kissed him on the cheek.

"No, Robin, I've told you. Save your kisses for a nice young lady. You'll find one you know, dear," his mother chided.

"Do you really think so, Mother? It seems unlikely that I shall be seen as much of a catch now." Robin looked angry, but Derek shook his head. He led Mrs Land away, holding her hand and chatting animatedly to her gently as they went up the stairs.

"Always good to see the old people treated as they should be," Lucky said to Derek as he returned.

The group was a little unsettled by Mrs Land's reaction to Robin's display of affection towards Derek.

The tensions in this house were becoming increasingly obvious to Gillian. She decided to try to defuse the stress and went to get her guitar. When Simon saw it, he fetched his fiddle from the corner of the living room.

"I don't play this nearly often enough, so I may be a bit rusty. But let's see if we can get the party started shall we, Gillian?" Simon said.

"Let's do that," she said.

"Do you still sing, Ailsa?" Simon asked.

"Try and stop me."

"Yes, do try and stop her, please," Tim teased.

Ailsa groaned at him and then started to sing,
"O the summer time has come.
And the trees are sweetly blooming."
She smiled as Simon and Gillian began to play and the others joined in.
"And wild mountain thyme.
Grows around the purple heather,"
Lucky applauded themselves loudly and took up the vocal baton with a reasonable rendition of *The Skye Boat Song*. Ailsa and Gillian added the descant. Then the group soon settled in to sing, eat, drink and talk well into the early morning.

Tim noticed that every time he looked at Derek, he seemed to be staring at him. He also noticed the nurse's pupils seemed quite dilated. He wondered if Derek was light sensitive, or if he were thinking about the close relationship Lucky had with Robin and Simon.

***

Bear was laughing and joking with the best of them; even if his singing did not always hit the right note, he was enthusiastic. It was always easy to underestimate Bear when he was on jovial form. That was usually a mistake.

Lucky did just that as he glanced around the room and believed nobody was paying him any attention. Lucky winked at Derek then caught Robin's eye. Robin moved his chair out of the living room and towards the back-kitchen door.

"I'm in agony. What's your excuse, Lucky?" Robin asked quietly.

Lucky shrugged. "Do I need one?"

Derek joined them. "I always think it's best to experiment with those who will be least missed," he said softly. "This should ease your pain, Robin."

"I'm counting on it," Robin whispered. He snorted the drug and then turned to Lucky.

Bear wandered through to the kitchen just in time to notice Lucky wiping white powder off the table. Bear smiled at Lucky innocently, but noticed the streak of white that led from his nose. Bear ignored it.

"I'm just getting another beer boys," Bear said. "Any of you need anything?"

"No, Robin and I are just going out for some air. And I want to make a call without disturbing the music," Lucky said. "It's a bit too hot in here, isn't it?"

"It is. Yes, it is," Robin giggled.

Bear acknowledged this by nodding and raising his bottle and then wandered back through to the others. He noticed Derek had followed him through when he flopped down beside Mel. "I think Lucky is using again and he's off out with Robin. They say it's too hot in here," he whispered. "He's up to something. I do not like that man, never have."

"Robin?" Mel asked.

"Him too, but Lucky is the dangerous one. He's manipulative and leads people astray. Always has with his money and personality."

Bear looked out of the window in time to see Lucky's Range Rover pull away from the house and drive towards the barn. "See? I bet they're up to no good and Lucky is the instigator."

"Does anybody else know he's using?" Mel asked.

"Who knows what the darling Lady Sophie Dalmore knows, or pretends not to know, Mel? After what she did to Tim when they were dating, I wouldn't trust her as far I could throw her."

Bear looked up to see Lucky and Robin return to the room. Lucky looked furious. Bear realised something had not gone his way.

Mel shook her head sadly, then kissed Bear gently then firmly on the lips. His response as she gripped his thigh was immediate and obvious.

"Will you two get a bloody room?" Tim laughed.

"Your wish is our command," Bear grinned, lifting Mel effortlessly and disappearing up the stairs with her.

***

Early the following morning a loud hammering on the kitchen door raised the household. It was an unwelcome alarm call for the guests who had stayed up into the early hours. Bear and Mel had spent little time sleeping. Nevertheless, Simon had already been to tend the animals and was sitting drinking tea in the kitchen with Robin. They exchanged glances at the thunderous roar that followed.

"Mr Land! Mr Land! Can you help?"

Chapter Eleven

"Christian, darling, how lovely to see you. How are you keeping, my dear? Busy as ever, I expect," Hunter's mother said. She stretched up on her tiptoes to give him a kiss on the cheek.

He smiled at her, then followed the plump bustling little figure into the new town flat she now called home. "I'm fine, Mum. How are you and Dad?" Hunter asked.

"I'm just doing away, but your dad is stressed. He's terribly worried about your Aunt Sandra. She's been in the hospital for two weeks now and seems to be getting worse rather than better. It's sad to see. We knew your Uncle Ross's death would take its toll on her, but she's not coping at all."

"I know. She came to the station last night. She left the hospital without any of the staff noticing, I think it was just blind luck that she found me."

"Oh dear, she really hasn't been herself since your uncle passed away. Let's go and see your Dad. You better tell him yourself."

Hunter followed his mother into the kitchen and found his father sitting at the table by the window with his face much closer to the page than necessary. The large room smelt of fresh scones and good coffee, the love of which was among the things Hunter and his father shared.

"I think you would see the page better if you wore your spectacles, Dad." Hunter smiled and shook his father by the hand.

"They keep slipping down my nose. I really should take them to the optician and get them tightened," Andrew Wilson said. "So how are you, Christian? The hospital phoned this morning to say you returned your aunt to the ward. Nice of you to take her out, though, son."

"That's not really how it was, Dad. So, I thought I'd come and have a chat with you," Hunter said as he took a seat opposite his dad.

"Would you like a coffee and a couple of scones, dear?" his mother asked.

"Yes, please," both men answered in unison and the three of them laughed.

"What did happen last night with Sandra, son?" Andrew asked.

"I was just about to leave the station, but I had one thing to speak with a colleague about. While I was looking for my colleague, Sandra came into the station reception wearing her pyjamas and with bare feet. She was clearly very confused. Is she normally that bad?"

"Well, she's been a bit forgetful since your uncle died, but not usually that bad," Andrew said.

"She kept confusing me with you," Hunter said.

"An easy mistake given my youthful appearance."

"Aye, right!" Hunter laughed. "Anyway, I warmed her up, gave her something to eat, then took her back and the staff nurse told me they think she has a bladder infection. I suggested they run the necessary tests and treat said bladder infection or whatever else is causing her confusion. She's very vulnerable right now. It's really shocking nobody noticed the poor old soul leave the ward."

"It might be that. Those kinds of infections can do that. It's quite frightening for the patient," his mother said quietly. "But you're right, they should have taken better care of her."

"Your mother is quite correct. But how did Sandra get to you and how did she know where you were?" Andrew asked.

"I was told no member of staff noticed her leave the hospital. As to her finding me, I think that was sheer luck. I believe she jumped in a taxi and asked to be taken to the nearest police station and that happened to be mine. When she got to me, she was adamant that the staff were mistreating her. But I doubt that very much."

"That was lucky she found you. Goodness knows what

would have happened to her otherwise," Andrew said. "Your mother and I will go to see her this afternoon and speak to the staff nurse."

"Good idea. And you'll make clear how dangerous it could have been, her leaving the hospital in that condition without being noticed?" Hunter asked.

"Of course, we will, son," his mother said.

"Thanks Mum," Hunter said. "She had bare feet and was terribly cold. If she had been out for much longer, I'd hate to think what might have happened to her."

"Do you still keep spare clothes in the bottom drawer of your desk, just in case?" Andrew asked with a grin.

"Yes. She was certainly glad of my thick woollen socks," Hunter laughed.

***

"Where the hell have you been, DI Wilson?" Sergeant Charlie Middleton asked.

"Visiting my parents. Not that it's any of your business. "

"Well you're bloody late for your shift."

"No, I'm almost forty hours early, I'm not due in until Monday morning, but I've got some paperwork to catch up on."

Charlie sighed.

"Anyway, what's rattled your cage?"

"It was that thing I wanted to tell you about yesterday."

"Oh God! Yes, I'm sorry. With all that hassle with my aunt I forgot to speak to you about it. What's the matter?"

"There was a call last night, came through from our wonderful call centre. They said it sounded like a young voice, possibly a child, whispering that they were frightened and ran away because someone hurt them, and the child said they saw the man stick a big pin into his mouth. The voice said they didn't want the man to get them," Charlie said. "Then there was a shout in the distance and the line went dead."

"A prank?" Hunter asked.

"The call handler didn't seem to think so."

"Where from?"

"A mobile number, but not one that's registered."

"Of course not! Can we trace where the call came from?"

"Within the general area. If you authorise it. If you think it's worth it?" Charlie asked.

"Probably not," Hunter said. "It's probably something and nothing."

"That's what I thought, but it's your decision, not mine."

"Of course, Charlie." Hunter smiled. Then, while he climbed the stairs to his office, his phone rang.

"Cameron. I thought you were away this weekend, driving Lucky about to a social event," Hunter said. "What's up that you want to talk to me? Or is this a pocket call?"

Hunter continued to walk upstairs towards his office as he listened quietly to what his son said. His information had an uncanny echo of the call that Charlie had told him about. He always worried about the very young, the disabled and the very old: the most vulnerable members of society.

"Slow down, son," Hunter said to Cameron. "You're rambling. Start at the beginning and take it slowly."

Chapter Twelve

I woke up with a groan. Daylight. I couldn't see much through my hair, but at least there was light. I felt sore all over and could hardly move. The airbag that had exploded from the steering wheel had squeezed my chest but at least that pressure was easing now as the bag was deflated. My foot was still fixed under a pedal. My hands were clinging to my seatbelt. It seemed as if I couldn't control them because they were so stiff.

My hair lay over my face. It was thick and matted that it was almost like a curtain. It felt dirty and hung in little ropes that seemed to be glued together. The broken glass from the window had scratched my face and hands.

I wrinkled my nose. There was a ghastly smell. I couldn't work out where it was coming from. I didn't know why there were so many flies. Where had they come from? They certainly weren't there last time I looked. Wasn't it too cold for them anyway? What was that on the windows? I closed my eyes again and hoped the nightmare would float away. Usually a bad dream went away when you opened your eyes, didn't it? But I couldn't see properly through my hair and that didn't work. I let my eyes fall shut and then, as my memories came back to me, the nightmare was resurrected by the darkest part of my brain.

I started to scream. "Bob! Bob! Speak to me Bob!"

I glanced over at the lifeless eyes staring at me.

"Help, somebody help me please! Bob needs help!"

I kept screaming for as long as I could, but the airbag had hurt my chest. I couldn't take deep breaths without pain. I stopped. I would have to get out of here.

The buzzing of the flies seemed vicious, scary. There was the sound of traffic was close at hand, somehow that was comforting. I could not work out how long I had been there, but it felt like a long time. Surely somebody must have seen our van roll off the road. Someone would have called for help, wouldn't they? Soon they would come for me. I thought help must be on its way. I lost consciousness again.

Chapter Thirteen

Jamie and Frankie arrived at the car showroom, in good time to have a coffee and a doughnut before they opened the doors. The phone was ringing as they walked in.

"Just leave it," Jamie said.

"I might as well answer it. I'm here and it might be important," Frankie said.

"What can be so important before 9 o'clock?" Jamie asked, heading for the office and the kettle.

"Thomson's Top Cars, how can I help?" Frankie answered the phone. He listened quietly for a moment. "Yes, we have a garage attached to the showroom." Frankie began to stand straighter and to look more serious. "Yes, we can certainly arrange MOT certificates and source any new vans needed.Red livery? That's just a paint job, not a problem. Yes, that will be fine. We'll look forward to meeting you. Yes, I'm Frankie Hope. I'm here all day. Goodbye now" He ended the call.

"What was all that about?" Jamie asked, wandering across the showroom with a steaming mug in each hand.

"If it works, it's the reason your pop won't close the showroom. It's a delivery company, DayGo. They've been taken over and want a better deal on the MOTs that their fleet of old vans need and want to be able to replace the old vans with new, greener ones as and when. They all need to be in the company's bright red paint colour."

"Brilliant. We can do all that," Jamie said.

"Aye, I know. Aren't you glad I answered the phone?" Frankie grinned before taking a big bite out of his doughnut and jam dribbled all down his chin. "The guy's coming over to meet with us."

"Now? Fuck's sake, Frankie. I'll have to wash my hands. You better wash your face and then tell Mark to get the garage tidied up so we can show this guy around. What's his name?"

"Don't remember. I got all excited," Frankie said.

"Arse!" Jamie exclaimed.

"No, it definitely wasn't that. I'd have remembered that," Frankie grinned.

Jamie shook his head and went to wash the sugar from the doughnut off his hands.

***

"So, Mr O'Grady, do you think we can do some business here with DayGo?" Jamie asked as he and Frankie started to turn out of the garage and back into the showroom.

"If the price is right, son, there's always business to be done." The businessman smiled. "We're looking to start the repair of our vans from a more economical source and they may need a bit of fixing as well as re-sprayed into our new red livery. Can you handle that?"

"Mark and his boys in the garage will take care of that for you. Won't you, Mark?" Jamie nodded.

"Well, what are the repairs and how much fixing are we talking about? We're already pretty busy, Jamie," Mark replied.

But Jamie ignored him and spoke straight over the top of his concerns, "Like I say, Mr O'Grady, Mark and the mechanics in the garage will take care of that. No problem at all. Frankie and me'll get a price list over to you and let's do some business."

The men shook hands and, as the boss of DayGo left the showroom, Jamie skipped and jumped up to thump the air, "High five, Frankie my boy," he said. "At least a hundred vans a year! No way Pop'll close us down now. So glad you took that call. This'll be the making of us! Let's go and sharpen our pencils, Frankie, lad."

"Should we run it past your pop, first, Jamie?" Frankie asked.

"No way! We're getting this business all on our own and then we'll surprise him with a done deal."

Chapter Fourteen

Hunter was on his phone to Cameron when he reached his office and stared at his coffee machine. He suddenly realised he had forgotten to bring in the supply of coffee he needed. He would be stuck with the tasteless offerings from the machine. Yuck! Then he noticed he had stopped listening to his son and Cameron was still speaking to him. His son was now repeating himself as loudly and as slowly as possible. It was as if he were talking to a deaf pensioner. Hunter was unimpressed by his son's sarcastic tone, but decided just to listen and not to interrupt. That would only cause an argument.

"So has the child shown up?" Hunter asked.

"No, and she's only five years old," Cameron said.

"Oh God!"

"Exactly. I know she's only been missing just over twelve hours, but she is so young. Still, Tim, Bear and Mel are here and have arranged us into a search party, but they asked me to call you so the missing kid was formally reported as missing."

"Yes, okay, son. I'll complete the paperwork at this end, but I'll hold off informing the major incident team until you've had a chance to have a thorough look for her. Get Tim to call me if they need any extra resources, won't you?"

Hunter got to the top of the stairs and noticed all the lights on in the incident room. He strode in hoping to find a biscuit left over by his team that he could use to take away the taste of the machine coffee. He was surprised to see Rachael Anderson, Colin Reid and Nadia Chan all at their desks and Angus McKenzie scrabbling around under his.

"I don't have any decent coffee. Do you have any biscuits to take away the taste of the machine muck?"

"I can do better than that, I brought in a flask of proper coffee. Do you want a cup?" Colin asked.

"Did I tell you that you thoroughly deserved your promotion to sergeant, Colin? You're a good copper and a fine human being," Hunter said.

"Yeh, yeh, sure, boss. Where's your mug?" Colin laughed.

"Tea for us, Nadia, I think," Rachael said, getting up and moving towards the kettle.

"Anyway, do none of you have homes to go to?" He looked around at the team. They all looked back at him.

"I suppose we could ask the same of you, boss, Rosie has a nativity play coming up. She has a starring role – the third camel – and if I hear "Little Donkey" one more time, I will not be responsible for my actions."

"They're rehearsing already?" Hunter asked.

"Oh yes! They started after the October break."

"Good Lord."

"As for me, Janey is off to the Museum of Modern Art," Rachael said. "Personally I'd rather get a few things tidied up here."

Hunter smiled and nodded. "Ah yes, that I do understand." He turned and looked at Nadia, wondering what her excuse could possibly be.

"If Uncle Fred hears I've got a day off at the weekend, he'll have me over at his takeaway making more sweet and sour pork than you can imagine," she said.

"I'm only here to pick up my football boots," Angus shouted from under his desk. "I left them here last night and I've got a five-a-side today, so I'm away again now." He held his boots up in triumph. "But what's your excuse, boss?"

"Paperwork, Angus, my boy. It's always paperwork," Hunter sighed.

Rachael handed a mug to Nadia.

"Thanks for the tea, Rache," Nadia said. "Did you just come in here looking for biscuits, boss, or is there something particular you need from us?" Nadia asked Hunter.

"No, I don't think so Nadia. I planned to finish yesterday's paperwork that didn't get done. But I've just had a call from my son, Cameron. There's a wee girl gone missing out at Landsmuir Farm. You know the one, off the M8 motorway on the way to Harthill? The little girl is only five years old. She went missing yesterday evening and still hasn't turned up."

"Oh dear. Same age as Rosie?" Colin asked. "Isn't that where the pal of Tim stays? Steve, Sam or something?" Colin asked handing Hunter a steaming mug of black coffee.

"Yes, it's the one where Tim and Bear both know the family, isn't it?" Rachael asked.

"Yes, it is, Simon Land," Hunter said.

"There's a group of them there for a Bonfire Night Party, isn't there?" Rachael asked. "We think Ailsa went too."

"That farmer, Simon Land. Decent guy helped me when I needed it. But Tim seemed to think the host has an eye for Dr. Ailsa Myerscough." Hunter smiled as he nodded his thanks to Colin for the coffee.

"Well from what I can gather, half our team is out there," Nadia said.

"Yes, it shouldn't take them long to find one wee girl," Rachael said.

"She's managed to evade her family and the members of our fine force all night so far," Hunter said. "If they can't find her, I'll need to involve Jane and her friends at the major incident team. Anyway, Tim has set up a search party to cover the farm and will keep me in the loop. I just hope they find her quickly."

Hunter's phone rang as he turned to leave the room. He noticed the call was from his father. Strange. His father rarely used his mobile number.

"Dad? How can I help?" Hunter asked.

***

Hunter wandered back to his office to ensure the missing child's details were fully logged in the system.

He did this carefully but with a heavy heart. He knew the chances of finding a little girl unharmed even after this short time were slim and diminished even further with every minute that passed. He never understood why people knowingly left very young children alone. He thought children were much too precious to take risks with, just for the sake of going out to dinner or watching a third-rate cabaret. He remembered the family holidays he and his ex-wife had spent freezing on the balcony of their room or huddled in the bathroom, reading, when Alison and Cameron were too young to stay up late. Hunter smiled to himself. Whatever differences they had had, at least the kids were always the top priority for both of them, even now.

Hunter turned his thoughts back to the little girl. Nicola Cowper, aged five, was from a travelling community. This just got better and better. Hunter could see the headlines already if the wee soul was hurt, or worse. At least he had three of his best detectives on the scene. That didn't happen very often.

***

Nicky couldn't stop shivering. Her teeth were chattering although she wasn't trying to speak. She was too cold. She was very tired. She wanted to stay awake because she didn't want Uncle Ian or that nasty man to find her. They were mean. They were talking in mean whispers. They didn't know Nicky knew it, but she'd be in trouble if they knew. Nicky thought they would hurt her too much, so she grabbed Uncle Jonny's phone and pushed 999 and said very softly, but Uncle Jonny heard her voice, so she dropped the phone and ran outside. "Just to play for a wee while, Unca Jonny," she said as she tripped down the caravan steps and slid past the nasty man who was scowling at her.

She ran across the field and climbed the biggest tree she could. She heard Pop calling her but didn't move. Then pretty people came out and built a big pile of sticks and branches. It was humongous. They laughed and carried torches and looked kind and happy. Nicky smiled down at them. But they didn't know she was there. Pop didn't see her. She heard Uncle Jonny tell Pop that he hadn't seen her all day. That was bad to say. He did see her.

When the pretty people went inside, Nicky was cold. She should have worn her jacket, but she didn't. She was frightened to go home. Uncle Jonny would be cross, and she'd heard Pop saying she'd get a skelp. She was hungry, but she wouldn't go home just yet. She would come down from the tree and find somewhere to hide, out of the wind. And she did. But it was still cold, and damp and she was shivering when she fell asleep.

Chapter Fifteen

"Stop moaning, Mark," Jamie said to the senior mechanic. "First you complain because my pop might shut this place and you'd be outta job. Now you're grumbling because we've pulled a fine big contract and you'll be too busy. Are you never happy, man?"

"Course he's not, he's a Weegie," Frankie said. "They all grumble all the time in Glasgow. If it's no the football, it's the weather, if it's no the weather it's the prices, and if it's no—"

"All right! Enough! But I'll need an extra mechanic. One who knows what he's doing. And he'll have to be full time." Mark looked across at Jamie and Frankie from under his fringe. He fiddled with his moustache, anxiously.

"Mark, we can do that. I suppose you know a man, who knows a man, who kennt your father?" Jamie grinned.

"Aye, I know just the chap we need," Mark smiled. "I'll give him a call."

"Frankie my man, I think it's time for lunch," Jamie said.

"KFC?" Frankie asked.

"You talked me into it, cuz."

As Jamie and Frankie crossed the road to buy their lunch, Jamie phoned his pop to tell him the good news about their chat with Mr O'Grady and the new DayGo contract.

"Aye. Good enough, boy. You didn't think to run it past your old pop first?"

"Wanted to get it in the bag and surprise you, Pop," Jamie said. "This'll keep us busy, you know?"

"But would it be a Mr Connor O'Grady?" Ian asked.

"Yep, Connor Malcom O'Grady, Managing Director of DayGo Delivery Services. He's just taken over the company, Pop. They deliver all over the country for a lot of the mail order companies." Jamie felt his chest swell with pride as he shared their new client's credentials with his pop.

"Oh, yes, he certainly does."

"Why do you sound like there's a problem, Pop?"

"All that is a great cover for the drugs he delivers for Arjun Mansoor, my boy. You've bloody well got us back into bed with that piece of shite. But by the back door. Connor's been after me for years to work with him, but with drugs it's nothing doing as far as I'm concerned. Mansoor will be laughing his tits off. Fuck!"

"Ah, naw, Pop. You can't mean that. Is this a joke?"

"It's no joke, son. It's a fuckin' catastrophe. Connor is involved with organised crime in the UK and Ireland. That is where the drug money goes. Why could you and that daft cousin of yours not just run it by me first?"

"Well you said you were thinking of closing down Thomson's Top Cars. That'd be grim Pop. Me and Frankie and Donna all work there. We just wanted to help, and we thought it would be great to get this big contract so that would keep the business so busy you wouldn't be able to close it down. We thought we were doing the right thing, Pop," Jamie grumbled as he finished the call with his father.

"Jamie? Is yer pop no chuffed with us?" Frankie asked looking at his cousin's miserable face.

"No, Frankie, he is not. It's fair to say Mr O'Grady didn't tell us about *all* the things he delivers," Jamie said wearily. "We're in the shit right up to our necks, Frankie boy. Right up to our necks."

"How come? Connor O'Grady seemed decent enough to me."

"Aye. I suppose most con men are charming when there's something they want. It turns out our Mr O'Grady is in bed with Arjun Mansoor and his drugs business and we are caught up in the middle of it all now. He forgot to tell us that," Jamie explained.

"Oh no, not bloody old Argy Bargy again. I've had enough of that man and his antics to last me a lifetime," Frankie complained.

***

When Jamie and Frankie got home to their semi-detached house in West Mains Road, Donna was already there. She was with the twins giving them their tea.

As soon as she saw Frankie, she knew something was wrong.

"What's wrong, Frankie? You and Jamie look right miserable," she said. She turned her attention back to the twins before he could reply. "Come on now, Kylie, don't spit out your fish pie. Eat it nicely like Dannii. It's good for you." Donna smiled indulgently at the little girls and then looked back at Frankie. She knew something was badly wrong. Frankie hadn't kissed her or the twins as he came in.

She watched Jamie go into the kitchen and take two cans of beer out of the fridge. He handed one to Frankie. "Will one of you please tell me what is wrong? I have had enough today. I've been calling my Dad all day and my calls keep going to voicemail. Don't you two add to my stress," Donna said sharply. Kylie looked at her and burst into tears. She continued to spit out the proffered fish pie. Donna lifted Kylie out of her highchair and cuddled her on her lap while Dannii happily stayed in her chair and accepted the spoonfuls of food coming her way.

Frankie looked over and patted the twins on their heads. He smiled at them. Donna knew his little girls always made him smile.

"Is there a problem with your pop, Jamie?" Donna asked.

"Not exactly. Sort of. Yes, I suppose there is," Jamie said.

"Thanks. That makes it all perfectly clear," Donna said.

"We got a fine big contract for Thomson's Top Cars," Frankie began.

"Well, that's good. Your Uncle Ian won't need to shut down the business if you've got lots of work," Donna said.

"That's true as far as it goes. But the contract is with a right dodgy character," Frankie said.

Donna laughed. "Why did you take him on then?"

"Well we didn't know he was dodgy, did we?" Jamie

66

replied.

"Your pop'll be fit for him anyway," Donna said. "He's not as clean as the driven snow himself, is he?"

"No, he's not. But he'll take nought to do with drugs and this guy distributes them for me pop's former manager, Arjun Mansoor. Pop says he's proper nasty – organized crime and everything. Shit! This is really shit," Jamie said miserably.

"I know that name," Donna frowned.

"Argy Bargy," Frankie said.

"That's it. How come you can call your pop when he's inside and shouldn't even have a phone and I can't get hold of my Dad at all when he's never done anything wrong, Jamie?" Donna asked.

She watched Jamie shrug then turned back to finish feeding the twins. She couldn't help wondering why her father hadn't answered his phone.

Chapter Sixteen

I looked over at Bob again and started to cry again. I felt so sweaty and could feel my heart pumping hard. I noticed his features had begun to change. His skin was ashy white. His expression was rigid, and his dear lips were no longer the cheeky plump pink ones that kissed me all over and made me moan. They were a brownish colour and looked dry and hard. Bob was gone forever.

I had never told him about his baby. Oh, I know he has a daughter, but she is grown up. Bob was never too pleased about her latest squeeze – a young man with twins already. Bob had tried to persuade her that this was a bad idea, but she's a nineteen-year-old teenager. I tried to tell him that when you are a teenager your parents know nothing. This only made him angry. "Donna and I always had a good relationship. We can talk to each other about anything and she values my advice," he would say. Then we would argue. I hated it when we argued, but how I wished we could argue again. Right now. Then Bob would be alive here with me. It would not be so scary as being here all alone with a dead man. Covered in blood and that powdery muck from that parcel I couldn't deliver. I looked over and began to sob again.

Chapter Seventeen

"I hear we're back in business," Arjun Mansoor said as Ian Thomson sat down near to him in the prison dining hall. "My associate has signed a contract with your son. So nice to be working with you again, my friend."

It was noisy. Bearing in mind that everybody was using plastic plates and cutlery, it was amazing how much noise there was. The tables had seats for eight, four on each side, but there were rarely more than five prisoners at any one table. Most people wanted their own space, others had secrets to share, the rest wanted to ensure that their superiority was acknowledged by the other prisoners.

A newbie sat in Scar's favourite seat at the back of the hall. Every prisoner in the room stopped and stared. Scar liked to have his back to the wall and watch proceedings. His place was non-negotiable amongst the inmates. Ian watched Irish Mick as he went over to the lad and whispered into the newbie's ear. (How was Irish Mick back so soon? He surely can't have been out a week this time!) Ian couldn't hear what Mick said, but he had been there long enough to know. Ian smiled as he heard the newbie say "No seats have got names on them." The newbie sat down.

"Maybe no. But you will be more comfortable over here," Mick said.

Ian saw Mick nod in Scar's direction. The newbie swallowed, almost audibly, and then followed Irish Mick towards a table at the other end of the hall. Ian smiled. Then Ian turned his attention back to Arjun Mansoor. Ian did not want to have to shout, so he moved along to sit down directly opposite the man. He leaned over the table and whispered into Arjun's ear. "You are no friend of mine. You've proved that over and over again. Let me make myself perfectly clear, you bastard. My fucking idiot of a son may have signed a contract with Connor O'Grady, but it is to fix up his DayGo vans and see them through their MOTs for motor tax. You get my boy, or my business, involved in any of your drug running and you'll have me to answer to. And believe me, you'll be crying for your mummy and wishing you'd never been born, Arjun. Do you understand me?"

"I understand you talk a good game, Ian. Good luck following through. But I should warn you, you talk too much. That mac and cheese looks cold now." Arjun stood up and spat in Ian's dinner.

"Bastard!" Ian shouted.

Arjun smiled and walked away with his tray without looking back.

"This seat free, Ian?" Sir Peter Myerscough asked.

"Aye, Sir Pete. But I'm just going. Fucking Mansoor just gobbed in me dinner."

"Yuck!" Sir Peter pulled a face. "I thought you two avoided each other as far as possible. What's up?"

"Not here. Too many ears. We'll talk later, aye?" Ian asked.

"Fair to say I have no other pressing engagements that would take priority," Sir Peter replied.

"No. That's true. We're both going nowhere fast, aren't we?" Ian sighed. "I think I've got a bag of crisps and a snickers bar back in my cell I'd rather eat that than Mansoor's gob-shite."

"Don't blame you. I'd feel the same." Ian was aware that Sir Peter watched as he left the dining hall and then saw him return his attention to his plate. Ian didn't blame him. Sir Peter had lost too many meals to the hard men around him in the past to allow his attention to be diverted for too long.

∗∗∗

Frankie and Donna sat with Jamie staring at the blank screen of the television. None of them had thought to turn it on since they had put the twins to bed.

"How could we get it so wrong?" Frankie asked.

"If you hadnae answered the phone like I said, it wouldn't have happened," Jamie grumbled.

"Don't be daft. He'd have just phoned back, Jamie,"

"Aye, probably." "Why is my dad's phone still ringing out?" Donna muttered.

"He's probably lost it," Frankie offered.

"Or had it nicked," Jamie suggested.

"But it's ringing. Dad's sim card is still in it surely?"

"I don't know, love," Frankie sighed.

"To be honest, no speaking to your pop sounds good to me right now," Jamie said.

"Only because you've been able to speak to yours and he's given you an earful," Donna said.

"Point taken. I don't see how signing up to paint and repair vans and getting them through services is that bad anyway."

"I know. It's no as if we've agreed to take his bloody drugs all around, have we?" Frankie replied.

"I think Pop was a bit harsh," Jamie agreed. "Youse fancy another beer? We could order pizza and watch Corrie?"

"Let's do that," Donna agreed.

"Pepperoni with extra cheese?" Frankie suggested.

"And extra pepperoni," Jamie grinned, handing out the beers.

Chapter Eighteen

"Dad, Dad, can you slow down? I can't hear you properly when you ramble so fast."

Hunter shut the door of his office and flopped down in his chair. He could hear the panic in his father's voice. His dad was not given to panic, so Hunter could gauge from this how upset his father must be. "Take a deep breath, Dad. Sit down and take three deep breaths. In, out. In, out. In, out. Now, are you feeling any calmer?"

"Not at all. But I can breathe better," his father said.

"At least I can understand you now," Hunter said. He took a sip of the coffee that Colin had poured for him and held the delicious, warm liquid in his mouth before swallowing. "Now, what were you trying to tell me, Dad?"

He listened to his father, but he did drone on. Hunter let his mind wander as he glanced around the room at the piles of papers, files and the old photograph of himself with his kids, Alison and Cameron. Kids, who was he trying to fool? Alison was married and living in Orkney while Cameron had a job working for 'Lucky' Lord Buchanan, Tim's pal. At least Cameron was clean again. Both kids were all grown up and fending for themselves now. Not like that little girl who had gone missing at Landsmuir Farm. But as a parent, you never stopped worrying. It just went with the territory. Then his attention was pulled back to his dad's voice.

"What? Oh, for goodness sake! Old lady dies in hospital. I'm very sorry for the family, but it's really not my problem. I have enough to do without worrying about this."

"No, it's not just that, it's bad enough about old Mrs Florence Roberts," his father continued. "Just listen to me, son. There is something odd."

"Mrs Florence Roberts, that name is familiar. An elderly lady by that name was a witness in a recent case I had," Hunter said.

"Well, her grandson works here at the hospital. He's a porter. He was visiting her during his break and was horrified to find her dead not forty minutes ago. When your mother and I arrived just now to visit your Aunt Sandra, we found her dead, too, and they've both got strange marks on their bodies that the nurses can't explain to me." The panic began to rise in his father's voice again. "Son, you've got to come. Come now."

"Aunt Sandra is dead? Oh no! Why didn't you tell me?" Hunter put his coffee mug on his desk and ran his hands through his hair.

"I was trying to tell you. I just got so upset," Andrew Wilson sighed.

"Of course, Dad. You should have told me about Aunt Sandra first, I'll be there as soon as I can. Look for me within half an hour."

Hunter sat, staring at his desk. Tears fell into his coffee. He didn't hear the knock on his door as Colin Reid walked in.

"More coffee, boss? My God, what's wrong? Can I help?" Colin asked.

"Sorry, Colin. I just got bad news. Not wholly unexpected, but sad nevertheless. My dad just called to inform me that an old auntie of mine has just passed away. Found dead in the hospital."

"Oh, boss, I'm so very sorry. You get away. Do you need me to cover that missing wee girl?"

"Aye, go on, Colin. If you and Nadia are going to be here anyway. It'll probably be something and nothing and the wee one will turn up safe and well, but I can't take any risks with such a young child. I've put her on the system."

"No problem, boss, don't give it a second thought," Colin said. He almost knocked Rachael over as he left Hunter pulling on his coat. Colin told her the news.

"Boss, is it your Aunt Sandra that's died?" Rachael stuck her head round the door. "I met her yesterday. She can't be dead, surely?"

"Yes, that's who it is, Rachael. My dad says there are strange marks on her body, and another old dear has been found dead in her bed with similar wounds," Hunter said. "Dad sees conspiracy. I doubt it's that exciting, though."

"Do you want me to come with you, just in case?" Rachael asked. "I'll just phone Janey and tell her she's on duty to cook the dinner."

"Thank you, Rachael. I'd appreciate that." Hunter smiled. "You drive, will you? I want time to think."

***

"I'll drop you at the door, boss, and find somewhere to park," Rachael said as she pulled up in front of the Anne Ferguson Building. "Ward 52 is on the second floor. I think my sister, is working today. Remind her who you are, and I'll be with you as soon as I can."

"It's Saturday afternoon, you probably won't get parked closer than Balerno," Hunter said as he closed the car door.

Hunter followed the signs in the building and took the stairs rather than the elevator to the second floor. He found his parents in the visitors' room with a young man. All three of them were extremely distressed. The young man stood up as Hunter entered.

"Oh, son, thank you for coming," his father said. "This is Andy, Andy Roberts. He works here as a porter but he's not on duty today. Just popped in to see his granny. This same ward as your Aunt Sandra."

"You're havering, love," Hunter's mother said. She took out a tissue and blew her nose loudly. Hunter thought that her red-rimmed eyes made her look sad.

"Andy? How do you do. I'm DI Hunter Wilson."He shook the young man's slender hand. His intense grey eyes swept across Andy, observing him closely. First, Hunter could not help but notice the young man's distinctive, wide brimmed hat. He wore it at a fashionable angle but still the wide brim hid the top third of his face assisted by his large-rimmed glasses. Behind the lenses, Andy's eyes were red and he looked dejected. He stared at Hunter and his mouth tried to smile, but the smile did not reach his eyes. He was clean shaven and more smartly dressed than most young men in their mid-twenties on a Saturday afternoon.

"Nice to meet you, Detective Inspector," Andy said. "I understand your father has told you about the strange marks on my gran and his sister."

"Yes he has, Andy. My colleague is joining me as soon as she gets parked and we'll take a look at the bodies," Hunter said.

"Parked? You'll be lucky if you see her this side of Monday," Andy said.

"Hi boss, I think I've got the last parking spot in the whole hospital car park," Rachael said as she arrived to join the group in the small room.

"Gosh you were quick, Rachael."

"Of course, boss, I do my best. Reverend and Mrs Wilson, I am so sorry for your loss," she said, turning to his parents. "Shall I see if I can find Sarah?"

"DS Rachael Anderson, may I just introduce Andy Roberts? His grandmother has been found dead today too."

"Oh, Mr Roberts, I am so very sorry," Rachael said.

"It's so sad. I thought Gran was on the mend. She seemed to be getting a bit better," Andy said as he and Rachael shook hands.

"Yes, Rache, see if you can find Sarah and perhaps a cup of coffee while these good folks are waiting." Hunter said.

"I'll see what I can do." Rachael smiled widely and left the room.

***

Rachael trotted along the hospital corridor to the nurses' room. She tapped lightly on the door and it opened immediately. "I'm looking for Staff Nurse Sarah Anderson," she said.

The student nurse who opened the door was a large woman in every sense of the word. She stood about five feet eight inches tall with a round face and light brown eyes. Her long blonde hair was tied up in a bun, but one strand had escaped, and she swept this behind her left ear as she screwed up her eyes to focus on Rachael.

"Oh yeh, her," she said, turning her head. "Sarah, it's someone for you. Don't know them."

"You don't need to know them, but you do need to be courteous, Angie." Sarah came to the door. "I thought that was your voice, sis," she said. "You here in your official capacity or just to visit your loving sister?" Sarah gave Rachael a hug.

"The boss and I need to see the bodies of the wee old women found dead today. One of them is his aunt," Rachael said.

"Shit, that is all I need at the weekend," Sarah sighed.

"And his folks and the other guy in the relatives' room could do with a cup of tea or coffee."

"Of course, Rache. Nothing is too much trouble."

"Thanks Sarah," Rachael said.

"You don't understand. I'm so short staffed, nothing *is* too much trouble," Sarah grumbled. "Angie, will you get some tea and coffee along to the relatives' room, please?"

"Aye, I suppose. It's really no my job, we've got a tea lady," the student nurse said. Then she switched the kettle on as Sarah and Rachael walked together to meet up with Hunter.

"Derek, I know it's your lunch hour, but do you mind eating it up here and if anything crops up will you cover for me while I show the police around?" Sarah asked.

"Of course, no problem," Derek said.

Chapter Nineteen

"There are enough of us to make search parties and look for little Nicky Cowper," Tim said. "Bear, you and Ailsa search the caravans and the surrounding areas. Mel, will you and Gillian search through the farmhouse? Simon and I can look around the barns and outhouses."

"No problem," Mel said.

"What can Sophie and I do?" Lucky asked Tim.

"Search that wooded area and around the bonfire, will you, Lucky?" Tim said without even glancing at Sophie.

"How can I help, big man?" Cameron asked Tim.

"Cameron, can you ask for a recent picture of the wee one from her folks? Take a picture of that with your phone and then call your dad and get an All Ports Warning issued for Nicky."

"No problem. I'll find out from her parents what she was wearing, too." Cameron jogged away in the direction of the caravans.

Bear and Ailsa marched smartly behind him in step. She wasn't as tall as Bear, but with her athletic build and long legs, she kept pace.

"It's very cold and damp today, isn't it?" Bear said.

"Yes, I hope the little girl was wearing warm clothes. It wouldn't take long for a wee one to suffer from hypothermia."

"I'm certainly glad of my fleece." He then pulled his ski hat more firmly onto his head. "You lose a lot of heat from your head, too, don't you?"

"Yes, about seven to ten percent."

"Is that all? I thought it was about half."

Ailsa laughed. "No, not so. I think that came from some erroneous tests done in the fifties. American military researchers exposed subjects to frigid temperatures. Although the subjects' bodies were all bundled up and kept warm, their heads were not."

"No wonder they were found to have lost a lot of heat through their heads."

As Bear and Ailsa arrived at the caravans, they saw Cameron was leaving Jock Cowper's home, wandering across the field talking into his phone. "Dad, this little girl has gone missing." There was a pause while he listened to Hunter's reply. "I know it's not that long, Dad. But she's only five years old!"

"Five is very little to be out all night," Ailsa said to Bear. "No way our parents would have left it until the morning to look for us,"

"The hours your dad worked, would he have noticed you were gone?" Bear replied. He knocked on Jock's caravan door and pulled a notebook out of his pocket. "Be prepared, like a good boy scout," he answered Ailsa's questioning glance.

"Hello Mr Cowper. I'm Ailsa Myerscough, one of the guests staying at Landsmuir. This is my friend, Bear. He is a police detective."

"Aye, lass," Jock Cowper said. "We thought Nicky was staying with the wife's brother, Jonny, in that van there. But this morning when I went knocking, she wasn't there. The wife's in bits and I just don't know where to start."

"Of course, that was why you asked Simon for help tracing your wee girl this morning," Bear said.

"Aye, so you're really a copper?" Jock asked. "We don't see many that look like you."

"Yes, I'm a Detective Constable. There's a group of us just staying with the Lands this weekend. Can I ask you a few questions and then Ailsa and I will check each of the caravans?"

"Well I don't think that's necessary. We've looked inside already, you know," Jock said.

"It's just to make sure," Ailsa said softly. "When did you last see Nicky?"

"Her mum saw her when she went off to the school. But

when she got back the wife was out, so Nicky just went next door to her Uncle Jonny. At first when I asked Jonny, he said he hadn't seen her, then he remembered," Jock said.

"When did she leave her uncle's?" Bear asked.

"Well, we don't really know."

"What do you mean, you don't know?" Bear asked.

"She must have slipped out of Jonny's when he was talking with Mr Robin or his pal. I asked Mr Simon if he had seen her when you were all out in the fields, because she hadn't come back for her tea."

"Did she come back later?" Ailsa asked.

"Her cousin said she and her brother were back in Jonny's, having a sleepover. So the wife and I were happy to have a bit of rumpy-pumpy, if you know what I mean? So little time to ourselves, ken?"

"Didn't you go next door and give the wee one a kiss goodnight, Mrs Cowper?" Ailsa's voice betrayed her horror and disbelief.

"Nope."

"Don't you think that might have been nice?" Ailsa's voice rose.

"Do you know how hard it is for the wife and I to get good old-fashioned sex, living with two kids in a caravan?" Jock Cowper said belligerently.

Bear put his hand on Ailsa's leg and shook his head. "Mr Cowper, was your son at his uncle's?"

"Aye, and the kids thought it would be a laugh just to say Nicky was there too. They don't know, do they?"

"What was Nicky wearing last time you saw her?" Bear asked the two parents.

"She was dressed for school," the mother said from the door of the caravan. "I always dress her right nice, white blouse, grey skirt, grey socks and bright red shoes. She likes her red shoes," Mrs Cowper sobbed.

"What about a jacket or a cardigan to keep her warm?" Ailsa asked.

"Aye, she had a jacket on when she went to school. But she must have left it in Jonny's when she slipped out. It's still there," Mrs Cowper said.

"Daft wee lassie," Jock said.

"She's only five. Someone should have been looking out for her," Ailsa said.

Bear frowned at her and signaled to be quiet. He didn't want the parents becoming defensive and withdrawing permission for them to intervene. He knew their current search was unofficial, but time was of the essence and he wanted to look in all the caravans to find out what Uncle Jonny and Robin had been talking about that was so important they missed a little girl running away. There was no way Robin could have got into the caravan, so they must have been talking outside.

"I think you have given our friend a photo of Nicky," Bear said.

"Yes, I had her new school photo. It was the clearest picture," Mrs Cowper sniffed.

"Thanks very much. His father is a Detective Inspector and will spread the word to all our officers." Bear smiled. "Just for elimination purposes, may we take a quick look around all the caravans?"

"You never know. The wee one may be hiding and thinking all this attention is funny," Ailsa said.

"She'll no think it's funny when I get hold of her," Jock growled.

Bear and Ailsa had a look around the Cowper's home. It was small but Bear was amazed at how much could be fitted into the space. Everything was neat and tidy, and it was clear Mrs Cowper had a place for everything and put each item away when it was not in use.

"What a pity they couldn't get rid of the smell of stale cigarette smoke and body odour," Ailsa whispered to Bear.

It did not take them long to look in all the caravan's nooks and crannies, in case Nicky Cowper was hiding in a tight corner. They followed Jock to the caravans owned by his brother and his wife, then to the one his cousin and her husband lived in. This one was a bit bigger than the others but, as the couple had four children, Bear thought it probably needed to be larger. He couldn't imagine having to entertain four restless kids on a wet weekend in January in this confined space.

"No sign of the wee one," Bear said to Ailsa.

"Yet," she replied. "Can we just pop in and have a look around your sister's home now please?" Ailsa asked Jock.

"I don't know if they're home, but let's see."

Bear and Ailsa followed Jock to the caravan at the end of the row.

Chapter Twenty

"Can we see the bodies?" Rachael asked Sarah.

"You can, but it's not very unusual to have old folks dying in these wards."

"I know, but it must be unusual for it to happen so close together?"

"I'm not sure exactly when old Mrs Roberts passed, but Mrs Button must have been very recently," Sarah said. "The doctors have confirmed life extinct and time of death for both patients."

"Don't worry about that for our part. We'll have to arrange postmortems anyway," Hunter replied.

"Surely that won't be necessary when they died in hospital?"

"I think it will be. They were found dead in such short order," Rachael said.

"Yes, there's close proximity of time as well as place," Hunter said.

"We found Mrs Button just after her teatime, I mean. She's got her tea and a piece of fruit cake. Mrs Button was partial to a piece of fruit cake. Oh God! This is awful. And with me as senior nurse. I mean, I know Derek is also a senior nurse, but he's on overtime so this happened on my watch," Sarah sighed, then looked at Rachael. "Who do you want to see first, sis?"

"Let's stop in at Mrs Roberts first, if it's alright with you," Hunter said.

"No problem. Then we'll need to get them ready for the relatives."

"That may not be possible, depending on what we find."

"What do you mean?" Sarah asked Rachael as she led them

down the corridor to Mrs Roberts' room.

"If we find evidence of foul play, we'll need the bodies just as they are before our pathologist makes initial inspections followed by postmortems," Hunter explained.

"I think foul play is highly unlikely, don't you, Inspector?" Sarah said coldly.

"Not from what I've heard so far."

The three of them entered the room in which Mrs Roberts lay. Although the hospital ward was extremely hot, Rachael felt a cold chill run down her spine, and she shuddered. The room was small with a little wet room leading off it to the right. There was a large window, but the room was dark because the blind had been lowered. The blinds had been closed over the window in the door and the internal window as well to prevent prying eyes staring at the corpse.

Hunter could not be sure what he was looking at, the room was so dark. That made it feel cramped and airless too. He crossed the room in a few steps and raised the window blind. Suddenly the dark, gloomy little room seemed bright again.

He stared at the body. "Why are there marks around Mrs Roberts' wrists?" he asked Sarah.

"There aren't," she said defiantly.

"There are, Sarah. See, here, and here." Rachael pointed out the marks to her sister. "It looks as if the old lady had been restrained. Would that be necessary?"

"I can't think why."

Hunter paused to think for a moment and then gently untucked the covers at the bottom of the bed. He grimaced at what he saw. "There are marks around the patient's ankles too, as if she's been tied to the bed or held tightly. And is that a mark at her neck?" he asked.

"Oh my God! Surely that's a shadow. I have no explanation for this at all." Sarah stared at the body in horror.

"Boss look at this." Rachael pointed to blood stains on the old lady's night gown.

"Sarah I'm sorry but we have to bring in our pathologist. At best this is a suspicious death," Hunter said softly. "Rachael, will you go and examine my aunt's body while I phone Doctor

Sharma?"

"Of course, boss."

"We'll need Dr Sharma, Dr Murray and the photographer Sam Hutchens. I'll phone Jane and advise her of the situation to keep MIT in the loop too. Then, I suppose, I'll need to speak to Andy Roberts and my folks to tell them what's going on."

"Would it be easier if I spoke to the family members, boss?"

"Easier for me, but not for you and not necessarily for them. No, as Senior Investigating Officer that unpleasant duty falls to me, but thank you, Rache. I'll do that bit." Hunter sighed and took out his phone to speak to Meera Sharma.

***

When Meera arrived with David Murray, they went directly to the relatives' room to express their condolences to Andy Roberts and Hunter's Parents.

"I am so very sorry for your loss," Meera said to Andy.

"I'm just so shocked. Gran looked like she was getting better. Did she suffer?" he asked Meera anxiously.

"I cannot tell until I have finished the postmortem. But I hope not."

Meera moved towards Hunters parents. They were sitting talking to David Murray. Tears were running down their faces and misery shone from their eyes. Angie, the student nurse, came in with refills of coffee, David thanked her and Meera sat down beside the Wilsons too.

"This isnae ma job," Angie said, belligerently. "We've got tea ladies to do tea. I'm training to be a nurse."

David repeated that they were grateful to her for the extra duties she was carrying out and then went to speak to Andy Roberts. He noticed the young man's horrified expression and tried to comfort him.

The pathologists talked to the relatives for over half an hour. Meera saw no reason to hurry away. They'd had a dreadful shock and deserved the time they needed from David and herself. If she was honest, it also gave Sam Hutchens time to take all the photographs they needed of both deceased women.

Sam knocked on the door of the relatives' room to tell Meera and David that she had finished her work. Meera introduced her to Andy and to Hunter's parents.

"I'm sorry, this is such a sad time for you," she said. Then she scuttled away to develop the photographs. Sam expressed herself better through her pictures than with words. Meera knew that.

Meera and David walked around the ward until they found Hunter and Rachael. Meera hugged Hunter.

"I am so terribly sorry, darling," she said. "I know how much your Aunt Sandra meant to you. This is awful for you, and for your parents too."

Hunter held her and kissed her hair. He breathed her in as if he never wanted to part from her. Then he became aware that David and Rachael were staring at the walls and the floor respectively. Hunter smiled and let go of Meera.

"Do you each want to take one corpse or do you both want to see both?"

"When we're both here, let's both visit both patients," Meera said.

"Good idea," David agreed. "Lead the way to Mrs Roberts first. She was found first."

Hunter began to lead the way. Then, suddenly, he stopped.Meera and David almost walked over him. "Rachael, will you ask Sarah for a list of everybody who had access to both Mrs Roberts and Mrs Button for the last forty-eight hours, and get uniformed officers out here to interview each of them?" Hunter asked.

"That'll be a lot of people, boss."

"Then you better get started," Hunter replied. He continued to Mrs Roberts' room with Meera and David.

Chapter Twenty-One

Sir Peter Myerscough was reading a well-thumbed copy of a book from the prison library when Ian Thomson entered his cell. Sir Peter looked up. "Hello, Ian. Have you ever been into St. Giles church?"

"What's that?" Ian asked.

"You know, the High Kirk of Edinburgh on the Royal Mile. It's about a third of the way down if you walk from the castle to Holyrood Palace."

"Aye, I know where it is, Sir Pete, but why would I visit, and why are we talking about that? I'm here to talk about Mansoor."

Sir Peter pointed to the title of his book, *The Traitor of St. Giles*. It was part of the Templar series of books by Michael Jecks.

"It's no about that St. Giles though, is it?"

"No, not that building. But it made me think about happier times, visiting the cathedral when the children were younger. I love that view looking down the Royal Mile, especially on a sunny day when the distinctive crown steeple is such a prominent feature of the city skyline. I like to let my mind wander when I'm sitting in here," Sir Peter said.

"I know what you mean," Ian said. "You got a minute to talk through a problem with me?"

"Come in, sit down. After all the help and advice you've given me since I was convicted, I could hardly refuse."

"Young Jamie and Frankie are doing their best, but they've managed to get Thomson's Top Cars attached to Arjun Mansoor again. Just when I thought I'd got rid of the bastard." Ian turned the hard-back chair around and straddled it. Sir Peter swung his feet from the bed and sat opposite him in the small cell.

"What's happened?" Sir Pete asked.

Ian looked at the wall behind Sir Peter's head and took a deep breath. He told his friend about the contract the boys had entered into with Connor O'Grady. He got to the end of the tale and finally looked Sir Peter in the eye. "What do you think? I need to keep the boys out of trouble. You know what they're like."

"To be honest, I think Jamie and Frankie are doing a great job running the business and caring for Frankie's twins. He's got girls, hasn't he?"

"Aye, aye that's all okay. But O'Grady is a serious slug. He's taken over supply of cocaine for Mansoor and he does it under the cover of his legit delivery firm. I just don't want him pulling the boys into that kind of dirty business. Drugs destroy so many lives. I can't tell you how much I hate the pushers," Ian said.

Sir Peter smiled. "You don't need to tell me about drugs destroying lives."

Ian nodded. "Aye, right enough. How the mighty have fallen."

"Thanks so much."

"Sorry, no offense," Ian said.

"None taken of course. As far as the boys are concerned, the only problems I can think of are, if the drugs were hidden in vans that they drive about to deliver. Or, of course, if Thomson's Top Cars was visited by the police and drugs were found on the premises," Sir Peter said.

"Either is perfectly possible, Sir Pete. You can see why I worry," Ian said. "Anyway, I can't sit here talking to you all day. It'll no look good for me to be mixing with a toff like you. Give me a cigarette and make it look like a useful visit."

"Here you go, Ian. Don't worry about the boys too much. They're not as daft as you think."

Sir Peter got back onto the bed and continued reading his book.

Chapter Twenty-Two

When I came to this time my fear was worse. I began to panic. What if nobody found me? What if I died? What if my baby died inside me? I knew Bob was already gone, but I didn't want to think about that. I loved him. I needed him now. Our baby needed him.

I sobbed and gasped. I held my breath and listened to my pulse. It felt like my heart was going to explode. It was pumping harder and faster now as I thought more about what might happen. I felt so thirsty. I chewed my bottom lip like I do when I'm nervous, unhappy or scared, but that didn't help. It tasted nasty, bloody, salty, metallic.

All of a sudden, I realised it must be Bob's blood. I realised how much I wanted Bob, and I wanted someone to find me, I wanted out. I wanted to save my baby.

I screamed.

Then I was overcome by a ghastly bout of diarrhea and the need to empty my bladder. I couldn't help it. I was just so frightened. It all poured out, liquid, smelly, sticky. Too horrible to think about. Ghastly.

Now the car smelt even worse and I was sitting in my own poo. It was too much for me. My muscles kept cramping as they were held in the same position. It caused me such a lot of pain. A wave of nausea passed over me. I swallowed the bile.

When would somebody find me? When would they come and save me, save my baby? How could anybody find me? I could hear the road, but couldn't see it. Maybe nobody would see me? Oh God, the panic began to rise inside again.

I needed someone to save me, like Bob had saved the rabbit. I needed someone to save me so I could save the baby. My baby. Our baby. Bob's baby. It was a relief when I passed out again.

Chapter Twenty-Three

"That's a biting wind for a wee one to be out in," Ailsa said.

"Yep. Very cold." Bear nodded. He, Ailsa and Jock strode across the field to the next caravan.

"My sister, Maggie, and her husband, Jonny live here with their kids."

Maggie opened the door before they arrived. "Hello, Bro," she said. "I saw you working your way down the vans and guessed you were coming to us. Have you found the wee one, Jock?"

"Not yet, Maggie. Mr Simon is getting all his friends to help us look."

"That's right good of him."

"Could we have just a quick look around your home in case Nicky is hiding and thinks of it as a joke?" Bear asked.

The woman looked over her shoulder. "Jonny, you okay for Jock and these folks to have a wee shifty here for Nicky?"

"What fur? She's no here, Jock."

"They just want to rule out all the vans so that they can start looking further afield with a clean slate, Jonny. They'll no' take a minute. Will ye?" Jock looked at Bear.

"No, not long at all. It's just a double check," Bear said as he started climbing the few steps into the caravan, despite the lack of an invitation.

Maggie stepped back to make way for him.

"Come in," she said belatedly.

Ailsa moved towards the bedrooms while Bear started opening cupboards in the kitchen area. Ailsa looked in the storage areas under the beds and in the ceiling above the shower room but found nothing. Bear finished his search in the kitchen and living areas and drew a blank. Just as he turned to thank Maggie and Jonny for allowing them in, Maggie saw his eye catch a darkened area in the kitchen ceiling which covered the reset lights. Her heart sank. She glowered at Jonny.

"Do you see that shadow in the kitchen ceiling?" Bear asked Ailsa.

"Oh, yes. A bit small for a wee girl though and not easy for Nicky to get into," she said.

"Quite right dear. Probably just a bulb that's broken. You must fix that, Jonny," Maggie said. She tried to move forward and get Bear and Ailsa out of the caravan, but Bear was standing below the shadow and was far too big a man to submit to her shoving.

He stood with his feet shoulder width apart and raised his arms. He moved the tile that covered the lighting and put his hand into the void. He pulled out a large bag that was filled with white powder.

"Oh my, oh my. What have we here?" Bear looked at Ailsa. She was standing in front of the door. "Have you any idea what this is or how it got here?" he asked Maggie and Jonny.

"What is that?" Jonny asked.

"I can't be sure, but I'd guess it's about a kilo of cocaine. That's worth somewhere around forty-thousand pounds, and you didn't know it was here?" Bear asked. The doubt in his voice was evident.

"Of course it's not fucking cocaine! It's flour for your baking, isn't it, Maggie?" Jonny asked.

"Don't you get me dragged into this, Jonny Baird," Maggie said. "If you're up to your old tricks, you're on your own. That's not anything of mine, son," she said to Bear. She looked terrified.

"How would we know it was there anyway?" Jonny said defiantly. "It was hidden, wasn't it?"

"Who has access to your home that might have hidden this if it wasn't you, sir?" Bear asked, turning the bag in one hand.

"Yes. Who are you going to drop in it this time Jonny?" Maggie asked as she burst into tears. Ailsa put an arm around her shoulders and the woman turned her back towards her husband.

"Well let's deal with this practically. The most important

thing right now is to find Nicky. I'll take this bag of powder and give you a receipt for it and get it tested," Bear said, holding the large packet in one hand. "But I have to say that, if I'm right, you'll need to explain how it got into your home and why you have it."

"You and your family have no plans to move on, Jock?" Bear asked.

"No, we'll be here 'til after Christmas. We have a stall at the Christmas market in Princes Street. Toys and jewelry," Jock said.

***

Mel and Gillian walked back to the farmhouse to begin searching each room

"The poor wee soul must be terrified, don't you think Mel?"

"Yes. Not to mention cold and hungry."

Robin came into the kitchen. "You girls back for a coffee already?"

"That would be lovely, but it's not why we're here. Tim has asked us to check that Nicky isn't hiding here somewhere," Mel said.

"The house is rather full. I think one of us would have seen her, don't you?" Robin asked, sarcastically.

"Well, we'll just take a quick look around to make sure, but that coffee would be most welcome," Gillian said.

She watched as Robin took mugs off the mug tree on the work surface and poured three servings of strong, filtered coffee out of the pot. She couldn't help but wonder how Robin had coped with such a sudden and drastic change in his life after his rugby accident. Most of the time he seemed to be very calm and always kept himself busy, but occasionally Gillian had noticed his expression change, sometimes to one of anger, other times depression and sometimes. When Lucky was around Robin became quite euphoric. Lucky seemed to be good for Robin. She noticed that each change came swiftly.

Gillian poured milk into each of the mugs.

"Do either of you take sugar?" she asked

"No thanks. I'm watching my figure." Robin smiled.

Mel shook her head. "Come on then. Let's take a look around and see if we can find this wee monster. I bet she's hiding out for a joke or something."

The women went upstairs to search through each of the bedrooms. They paid particular attention to the areas under the beds, in the wardrobes and on top of the wardrobes in case Nicky had found a good place to hide there. They checked in baths and shower cubicles and even took everything out of the airing cupboard in the hall. But they found nothing even remotely like a child anywhere. So they repacked the cupboard and came back downstairs.

They checked the two downstairs bedrooms. The larger of the two was en-suite, used by Robin. They found a stack of 'lads mags' in there. They acknowledged them between themselves but said nothing to Robin. The smaller bedroom was little more than a cupboard. It had no window and was probably a larder or storage room when the farmhouse was built. Above the kitchen, Cameron had a room with sofa bed at the top of the steep stairs. There was a shower room, too, but no Nicky Cowper was to be found.

Mel and Gillian returned to the kitchen and placed their coffee mugs on the table.

"Any joy?" Robin said.

"No. To be honest we didn't expect to find her, but we had to make sure she's not here. We'd all look really stupid if we set up a full police search and found her in the bathroom!" Mel said.

"Of course. Don't let me stand in your way. I'm off to make some lentil soup for lunch. Have you seen my mother on your travels?"

"No, no sign of your Mum. Maybe she's out with Simon or Derek."

"Must be." Robin rolled himself into the back kitchen to start preparing the soup.

Mel and Gillian followed him. They looked in each of the cupboards and even in the oven, but no Nicky. They checked every cupboard in the main kitchen.

Mel pulled the cushions off the furniture in the living room. Gillian even looked behind the sofa, but Nicky was nowhere to be seen. Somewhat dejected by their lack of success, they went to say their goodbyes to Robin.

"Just before you go, could you get me another loaf of bread out of the freezer?" Robin asked.

"What, you don't make it fresh every day?" Gillian smiled. "Is this it?" She showed him an oblong shape wrapped in cling film and a plastic bag.

He looked over. "No! Put that back," he said sharply. "It'll be bigger than that and on a higher shelf. That is nothing to do with you," he frowned. "Yes, that's it," he said to her second attempt.

The women left the house and Gillian turned to Mel." Robin was a bit short with me about that bread, wasn't he?"

"I think I would be a bit short sometimes, if I were stuck in a wheelchair," Mel said. She and Gillian headed outside to find the others.

Chapter Twenty-Four

Jamie was in the showroom of Thomson's Top Cars when he saw Frankie walk in from the garage. Neither of them felt very clever about making a deal with Connor O'Grady.

"How could we have taken on that bastard O'Grady without running it passed my pop?" Jamie asked.

"Because your pop was talking about closing us down and we tried to do right by saving the place."

"We should have known better."

"True enough," Frankie sighed.

"Do you want the good news or the bad news?"

"There's good news?" Frankie looked surprised.

"The garage part of the business will be busy all week."

"That's good. Not so much pressure to sell cars. What's the bad news then?"

"The work is ten re-sprays and five MOTs for our friend Connor O'Grady."

"Fucking brilliant."

"My thoughts exactly when he arranged to bring them in this afternoon, cuz. He says he needs them done quick as two of his vans have gone missing."

"Missing? How do you lose a bright red van?" Frankie shrugged.

"Dunno. He says the drivers havenae come back either."

"That's just weird."

"Aye. D'you think we should go and see my pop and talk it over?"

"Probably. Maybe we could get an emergency visit today."

"That doesn't happen very often, but we can try. After all, we're regulars." Jamie chuckled.

"We are. And so is he," Frankie joked. "Is that a good thing?"

"It might be, today."

***

"Hi Pop." Jamie smiled at his father.

"Jamie, lad. Frankie," Ian nodded at the chairs on the other side of the table in front of him. "I've been thinking about Connor O'Grady."

"You've probably thought about it a lot, Uncle Ian. We weren't trying to cause a problem. We thought it would help getting new business in the doors."

"And from anybody but the wanker, you'd have been right, Frankie. Now I was talking about it to Sir Peter," Ian said.

"Blondie's pop."

"Aye, they big cop. Well, he thinks that you should be okay as long as you check the vans when they're brought in. Check them right carefully. Only you two can do it. If there's any stuff in those vans when they get to you, don't take them. Right?"

"Right," Jamie said. "But what if they're already there?"

"What's that? He's got vans to you already?"

"Yes, Pop."

"And where have you to get them back to? All to his main depot?"

"Five to the main depot, the others are to be taken to places all over the city."

"Fucking, shitting, bastard." Ian held his head in his hands. "Those ten are the most likely to be dirty."

"We don't even need to look inside them. They're only in for a respray black to red," Jamie said.

"How convenient. You don't have to open up the engines or inspect them for that Then you move them around the city and risk getting caught rather than him or his men," Ian said. "He's clever. I've got to give him that, he's clever."

"And he's got a couple of vans gone missing. He's raging about it," Frankie added.

"I don't doubt that he is. Some driver'll have found a dirty parcel and vamooshed with it," Ian said. "Right, only do what you need to do to get the spraying done, then get those vans out of my place, pronto. You hear me?"

"Aye, but should we no' just give the police a shout, Uncle Ian?" Frankie asked. "We could come clean to Blondie. He's one of the good guys."

"He is, but he's straight, not like his pop was," Jamie said.

"Exactly, my son. It was coming clean to young Myerscough that got me banged up in here the last time."

***

Jamie and Frankie talked about their meeting as they drove home. Jamie was not even breaking the speed limit, so Frankie knew he was concentrating on the jobs for O'Grady. As he looked around, Frankie saw the roof of a bright red van off the road. He couldn't see much of it, but some of the grass and bushes at the side of the road seemed to have been squashed. He was just tall enough to see the roof over the top.

"Jamie, is that a DayGo van? It's the right colour."

"Where? I cannae see it. Mind you it's about where we saw that van roll when we were coming home with Donna and the twins the other day," Jamie said.

"Shall we go and take a look?" Frankie asked.

"I really want to get back and see what's happening with those vans. If Mark's fine we can always come back."

"Fair enough. Cos I'm sure that's the DayGo red colour. We might get a reward from Mr O'Grady for finding it."

Chapter Twenty-Five

No wonder babies cry when their nappies need changed. It feels awful just sitting in shit. It's bad enough when it's warm, but when it goes cold it goes hard and folds into your skin. It is truly revolting.

And then I looked at Bob's eyes. Bob's eyes were still staring at me, but the colour had gone all cloudy and the black bits in the middle, whatever they're called, didn't change. It was scary. I decided to close his eyes, but I found I couldn't move my hands. My fingers were gripping the steering wheel so tight that I couldn't let go. Fight or flight, I thought. Well there wasn't going to be any flight, I could guarantee that, because Bob was dead, and the steering wheel and that horrid tree branch had me pegged well into place. The engine was tight up against my legs. I had even less chance of moving them than my hands.

I have no idea how long I sat there. I stared at the dried blood all around me. My mind wandered, like I was in a set of a horror movie. Bob always liked horror movies, but I never did. 'This one's not suitable for my wee Linda,' he would say. The blood that was red when we crashed was turning a funny shade of brown now. There were flies, big fat flies, all around me.

And I was so thirsty. How long can you live without drinking? I know you can live for two or three weeks without eating. And I didn't feel hungry. The smell of the blood and the shit and the piss was too awful to make me think about eating. But I was thirsty, so thirsty. I licked my lips but just tasted the dried blood.

Yuck!

How I would love a big cool glass of Magners over ice, or a Bucks Fizz. But Bucks Fizz was for a celebration and there was no celebrating going on here. Even a soda water and lime would do.

Why didn't someone come and help me? Work must have noticed I was missing by now. Somebody had to be looking for me. Surely somebody would find me soon.

Chapter Twenty-Six

Tim and Simon strode across to the outbuildings. They were dressed warmly because the morning was sharp.

"Do you see much of Lucky, nowadays?" Tim asked.

"A fair bit. When my father died, the farm was in trouble. We had arrears of taxes to pay and Her Majesty's Revenue and Customs were not for waiting. Lucky lent us the money. He just needs to store a few things in the old outhouses from time to time," Simon said. "And to be honest, we rarely use them now."

"What sort of things? He's got that huge estate. He can't be tight for space?"

"No, of course not. It's just that he's a bit away and we're closer to Edinburgh and Glasgow if something needs transporting. His driver Cameron often picks up the packages or drives away the vans. He seems a nice enough lad."

"He is. He's my boss's son, but both Cameron and Lucky have had their issues, you know?"

"Oh, I know. Lucky was very open about that. It was good for Robin to hear that someone else we know has a life-long struggle ahead of them," Simon replied.

"I know what you mean. Misery loves company."

"Yes, something like that."

"How does Robin cope? I mean, he was so active and a real sportsman before his accident," Tim asked.

"Oh yes, he was Mr Party Time, no doubt about that. Life is much quieter for him now."

"How did he and Derek meet?" Tim asked.

"He was in hospital for about a year and sometimes I would pop in to visit him and I'd take him down to the cafe for a drink or a bite to eat, just for a change. One day when I was with him it was so busy. Derek was in for his lunch and asked if he could join our table. We all got talking and the rest, as they say, is history." Simon looked at Tim. "Derek has been really good for him and he's a gem when it comes to caring for Mum."

"It must have been really difficult since your dad passed away," Tim said.

"Yes. Mum has just been going down and down. I can't tell if it's depression or some form of dementia."

"Can't the medics tell you that? I'm sure there are tests they can do."

"You try and get her to go!"

"Fair enough," Tim smiled. "I'm not sure I would want to know if it were me either."

"Enough procrastinating, Timmy boy. Let's find that wee girl."

***

Tim followed Simon into the first barn. He climbed swiftly up the ladder to examine the loft. Simon went in and out of stalls poking at bundles of straw. He hoped they would find Nicky fit and well l.

In the second barn, Simon went up to the loft. Tim searched down below. In the third stall he could not believe what he was seeing. "Simon! Come down quickly! It's your Mum!"

"What are you talking about, Tim?"

"Your Mum is here. She's on the ground. Are you all right, Mrs Land? Did you trip or fall? What were you doing out here?" Tim asked.

The woman's skin was cold to the touch and her lips were quite blue. Tim felt for a pulse. It was weak, but it was there. He tried to wake Mrs Land, but she just groaned.

"Oh God! Mum, wake up, Mum. Come on!" Simon shouted as he entered the stall.

Tim glanced at Simon and took out his mobile phone. He called Ailsa and asked her to hurry back over to the house. He explained that he had found Mrs Land unconscious and cold in the barns.

"Take her to the farmhouse, Tim. I'll meet you there. And call an ambulance, bro, will you? We'll need paramedics and their equipment," Ailsa said. "Bear, can you finish up here with Jock and Jonny? Tim and Simon have found Mrs Land in one of the barns and she's in a bad way."

"How did she get there?" Bear asked. "And why was she there alone?"

"Lord alone knows!" Ailsa exclaimed. "We'll deal with the incident first and do the whys later."

"Shouldn't you call an ambulance first, lassie?" Jock asked.

"Yes, my brother will do that, but I'll get there sooner.""I'm an emergency doctor."

"Ooh, la-di-dah," Jonny said sarcastically.

"No, not 'la-di-dah'. It's just what I do." She turned and jogged at a steady pace back to the farmhouse.

"You're on thin enough ice as it is without wanting to make any extra enemies, Jonny," Maggie said to her husband.

Jonny stormed back into the caravan and slammed the door.

"He's going to break that door if he's not careful," Bear said.

"It'll not be the first time, son," Maggie said. She pointed to the repairs on the hinges of the door.

"Maggie, I need to give a receipt for this bag of powder. Do you have a set of scales we could use to weigh it?" Bear asked.

"Of course. Come on. Let's do this," she said.

Chapter Twenty-Seven

Hunter walked into the relatives' room. He looked around and sat down in an empty chair opposite his parents. They looked so miserable. They looked old. It made him feel sad. He felt responsible for their sadness, although intellectually he knew the fault was not his.

"Would you like more coffee?" Hunter asked his parents.

"No, son. I think your mother and I will twitch if we drink any more coffee," his Dad said.

"What about you, Andy?"

"No, mate. I'm like your folks. I've had far too much caffeine today already. What's going on now?"

"The pathologists are carrying out initial examinations here and then your grandmother and my aunt will have to be taken to the morgue for postmortems."

Andy Roberts stared anxiously at Hunter. "I didn't think you needed a postmortem if the person died in hospital. That's what my dad told me anyway. I phoned him. He can't believe this."

"Normally that's true," Hunter said. "The problem we have here is that there are marks on the bodies that neither we, nor the nursing staff, can explain."

"What on earth does that mean?"

"Please don't cry, Mum. I hate to see you cry," Hunter sighed.

"Christian, son, your Aunt Sandra has been my best friend for nearly fifty years, your father's only sister. Of course her death is going to make me cry, especially when you say strange things like that."

"I understand, Mum," Hunter said. "Meera has confirmed that the marks Rachael and I found are unusual. That means that we must consider the deaths as unexplained. When we have to treat the deaths as unexplained a full postmortem examination on each body will be required."

"When will we be able to bury my gran then?" Andy asked.

"Her body will be released as soon as possible, but I honestly can't give you a time-scale. It really depends on what the pathologists find," Hunter said.

"What on earth do I tell my dad? And my auntie will go mental. What do I tell her?" Andy asked.

"If they need to speak to me, please ask them to call. Here's my card. I'm so sorry for you and your family about all of this," Hunter said.

David Murray popped his head around the door. "That's us finished here, Hunter. Does anyone want to say goodbye to their loved one before the bodies are removed?"

Hunter, his parents and Andy Roberts all walked back along the corridor. The nursing staff hadn't been permitted to clean up the bodies or dress them. Still the families found comfort in the visits.

"Will my dad and aunt be able to see my gran?" Andy asked.

"They might if they contact our office at the mortuary soon enough. Are they local?" David Murray asked.

"Dad's in Musselburgh and Auntie Helen is in Wallyford, so they're not far," Andy replied.

"Here's my card. That phone number is for the office Dr Sharma and I share at the mortuary. Your family are free to contact us," David said.

Andy nodded and walked back with Hunter and his parents towards the exit of the ward.

"Do you need a lift home?" Hunter asked him.

"No, I've got my bike. I'll be fine. But thank you."

Hunter's Mum took his hand. "We would appreciate a lift if you're offering, son."

"Of course, Mum. That goes without saying. I'm not sure where Rachael parked the car. She is making a list of everybody who visited or treated Mrs Roberts and Aunt Sandra. You have a seat over there and I'll go and find her. Then she can go and get the car and bring it to the main entrance of the building," Hunter said.

"Son, we've spent such a long time sitting. I think we'll just stand and wait at the entrance to the building. There's a bench outside the Anne Ferguson Building, we can sit on that if we need to. It'll give us a chance to get a bit of fresh air and a change of scene," his Dad said.

Hunter gazed at his father. He seemed to have aged ten years since they had last been together, enjoying his mother's scones and squabbling about the crossword in the newspaper. Now, facing up to the death of his little sister was too hard for the old man, that was clear from his expression, his stance and the pallor of his complexion. Hunter patted his dad on the shoulder and went to look for Rachael.

Chapter Twenty-Eight

Just as Simon lifted his mother from the cold straw, Gillian and Mel arrived from the house.

"What's happened?" Gillian asked.

"We found Mrs Land out cold, in the straw of that second barn," Tim said.

"Oh no. Is she going to be okay?" Gillian asked.

"I hope so. Ailsa is going to meet us at the house. I've phoned an ambulance to get Mrs Land to the hospital but, no matter how fast they get there, Ailsa will be there faster. Could you and Mel finish searching the barns for little Nicky while I help Simon?"

"No problem," Mel said. She turned to Gillian and they moved towards the next barn to take over where the men had left off.

"Let me help you carry your Mum," Tim turned to look at Simon, but the farmer had already started walking determinedly to the farmhouse. It would start getting dark soon. He didn't like to think what would have happened to Mrs Land if they hadn't found her.

***

Ailsa was in the kitchen filling hot water bottles with warm water, when Tim and Simon returned.

"Robin told me your mum has an electric blanket, but these will give her immediate heat, whereas the electric blanket will take a while to warm up. We may not have time."

"Don't use the electric blanket with those," Robin said.

"I wasn't going to," Ailsa said sourly.

"Can you take your mum up to her room? Put her under the

covers on her bed," Ailsa said to Simon.

She watched him carry his mother gently up the stairs. She wrapped the hot water bottles in tea-towels and handed two of them to Tim.

"Did Mrs Land regain full consciousness at all when Simon was carrying her?" she asked Tim.

"I'm honestly not sure. He was well away before I even turned around." Tim left to take the hot water bottles upstairs. He watched as Simon tenderly put them on either side of his mother.

"Make your mother a cup of hot sweet tea, will you, Robin?" Ailsa asked. She turned and bounded up the stairs and into Mrs Land's room with more hot water bottles.

"Will she be alright, Ailsa?"

"I hope so, Simon. I'll do my best until the ambulance gets here." Ailsa loosened the older woman's clothes so that her blood could flow more freely. She put one hot water bottle at Mrs Land's feet and wrapped another firmly before putting it on her stomach.

"Her breathing is stronger than when we found her. And she did stir a little in my arms."

"To be honest, just the warmth of your body will have helped." Ailsa smiled. She pulled the covers more tightly around Mrs Land. "How long is it since you called the ambulance, Tim?" she asked.

"About ten, fifteen minutes, maybe." He looked at his watch. "Yes, nearer fifteen."

"Of course. We're out in the sticks here. It takes a while for them to get to us," Simon said.

"Tim, could you go down and get the tea Robin made for his Mum?" Ailsa asked.

"You can't give her tea when she's unconscious."

"No, but it's something Robin can do. And it will be here when she does wake up."

Tim nodded and ran down the stairs three at a time as he left to fetch the tea.

"Has Mum woken up yet?" Robin asked, as Tim reached the kitchen.

"Not yet, but she did stir." Tim replied. "That's got to be a good sign, hasn't it?"

"I hope so," Robin said. "Look, there's the ambulance now. That's quick to get out here." He opened the door and directed the paramedics to his mother's bedroom. "I haven't been able to get up those stairs in almost ten years, and never missed getting to the upper floor of the house until today," he told Tim.

It was almost twenty minutes until the paramedics had finished the work Ailsa had started. They stabilised Mrs Land on a drip and wrapped her in a foil blanket to get her body temperature higher, faster.

"How's Mum?" Robin asked Simon when he came downstairs.

"Holding on."

"I know she drives me crazy. But I do care," Robin said.

"I know you do! She knows that too," Simon replied. "Ailsa is going to go in the ambulance with Mum, and I'll follow in the car. Will you hold the fort here?" Simon asked his brother.

Just as the ambulance was leaving, Lucky and Sophie wandered back into the house closely followed by Cameron. They looked around the room at the anxious faces.

"We saw an ambulance arrive. What's happened? Has the girl been found?" Lucky asked.

"No, but they found my mum out in one of the barns, unconscious," Robin said. "Ailsa and Simon have gone with her to the hospital."

"God, that's awful. Your poor mother. How did she get there?" Sophie asked.

"Who knows? But she'd been there a while. She was blue with the cold, and her pulse was very weak," Robin said. "Ailsa was able to warm her up until the ambulance got here."

"Nobody in rest of the barns. Just a DayGo delivery van in one and a couple of cows in the other," Mel said as she and Gillian walked into the kitchen.

"Has everybody finished their areas?" Tim asked.

"Yep, nobody in the trees or around the wooded bit," Lucky said. "Shall we have a coffee?"

"Lucky, we forgot to look around the bonfire," Sophie said. "We forgot when we saw the ambulance, didn't we? We got side-tracked."

"No doubt you did," Tim said sarcastically. "And caring for the younger generation has never really been your thing, has it, Lady Sophie?"

Sophie blushed. "How many times do I need to say I'm sorry, Tim? I made a mistake."

"An abortion is a bit more than a mistake, Sophie," Tim whispered in her ear.

"Oh, come now, my man. There's no call for that," Lucky said.

"My man! Good God, Lucky, what century are you from?" Bear laughed.

"Don't you my man me," Tim said, standing straight and staring down at Lucky. He whispered into Lucky's ear. "Believe me, I have every call for that, and she bloody knows it. I just hope for your sake she doesn't do the same thing to you."

Tim moved away from Lucky and spoke in a louder voice. "Anyway, you've always been a nosy, lazy sod, Lucky. You enjoy your coffee. Bear and I'll clean up after you and Sophie and go and check the bonfire. Come on, Bear. We've spent all bloody day on this, but Sophie and Lucky can't be bothered to finish their piece of the puzzle."

The big men walked out of the door and the room fell silent.

"What on earth did you do to Tim to make him react like that, Sophie?" Robin asked. "He is usually so calm and polite, I have never, ever seen him behave in that way."

Sophie blushed again. "This is so embarrassing. It was a long time ago. He really should have moved on."

Lucky pulled her into his arms and held her tight. "Of course he should, angel."

"Tell, me, Sophie, how exactly do you move on when your girlfriend aborts your child?" Mel asked flatly.

Chapter Twenty-Nine

Frankie watched as head mechanic Mark took off his protective gear to speak to him. The DayGo van was getting re-sprayed from its original black to the virulent shade of red that was now the company's colour. The more Frankie thought about it, the more certain he was that this was the same colour as the bit of the van he had seen on the way back from visiting his Uncle Ian.

"What's the problem, Frankie?"

"Did you check all the vans were empty before you accepted them in?"

"Not really," Mark said. "But there's nought valuable in any of them. The odd CD or that. Anyway, my boys won't steal out the vans Frankie." The mechanic wiped his gloved hand across his forehead, leaving a vivid red streak. "Blast. I've done it again, haven't I?"

Frankie nodded. "No, it's no that, Mark. It was just that Jamie thinks we should make a note of anything that's in Mr O'Grady's vans when they come in. Because he's going to be such a big customer, like."

"Oh aye?" Mark said.

"Just to keep ourselves right, so he cannae say ought's missing when it's not."

"Aye, fine. But I havenae got time for that, Frankie. You or Jamie'll have to do it," Mark said.

"No trouble. I'll just start now."

"Well they're in the books already, Frankie. Shall we come in early tomorrow and check these vans out?" Jamie walked into the room. "You want to go and take a look at that other van at the side of the motorway on the way home, don't you?"

"It's no even five o'clock, Jamie," Mark complained.

"If you get a run of punters banging on the door in the next ten minutes, give me a call and I'll come back," Jamie said. "Remember to close up the garage, Mark. I'll lock the showroom. Come on, Frankie," Jamie smoothed his designer stubble. It wasn't necessary, but he was still conscious of the new look. Donna had said it made him look hot. He liked that.

Frankie caught Mark's eye and shrugged. He saw the mechanic put his eye protectors back on and carry on with the respray.

"Mark will be at that at least another half an hour, you know, Jamie?" Frankie said. "We should at least wait till the proper closing time. It doesn't set a good example."

"You're beginning to sound like an old woman, Frankie. Or my pop. I don't know which. Either way it's no a compliment," Jamie said. "This time of year it gets dark earlier and earlier. If we want to be able to see where this van is, and if it's a DayGo van, we still have to have some light, don't we?"

"You're right. We do," Frankie said.

"Then stop bleating and let's get going."

***

Jamie had his headlights on. He took the first turn-off past the red thing that Frankie said he could see behind the grass and shrubs on the embankment. Jamie was becoming less convinced that this was a DayGo van, or anything else interesting. Far from getting praise or even a reward from Connor O'Grady, he was sure this was a wild goose chase. Light was beginning to fade and what had been a grey, cloudy day was fast turning into a dark cloudy night. He couldn't see exactly where the van was from here off the motorway anyway. Still, he had told Frankie that they would go and look, and he was a man of his word most of the time, where Frankie was concerned, anyway.

"I'm just going to stop here and we can go over there and check out what's what. It must be around here somewhere," Jamie said.

"Thanks, cuz. I hope this isnae something and nothing,"

Frankie said.

"My thoughts exactly."

"It's just that I'm sure we saw that van go off the road about here."

"Aye but that was ages ago, Frankie. That'll have been towed by now. You called the police remember?"

They climbed the embankment from the slip road and began to stumble about in the undergrowth. Jamie's new trousers got caught on a bramble. He could hear they had snagged as he pulled away from the thorns. He heard Frankie shout.

"What's up with you, cuz?" Jamie called out.

"I've twisted my ankle. Oh, and I've been stung by nettles on my hand. Fuck that's right sare," Frankie said.

"Oh, poor wee Frankie is terribly sore," Jamie said sarcastically. "I don't mean to sound harsh, but I don't give a fuck. This was your idea, let's get on with it."

Jamie plodded on up the hill. He knew it wasn't a steep hill, but he was getting increasingly out of breath and cross. He hoped there was going to be money in this from Connor O'Grady if they did find his van and get it back to him. But so far things didn't look too hopeful. Being out climbing any hill on a cold windy evening in November, for no good reason, like heading to a pub or a nudist hen party at the top, was not his idea of fun. Frankie would have to see a bloody red thing and want to check it out, wouldn't he? Why couldn't he just mumble about it over a beer, like anybody else would? Jamie decided to give this effort another two minutes amongst the bushes and stinging nettles, then he was going home.

"Jamie, did you hear that? Somebody is shouting. Can you hear them? It sounds like it's coming from in front of us," Frankie said.

Chapter Thirty

It was almost dark when I came around again. I was so very thirsty, and I had pissed myself again. Was that just the flies buzzing about or could I hear voices?

"Bob, Bob, I think someone's coming. Listen. Can you hear them?"

Bob didn't reply. He couldn't, could he?

"Help! Help! Over here!" I said. Then my voice gave out. My throat was so dry.

I heard someone say, "Fucking shit, Frankie. It *is* a DayGo van. If it's that one we saw go off road they'll be dead. I don't want to see that."

I had to make them hear me. Just one more try. "Help!"

The door nearest me swung open. A big draft of cold air blasted from the side and the most beautiful man I have ever seen, with designer stubble, spoke loudly.

"Jesus Christ, Frankie. What a fucking honk. She pongs of piss, and she's caked in blood. But she's alive!"

"This one isnae," the reply came back. "Shit, this dead one's Bob, Jamie!"

"Who the hell's Bob when he's at home?"

"Donna's pop."

"This is just our fucking luck, Frankie," designer stubble said. "We come out looking to make a few quid by tracking down Mr O'Grady's lost van and we find Bob's bloody corpse. No wonder he didnae answer his phone. Well, you can tell Donna. I'm no carrying the can for this. And, come to think of it, neither are you, cuz. This is just insane."

The one, whose name must have been Frankie, asked, "if we don't call the ambulance right quick and the other one dies, we may end up carrying the can for that, Jamie. Stop gassing and get on the blower. The other one needs help. Should we call the cops too?"

"I'm no phoning any bloody cops today. We might get the blame!" Designer stubble, who must have been Jamie, said, "how? We did nothing wrong," Frankie whined. "We could always phone that big blond one, he's all right."

"Help! Just help me for pity's sake," I called out. The one with the designer stubble stared at me.

Chapter Thirty-One

Hunter let Rachael drive him and his parents back to their New Town flat. He remembered the arguments he'd had as a teenager with his father when the Coates Crescent flat had been purchased. It had been a struggle to pay a mortgage on such a fine property from the stipend his father received as a Church of Scotland Minister. Hunter felt then that he and his brother were hard done to enough as they didn't have the best football boots and had to wear the less fashionable jumpers that his mother knitted rather than the brands that their friends wore. Then, on top of all that, Dad had bought this run-down old property on the west side of the city centre. Hunter and his brother had to earn their pocket money by stripping wallpaper, sanding floors and painting skirting boards. They had to help further by cutting the grass in the mutual gardens and mopping the stairs in the close when it was their turn. His father even got them to help put up the wallpaper. That was the one job that Hunter enjoyed, it was satisfying and it was fun.

Only when the flat was fully decorated and smartly, if inexpensively furnished, had Hunter realised that their family were not going to live in the place then. The New Town property would be rented out and they would continue to live in the manse in Leith while his father remained a minister there. The New Town flat in Coates Crescent was to provide a home for his parents after his father retired. As a teenager, Hunter had never thought about his parent's retirement: nor where they would live when their tenure at the house tied to his father's job came to an end.

Now Hunter was delighted that his father had shown such foresight, and he knew Fraser was too, even if his brother and he had had to work on this flat but never lived there. His parents' home was now in the centre of Edinburgh and, as they grew older, they lived in a relatively safe part of the city, with good access to transport, the beauty of Princes Street Gardens and a church. Hunter knew his parents really didn't look for much more than that.

"Rachael, I think I'll just get out here and see my folks settled. If anybody is looking for me, please tell them I have taken back a couple of hours of the unpaid overtime that I've worked," Hunter said. "I think we should have a briefing tomorrow about Mrs Roberts and Mrs Button and, if Tim's search parties haven't found her, that missing child too."

"I'll tell DCI Mackay, boss. Do you want me to call Tim, Mel and Bear and get them all back from their weekend off?"

"I think we need to, although I don't like to do that. We all work so bloody hard. They need their down time. But let's call the briefing for ten o'clock tomorrow, shall we?"

"Of course, boss. If you're sure you want to be there, I'll see you then," Rachael said.

Chapter Thirty-Two

Tim and Bear jogged back to the enormous pile of twigs, branches and wood that had been piled together to form what the group of friends had jokingly called 'the biggest bonfire on the planet'. The men both wore their thick Aran sweaters and shower-proof jackets. They kept step together and Bear told Tim about the plastic bag of powder he and Ailsa had found in Jonny's ceiling.

"That's funny because Gillian mentioned that Robin got quite cross when she and Mel took a similar package out of the freezer. He had asked them to look for bread, but they took out the wrong thing first."

"It's not very funny, Tim. It seems Robin was talking to Jonny when little Nicky ran away from his caravan," Bear said.

"Where would they get cocaine from? That size of bag would cost a fortune. Simon told me things haven't been great financially since his father died, so Robin couldn't afford it. Also, a traveller like Jonny hardly has the wherewithal to pay for that amount of snow," Tim said.

"Sorry to hear about Simon's money worries. My gut feeling is that Lucky has something to do with this," Bear said.

"I agree. Simon went to Lucky for help. He should have come to me," Tim said.

"Yes. because I have a horrible feeling Lucky has fallen off the wagon. I'm sure I saw him using again," Bear said.

***

The light was fading, but it was not completely dark when the two big men arrived at the bonfire site. Dried leaves on the ground scrunched underneath their feet. They began to call out Nicky's name. Then they stood stock still and listened to the wind rustling thorough the trees. Tim pulled a small bright torch out of his pocket and swept the beam across the area.

"I don't see her here. Could she have climbed a tree?" Tim asked.

"It's possible, but these are high trees and branches mostly start much higher that a five-year-old could reach." "She must be somewhere."

"Thank you, Captain Obvious," Bear said. "Wait! Did you hear that?"

"Hear what?" Tim stopped to listen again. "I can't hear anything but the wind."

"That's probably it. I thought I heard a squeak," Bear said. "Well, before we go back with no news, I'm going to follow my father's advice about bonfires."

"Remind me." Tim smiled.

"Never light a bonfire until you've poked about for hedgehogs," Bear said matter of factly.

"Bear, may I just remind you that one, we are not looking for hedgehogs, and two, we are not going to light the bonfire." Tim smiled and shook his head at his friend.

"True and true, but let's find a big stick anyway, it's fun to poke the bonfire, believe me! Wait, I did hear something that time."

"Yes, I did too," Tim got down on to his hands and knees to be nearer the source of the sound. "Nicky? Nicky? Is that you? Can you hear me?"

"No. No sticks. Too sore," a little voice said as Nicky crawled out of the centre of the bonfire. Her teeth were chattering, and her clothes were dirty and torn.

"No sticks. Of course, no sticks. My friend was joking," Tim said softly. "He thought you were a hedgehog."

Tim was glad to see the little girl grin. "I'm not a hedgehog, silly. I'm a girl. Hedgehogs can't speak."

"I'll tell him," Tim said.

He knelt down in front of her and smiled to encourage her to crawl towards him. She seemed too frightened to want to do that, but the space was far too tiny for either him or Bear to have clambered in. They would have had to deconstruct the bonfire before they would have had a chance. Tim knew that would take too long because the little girl sat and shivered, gazing at him. She bit her fingernails.

"No sticks," she confirmed.

"No sticks," he agreed again.

Tim stared back at the little one. He was worried about her. She must be hungry and very cold, he thought. He smiled at Nicky and put his hand in his pocket. She started at the movement.

"Don't worry. I just wondered if you would like this." Tim pulled an energy bar out of his pocket, unwrapped it, and held it out to the little girl.

She nodded and put out her hand, but Tim held the bar just out of her reach. She would have to leave the safety of her hidey-hole to take the food. She looked at him quizzically and, still shivering, she shuffled forward and took the bar from his hand.

Tim held her other hand and, without hurting her or causing any signs of panic from her, pulled her towards him then gently lifted her into his arms. He held her in the warmth between the Aran wool of his jumper and the inside of his jacket.

"You're pretty and you smell nice," she whispered to him between chattering teeth.

"Well, thank you. That's very kind. You're pretty too, Nicky. Bear, I think we need to get this little girl to hospital for a check-over. I'm sure, like Mrs Land, she is suffering from hypothermia. I'll take her back to the farmhouse to wait for an ambulance. It'll be warmer than any of the caravans. Will you go over and get her folks? I'm sure they'll want to go with her to the hospital."

"No problem. I'll call the ambulance on my way to the caravan, Tim."

***

When Bear got to Jock Cowper's caravan, the reception that he received was not what he had expected. Jock Cowper and his clan seemed furious with Bear that he and Tim had found Nicky but not brought her home to them. Bear was quite startled.

"What in God's name gives your fancy friend the right to take my wee girl away and not bring her back here to me?" Mrs Cowper shouted. "You say you'll help find my wee Nicky and then you take her in the opposite direction. And give my family a hard time for a wee bag of stuff you find in their caravan. What's going on?"

"Mrs Cowper, please don't shout at me," Bear said. "My friend and I found your missing child. She appears to be suffering from hypothermia and hunger and needs medical attention. We thought the farmhouse would be easier for the ambulance to find than these caravans in a field. We also thought it would be warmer there. We tried to do the right thing. Nicky is very scared. She is also bruised, scratched and cold after running away from her uncle Jonny's caravan. She needs to be checked out at the hospital."

"Oh no, lad, I don't think so. Nicky's not going anywhere. They social workers'll just use this as an excuse to take her away from us," Jock Cowper said.

"They will that, Jock. Go and get her now before they get any information out of her," Jonny said.

"Information? Like what? She's five years old, Jonny," Jock said in disbelief. "You were meant to be watching her in the first place. If you hadn't been outside talking with Mr Robin, all this would never have happened. You spend too much time with his fancy friends too."

Bear watched as the travellers marched off across the fields to claim Nicky back to her family. He understood their point of view, but also knew the farmhouse would be much warmer than the caravans and the ambulance men would emphasise the benefits of Nicky getting proper care in the hospital.

***

"Hello, Nicky," Robin said when Tim walked in carrying the little girl. "How nice to see you. We were very worried about you."

"Not like him or the other man," Nicky said, looking at Robin, then at Lucky.

"Where have you been?" Robin asked.

"Away from you and Unca Jonny and him," Nicky pointed at Lucky and cuddled into Tim's chest. She sucked the remnants of the energy bar off her fingers.

"Would you like some hot chocolate?" Mel asked.

The little girl nodded.

Tim sat down in the chair nearest the fire but kept her tucked inside his jacket to keep up her body heat. He could still feel her shivering against his chest. He asked Gillian to bring down her hat to lend to Nicky. It would keep the heat in her head, and it was also full of bright colours. Nicky would like it. He could always buy Gillian another one.

Tim watched as Gillian brought the pretty woollen hat towards Nicky. The little girl was delighted with it but no sooner had Tim put it on her head and admired it, than the door opened with a crash.

"Where's my wee girl?" Jock shouted.

"Nicky, darling," his wife said.

"She's right here. I'm trying to keep her warm," Tim said quietly, smiling at the little girl.

"Mummy, Mummy," Nicky called.

"What's that stupid thing on your head?" Jonny pulled the warm hat off Nicky's head, and threw it onto the floor. He pulled a handful of her hair as he did so.

"Jonny be careful! Don't hurt her," Jock said.

Nicky started to cry and burrowed deeper into Tim's sweater; her face hidden in his jacket.

"Would you like your hat back?" Tim asked.

Nicky nodded.

Tim retrieved the hat with one sweep of his long arm and smiled at the little girl as he and Nicky worked together to get the angle of it to her satisfaction. He could understand the child being angry with the uncle who had caused pain and pulled her hair, but Tim was curious as to what Robin and Lucky had done to cast them into the same category, as far as Nicky understood it.

"Don't like Unca Jonny, or you," she said again looking at Robin.

"Goodness me. I'm sure your uncle loves you, and what on earth is wrong with Robin? He's a good friend of mine. A fine chap," Tim said.

Nicky looked quizzically at him and shook her head.

"Right, thanks for finding her. We'll take her and sort her out now," Jonny said abruptly.

Tim heard the ambulance pull up outside the farmhouse just at that point. He looked at Robin. Tim saw him nod and watched as Robin went to the door to greet the paramedics before they had knocked at the door. Tim held Nicky a little closer to his chest in case Jonny grabbed her. Tim had not met the man before, but he did not like him, nor his attitude towards his niece.

The female paramedic walked towards Nicky and knelt down, so her face was opposite Nicky's. She smiled, firstly at Nicky and then at Tim.

"You've had a bit of an adventure, young lady, haven't you?" she said. "My name is Erin. My friend Devinder and I are here to try and see if you're alright. Would it be okay for me to have a little look at this lovely little girl, Daddy?" Erin gazed up into Tim's bright blue eyes and the big man blushed.

"I'm not Nicky's dad," he said. "If I had a little girl, I'd hope she would be as pretty and clever as Nicky. But Daddy and Mummy are Mr and Mrs Cowper, over there by the table. My friend and I just found her, and I've been keeping her warm under my jacket."

"What a nice place to be," Erin smiled into Tim's eyes.

Gillian looked heavenward. Why did all the women flock to Tim? And she hoped he was joking about having a wee girl. Kids had never figured in Gillian's life plan for herself. Gillian cleared her throat and moved across the room to stand close to Tim. She laid her hand on his shoulder.

Erin blushed.

"You can have a look at her, and then can we take her home?" Jock asked.

"If she's well enough, of course, Mr Cowper," Devinder said.

"They live in a caravan. Will it be warm enough?" Tim asked.

"Let me check her over first and then I can inspect the housing arrangements. Caravans can be lovely and cosy, though, can't they?" Erin said to Nicky with a smile.

"Can I get my hot chocolate first?" Nicky asked, staring at Mel.

"I'm so very sorry, I forgot about it. Let me go and make it now. Anyone else?" Mel asked.

"I'll take one, just to be polite," Bear said.

"You must have the best manners of anybody I know, then big man," Mel laughed as she went to make the drinks.

Nicky insisted on sitting on Tim's lap while Erin examined her. She watched with interest at everything Erin did, as the woman took her temperature, checked her blood pressure and examined her little body for scratches and bruises. When Mel re-entered the room a few minutes later, Nicky gratefully accepted the mug of hot chocolate and a home-made chocolate chip cookie to dunk in the warm liquid.

"Hmm, a cookie too. This looks good doesn't it, Nicky?"

"You're very black," Nicky smiled, waving her biscuit at him.

"Oh, no. Am I? Don't tell anybody"

Nicky giggled.

"And don't wave your cookie at him or he'll have it," Tim smiled.

Nicky held her biscuit tight but waved it at Bear, and he pretended to grab for it. She laughed with him, enjoying the joke.

Erin stood up and walked towards Jock and his wife. "Well, Mr and Mrs Cowper, your friend's quick thinking has probably saved Nicky's life. I understand she was outside all night. Her body temperature must have dropped dangerously low, but she has gained warmth from his body heat and being inside your friend's jacket."

"He's not a friend," Jonny said quickly.

"He saved their daughter's life. I'd say that makes him a very good friend," Devinder said sternly.

"However, Devinder, she's not out of the woods," Erin said. "Nicky's temperature is still lower than I would like and her heart rate, breathing pattern and blood pressure are all raised. She also has some bruises and cuts that I would like to have checked at the hospital."

"She was out all night clambering about and tripping over things. Of course, she's got bruises and stuff," Jonny said.

"And whose fault is that, Jonny?" Jock demanded.

"These look like historical bruises, sir. They did not occur in the last twenty-four hours, and the shapes of the marks are unusual," Erin said. "You are welcome to come in the ambulance with your daughter, Mrs Cowper. But she is likely to be in hospital overnight."

"Yes, of course I'll come with Nicky, won't I pet?" her mother said. "Have you finished your drink?"

Nicky nodded and handed the mug back to Mel.

"You coming too?" Nicky asked Tim.

"No, Nicky. Your Mummy will go with you and Erin will be with you too."

"Can I keep this?" Nicky pointed to the hat.

Tim looked at Gillian who smiled and nodded.

"Of course, you can," Gillian said.

"Yes, you keep it. You look lovely in it," Tim said.

"I like you," Nicky told him, as she clambered down from Tim's knee and took her Mummy's hand.

Chapter Thirty-Three

It was a busy night for the ambulance service. Not that Jamie or Frankie knew that, but it seemed to take ages for the emergency phone line even to get answered.

"Should we get her out?"

"Probably not, Frankie. They always say on those hospital shows that you shouldn't move them in case you cause more damage, don't they?" Jamie said. "I'll call Blondie and see what he says."

Jamie let the number ring ten times, eleven, twelve. "There's no answer. It's no like him to blank me. Come on, Timmy boy, where are the coppers when you need them?"

Frankie tugged at his cousin's sleeve. "Jamie, there's a panda car turning in, here, see? Let's skedaddle, I've got the twins to think of. They need their dinner and I don't want to end up in a cop shop talking to numpties."

"Right enough. Sorry lass, we'll have to go," Jamie and Frankie ran towards their car and drove off as quickly as they could.

***

I started to cry again. I really thought Designer Stubble would save me, Jamie and Frankie as they called themselves. Fuck! Now, I really was going to die with Bob's corpse beside me – and the other one knew Bob and Donna – but he still left me.

Chapter Thirty-Four

Tim and Simon watched the ambulance drive away with Nicky and her mother safely inside it.

"Where'll they take her?" Jock asked.

"Sick Kids up in Marchmont, I'd guess," Bear said.

"Where?"

"The Royal Hospital for Sick Children. It's in the Marchmont district of Edinburgh."

"I better follow her up," Jock said.

"Far be it for me to comment, but you smell like you've had a glass or two of ale this evening," Lucky said.

"Aye. So?"

"Well, I just wondered, if, rather than risk being pulled over for being under the influence, you might like my driver to give you a ride to the hospital?"

"That's right nice of you, sir. Thank you."

"Lucky, if you've no other plans, can I stop by and see my grandparents on my way back?" Cameron asked.

"Why would you want to do that?"

"I've had a call from my father. There's been a bereavement in the family. I just thought I might stop in to see them. Briefly, of course."

"On you go, Cameron. It sounds like you are needed more there than here. See you tomorrow."

"Who's passed?" Mel asked.

"My great aunt, Sandra. She was a nice old bird and my dad was very fond of her."

"If you see your dad, tell him we send our condolences," Bear said. "Robin, I'm sorry to say this, but with everything else that has gone on, Mel and I have had texts from the station, we have to report for a briefing at ten tomorrow

125

morning. Have you heard anything, Tim?"

"I don't know. My phone's charging upstairs. I'll go and get it," Tim bounded up the stairs two at a time and came back again staring at his screen. "Yep, me too, Robin."

"Then I doubt this bonfire party we planned will be much cop. Should we just give it up as a bad job?" Mel asked.

"We could do, but we should eat, anyway, and the bonfire is built. Why don't we light the bonfire and cook dinner on it, tonight?" Robin suggested. He rubbed his face as if something was irritating him.

"Seems a bit harsh with Ailsa and Simon away with your mother and Derek not back from work yet," Mel said.

"And Cameron away," Sophie said.

"Well Cameron is staff, not really a guest, pet," Lucky said.

"You pompous arse, Lucky," Mel said.

Tim looked around the group carefully. He understood Mel's point of view but was also conscious that Robin would have been looking forward to the social event and the company that went with it. He saw Robin rub his cheek and frown, as if in pain. Tim thought he must suffer a great deal now. He remembered him at school, vice-captain of the rugby team at only seventeen. Robin was a year younger than most of the boys, but he was strong, and fast and immensely popular. The lads enjoyed his blokish humour; the girls loved his good looks and charm. Robin had been the centre of everything. Tim had never thought Robin was gay but hoped he had found happiness with Derek.

Tim remembered how suddenly that had come to an end. One afternoon it all stopped. The accident Robin had suffered when the rugby scrum collapsed had changed his life overnight. Robin was in the thick of it as usual but, at the bottom of the pile, with his head in an awkward position, he had broken his neck and never walked again. He sometimes needed oxygen to breathe. It was no wonder he suffered from depression. Who could blame him if he sought relief from his constricted existence, even if it were by using Class A drugs? Tim wasn't sure how he would cope in Robin's place. But what on earth had happened to make Nicky feel so strongly

126

against him?

Tim moved his glance around to Lucky. The man seemed more vivacious and louder than usual. He certainly appeared to regard the farm as his home territory, helping himself to whatever he wanted without hesitation. Tim noticed that Sophie had distanced herself from Lucky a little bit and, as she did not have a strong bond with any of the women in the group, spent much of her time alone, watching him. He knew his inclination would have been to extend his and Gillian's company if it had been anybody but Lady Sophie bloody Dalmore.

Tim walked over to join Mel, Bear and Gillian who were standing in a little group discussing the pros and cons of Robin's suggestion.

"What do you think, Tim?" Bear asked, making space for his friend to join the group.

"I think Robin is right. We might as well use the food set aside for the bonfire because we do all have to eat. It'll be fun too. We could do with some of that today. And when Derek shows up, the food will be cooked."

"And if Ailsa and Simon get back, there will be plenty for them too," Robin wheeled up to the group. "Come on then. Tim, Bear, grab that old metal table and take it over towards the bonfire. Lucky and I will get the beers and the rest of you idlers bring the food."

"Let's do it, Robin. But tomorrow morning we'll need to get back to real life." Tim smiled and slapped Robin lightly on the shoulder. "Come on folks."

***

"Everything okay?" Bear asked as he and Tim made their way across the field with the table between them. "You look puzzled. You got a message?"

"Yes, I have two. There's a voicemail from Jamie Thomson, a rather garbled one, about a DayGo van driver. And one from Rachael, same as you and Mel had, I'd guess. We're needed back at the station for a ten o'clock briefing tomorrow morning, suspicious deaths of two elderly ladies - Cameron's great aunt, Sandra Button, and one called Florence Roberts."

"Oh no! Not poor wee Mrs Roberts? She was lovely. She was a witness on a case a few months ago. I liked her. Our messages didn't say why the meeting had been called," Bear said.

"It's sad. And when Cameron said his great aunt had died, he didn't mention the death was being treated as suspicious."

"That must be the boss's aunt. Oh no. This is all a bit close to home," Bear said as they positioned the table near the bonfire. "You going to call Jamie back?"

"No, that'll be something and nothing. But I'll need to stay sober if I'm driving us all back to Edinburgh tomorrow."

"True. But I don't."

"I've just heard from Simon," Robin called over. "Our mother has been made comfortable and is out of danger. He and Ailsa are on their way back. We better get the potatoes, chicken and sausages into the fire. Don't worry, I've got veggie sausages for you, Gillian."

Gillian grinned and began to help pushing the food into the blaze of the bonfire.

Chapter Thirty-Five

Hunter gazed at the large plate of food in front of him. Whenever his mother was worried or upset, she cooked. Today he knew she was thrilled to have himself and Cameron to feed as along with his father. Hunter knew he had to clear his plate. He looked across the table to his son and nodded that he, too, should finish all that was on offer.

Hunter smiled as Cameron raised his eyebrows and continued to shovel the food into his mouth. He wanted to start a conversation that would bring some comfort or peace to his parents, but what could he say when a dear loved one had just died in suspicious circumstances? He chose an easy subject, her cooking.

"This chicken is delicious and moist, Mum," Hunter said. "I always like your roast potatoes, too. It's a real treat to sit down and eat a proper meal with you all."

"Yes, especially having you here Cameron. That allows us to look forward, not dwell on the past. What are you busy with just now, dear?" Cameron's grandmother said softly.

"Are you enjoying your job with Lord Buchanan?" Hunter asked his son. Despite the fine trappings that went with Cameron's job, Hunter remained unsettled that his son had met his employer while they were both in rehab, both getting over cocaine addiction.

"I love it," Cameron said. "I work as the driver for this landed chap, Gran, and he's put me up in Frederick Street, just a short walk from here. It's great living in the city centre. Really handy. Maybe I could stop in for tea sometimes."

"That sounds grand, dear. You're welcome any time," his grandmother smiled.

"You passed your driving test first time, didn't you? You've always liked driving," his grandfather said.

"And you and Lord Buchanan both found rehab successful?" Hunter asked

"Yes, yes, Dad. That's in the past."

"I'm glad to hear it," Hunter said.

"He's got some fab cars. Sometimes I get to drive really flash ones, but other times I just have to drive scruffy old vans around. That's not such good fun," Cameron said. "Can I have a bit more chicken and a few carrots, Gran?"

Hunter gave his son a discreet thumbs up.

"I need to leave space for a bit of apple crumble too, so I won't take any more chicken, Mum," Hunter said.

"Oh, yes, your mother's apple crumble is not to be missed. And she's made her custard," his father said, smiling. Changing his expression, he asked softly, "When will Meera tend to your aunt? I need to know what happened, son."

"I've asked her to carry out the postmortem tomorrow. It is rare for her to carry out the procedure on a Sunday, but I agree with you, Dad, we need to know," Hunter said sadly.

Chapter Thirty-Six

Designer stubble or not, Jamie left me. Still stuck in the metal cage that had held me for so many hours. I just wept. I didn't know what else to do. And Bob's phone was ringing. It still kept ringing every now and then. I wanted to scream.

"He's dead! And I can't reach his phone to answer it. Fuck off! Life is bad enough," I shouted.

Then I heard more voices. I called out for them to help me. I could see their uniforms. Police. Designer Stubble Jamie wanted to avoid the police, didn't he? Why?

"This one's still alive, Neil. Call the medics and see how far away they are. I think we can save this one if they hurry." The officer looked at me and said, "Don't worry now, love, we're going to get you out of here."

"And Bob?" I asked.

***

"PC Neil Larkin to control. Yes, Sarge, we've got to the van accident reported today. Scott is at the van now. He tells me one of the occupants is dead, but the woman in the driver's seat is still alive. Tell the ambulance to get a shift on. We don't want to lose her too. There's just one more thing, Sarge. This isn't a recent RTA. No, this road traffic accident must have occurred several hours ago. Maybe even earlier than that. Easy, I can tell because the blood on the inside of the van is dry and the corpse is covered in flies."

Neil's colleague, PC Scott Clark, watched him as he screwed up his face and spoke into his phone again.

"Yes, it is disgusting, Sarge. The survivor is sitting in her own pee, not to mention her poo and the effluence from the corpse."

"What I want to know is why nobody called it in," Scott said.

"Scott wants to know why nobody called it in because the car must have veered off the road quite spectacularly," Neil went on. "Lovely as it is to chat, Sarge, could you chase up the ambulance?"

"He got it sorted?" Scott asked.

"Bloody Charlie Middleton will be the death of me, or more likely the death of her." Neil nodded at the woman still strapped into her car seat.

"Luckily neither is in his hands," Scott said. "I can see the ambulance now."

"Right boys, what do we have here?" the first paramedic asked Neil and Scott as she jumped out of the ambulance.

"RTA looks like the van rolled as it came off the road if you look at the damage," Neil said.

"We're not going to carry out a report for the motor insurer. I'm really more interested in the occupants," she said.

"The driver's still alive. Can't say the same for the passenger," Scott said.

The paramedic rushed around to the driver's side. She saw her colleague had moved towards the passenger door. She crouched down and looked into the car and witnessed firsthand the dried blood and the dreadful smell of death, dirt and decay that permeated the site.

"This accident didn't just happen. Why wasn't it reported sooner?" she asked.

"Dunno," Neil said. "But that's what I said to our sergeant, didn't I, Scott?"

Scott nodded.

"What's your name? I'm Erin," she said to the passenger.

"Linda," the driver said. "And that's Bob."

"All right. I don't think we can help Bob, but my colleague Devinder and I are going to look after of you and help you out of here. Then we'll take you to hospital so they can take care of you and get you better."

"Erin, they're right. This one's gone," said Devinder.

"Bob is dead, isn't he?" the driver said. She started to cry.

"Yes, he is, Linda. Now shush. Devinder. Come and give me a hand."

"Let's get the driver out and to hospital," Erin said. "You boys call in the deceased and start your investigation. You'll probably want to get hold of the medic who'll carry out your postmortem and a police photographer," Devinder said.

"Thanks, I'll go and suck a few eggs while I'm at it," Neil said. "Whose bloody phone keeps ringing? Is it yours, Scott?"

"No, it must belong to one of them. It's in the footwell below the passenger." Scott nodded at the offending phone. "Should I get it?"

"Don't touch anything without gloves. It's manky in there and you'll leave fingerprints," Neil said.

"Good thought. I won't touch it." Scott glanced to the back of the van. "Hey, Neil, there's still a package in the back of this van. I wonder why that wasn't delivered?"

"How would I know? Anyway, stick it in an evidence bag and we'll pass it up the chain. More bloody paperwork."

"Aye, Sarge, it's Neil again. No, I didnae swipe right for you on tinder. There's a mystery package in the back of the van. It's ripped but it's there, so Scott and me'll stick it in an evidence bag. No, how would we know what's in it? I don't think this is the time to question the driver, Sarge.

"The paramedics have confirmed the passenger is dead. We'll need Doctor Sharma or one of them to do the needful and Sam Hutchens to take a few snaps of the scene. And could you call a private ambulance to remove the body when they're finished. Will you set the wheels in motion?"

"Was that an RTA joke?" Devinder asked with a smile.

"No, course not," Neil said.

"Good. It was rubbish."

"Do you hurt anywhere, Linda?"

"All over. I can't move my hands, they're stuck, and my leg is squashed and my baby," Linda said, starting to cry again.

"Your baby? Are you pregnant, Linda?" Erin asked.

Linda nodded. "And my hands, I can't move my hands. I must have done earlier because I switched the car off, but now they won't release. I'll be stuck here forever!"

"No, I promise you won't be stuck forever. You've just suffered emotional shock resulting from the crash," Erin said. "Could you tie this branch back somehow so I can get to Linda properly, Devinder? Then bring your bag and get the stretcher ready."

Erin gently massaged Linda's hands and fingers until she was sufficiently relaxed to move their tight grip on the steering wheel. Then she fitted a neck brace before she fumbled with the steering wheel shaft until Linda could move her leg. Erin noticed Linda wince and realised that her leg may be fractured. She wanted to move the patient causing as little pain as possible.

Erin adjusted the seat backwards and Linda gasped. "I'm sorry Linda. I just want to be able to get you from the van without causing you any more damage."

"Would you like some pain relief?" Devinder asked.

"Yes please. And a drink. I'm very thirsty."

"Pass me a sponge to wet her lips, Devinder."

"Here you go, Erin. Now I'll just have to put a cannula into your hand, and we can get both painkillers and fluids sorted for you," he said gently. "Just a little scratch."

The paramedic administered the pain relief quickly and then deftly removed the container and attached the saline drip to give Linda the fluids she needed.

"It's no wonder she's dehydrated," Erin said to her colleague. "She says they came off the road and rolled to this point about six o'clock last night."

"Poor lass. That over twenty-four hours," Devinder said. "Now, Linda, I'm just going to help Erin move you onto this stretcher. We've had to put this collar around your neck so that your head stays still, and we don't want to risk any damage to your spine. I know it is awkward and uncomfortable, but you are doing really well."

"You won't feel any pain because the pain relief Devinder gave you will be working by now," Erin said. "All right, Devinder, one, two, three, now."

Erin and Devinder drove Linda to the Accident and Emergency department of the Royal Infirmary of Edinburgh. Just then police photographer, Samantha Hutchins and pathologist Meera Sharma drove up to inspect Bob and the site of the accident.

"Where's the boss?" Neil asked.

"DI Hunter Wilson has had a bereavement in the family. He's with his parents right now," Meera said. "I believe DS Colin Reid and DC Nadia Chan are on their way."

"No way this can be left with a DS, Doc," Scott said. "It happened yesterday, and this bloke died, and we've only had it called in now. Anonymous call, though,"

"Would it be all right with you if I decided on the timing and cause of death after the postmortem, Constable Clark?" Meera asked sourly. "Also, my guess is that DS Reid will meet with DI Wilson or DCI Allan Mackay tomorrow to settle the chain of command. Don't you think that likely?"

"Yes, Doc, of course," Scott said wandering back to Neil and raising his eyes heavenward. "What rattled her cage?" he said in a stage whisper.

"Idiot comments from constables. But that hasn't adversely affected my hearing, DC Clark," Meera said as she stood back to allow Sam to take her photos.

***

When Meera's examination was finished and Colin and Nadia had completed their preliminary investigations, Neil and Scott tossed a coin for who would stay and guard the crime scene. Scott lost and returned to the car to sit and watch. His job was to make sure the van remained undisturbed. Neil gathered the items left in the car, including Bob's phone and put them in evidence bags. He perfected his royal wave to Scott as he climbed into the back seat of the car. Colin and Nadia gave him a lift back to the station.

"Briefing at ten tomorrow morning, DCI Mackay says,"

Colin said to Nadia. "He's going to call Tim, Bear and Mel back from their break, so they should be there but I'm not sure about the boss. His aunt died earlier today. Suspicious circumstances, they say."

"What's the aunt's name? An old crazy woman came into the station yesterday when I was on duty with the inimitable Sergeant Charlie Middleton. Turns out she's Hunter's aunt who got out of the Western General Hospital without anybody noticing."

"Well, this one died in the Western. Must be the same," Nadia said.

"Funny old bird she was," Neil said. "Shame."

Chapter Thirty-Seven

Tim and Bear loaded the bags and Gillian's guitar into the back of Tim's car. Simon watched them from the doorway of the farmhouse.

"I'm sorry the weekend wasn't as we had planned, but maybe another time?" Tim said. "Just be careful with Lucky around so much, he's not always good news."

"I know, Tim, but what can I do? Apart from Derek, he's the only one who cheers Robin up at all," Simon said.

"Maybe. Just find out why Lucky has an interest in DayGo delivery vans. For any to come and go from your farm property is not normal. There's even one parked up in one of your barns now."

Bear stood quietly until Tim mentioned this. "I think you should know, Lucky is back on the cocaine, Simon," he said, finally.

"Oh God, no!" Simon said. "Fuck, I hope Robin hasn't started that."

"And I spoke to my dad last night. Apparently DayGo has been taken over by one Connor Martin O'Grady," Tim said.

"Even I know that name," Simon sighed. "Isn't he that Irish gangster who was in all the papers last year?"

"He is. But they couldn't pin a thing on him. Too clever," Bear said. "How do you know about him taking over that delivery company, anyway, Tim? I never heard about that."

"Ian Thomson confided in my dad. O'Grady is working with Arjun Mansoor and has signed a contract with Thomson's Top Cars. Ian was looking for advice from my dad."

"My advice would be to steer clear of Connor O'Grady and Arjun Mansoor," Bear said. "Anyway Tim, if we're going to be back to the station, and are to be in time for this briefing, we better round up the girls."

"Yes, just watch Robin won't you, Simon? He seemed to have some pain or irritation around his face yesterday, but he seemed to forget about it when Derek arrived," Tim smiled.

"He always does. Don't be a stranger, Tim."

Just then, Mel came out from the kitchen wearing gloves and carrying what looked like a large frozen bag of baking powder from the freezer. She sidled up to Simon and said softly, "Do you mind if I take this for testing? It's the same size and weight as the parcel Bear found in the caravan and Robin was very tetchy with Gillian and me when we accidentally took it out of your freezer yesterday."

"Oh God! Whatever," Simon said in a resigned tone of voice. "Just don't make any more trouble for me and Robin than you need to, please."

"Thanks Simon. I'll leave you with a receipt for it," Mel said. Then she climbed into the car to wait for the others.

***

Tim, Mel and Bear were last to arrive at the briefing. Tim entered the room and scanned the others present. No sign of DI Hunter Wilson. No surprise there. The room was already warm, so he pulled off his Aran jumper. As he did so it lifted his shirt to reveal a six pack. His tight-fitting jeans also emphasised his physique.

Mel gave a wolf-whistle and Tim blushed.

"Don't kid yourself, bro. That cat call was aimed at me," Bear whispered. "All you've got that she wants are the designer labels."

"Thank goodness! I would hate to have to break the rivalry to Gillian. Can you imagine the look on her face?"

"Sheer relief, that's what it would be, Timmy, boy. Sheer relief."

Tim feigned a punch at Bear's arm as DCI Allan Mackay called the meeting to order.

"If DCs Myerscough and Zewedu could refrain from fighting each other in the back row and concentrate on the matter in hand, we'll get started," Mackay said. "DI Hunter had intended to join us this morning, but there has been a bereavement in his family. His aunt has died, and the death is being treated as suspicious. He, of course, must be with his family today."

"I understand DS Reid and DC Chan attended a road traffic accident last night, but it appears to have happened some time ago."

"Yes, Sir, that's right," Colin Reid replied. "The driver was still alive, but severely hurt and in shock, so we were unable to get anything sensible from her at that time. However the passenger was dead and, although Doctor Sharma was unable to give an estimated time of death at the site, of course, DC Chan and I noticed the blood from the passenger's wounds was dry and there was other evidence that some time had passed since the crash and apparently the survivor told the paramedics that the van veered off the road on Friday evening about six and rolled over several times."

"Why was it not reported?" Mackay asked.

"I don't know, Sir. It was a bright red van with the DayGo company logo on it. The van must have left the road at some speed because the vehicle looked like it had rolled," Nadia said.

Tim looked at Bear and then at Mel. They both nodded at him.

"If it's the same one, we saw that van leave the road. It was about five or six o'clock on Friday when we were on our way to a bonfire party at a farm," Tim said.

Bear and Mel nodded.

"Three police detectives in a car witness an RTA, and you didn't think to stop or phone it in? Are you mad?" Mackay exploded. "The press will have a field day if that gets out."

"We didn't stop because we were on the other side of the road and I thought I would cause another incident by stopping or turning. However, we did phone it in. My girlfriend, Gillian, did it right away."

"Yes, I've met Dr Pearson, a very able young woman. Speaks Ukrainian, you know," Mackay muttered.

"Yes, I know, sir. But we *did* call it in," Tim said.

"Fuck, that's worse. DC McKenzie find out what happened to that call. Bloody mess getting rid of local caller handlers. Anyway, you do that, McKenzie," Mackay said.

"Yes, Sir," Angus McKenzie said and then scribbled some words onto his notepad.

"Now, if that weren't bad enough, we have some tragic news within our team. Two women died yesterday at the Western General Hospital in unexplained circumstances. One of them was the much-loved aunt of DI Hunter Wilson. The other was an elderly lady who acted as a witness in one of our cases some months ago."

"Yes, Sir. That's correct. Mrs Florence Roberts," Colin Reid said.

"Buggeration! McKenzie, find out from the hospital which professionals dealt with both Mrs Button and Mrs Roberts in the forty-eight hours before they died."

"Yes, Sir."

"I've already got that information, Sir," Rachael said. "I'll liaise with DC McKenzie."

"Yes, do that, DC Anderson," Mackay said. "DS Reid, I believe you have been assisting DI Wilson during this difficult time."

"Yes sir. There was also a report of a little girl going missing in North Lanarkshire," Colin began.

"Surely there's someone closer, even in the extended family of Police Scotland, who could have dealt with that?" Mackay raged.

"Indeed, Sir," Tim said. "However, DC Bear Zewedu, DC Mel Grant and I all happened to be attending a social event at the farm where the girl went missing and, as we were on the spot, we volunteered to search for her. DI Wilson's son was there in a professional capacity and offered to contact his father to get the child's picture circulated and an All Ports Warning put in place."

"However, when DI Wilson discovered about his aunt's death, he asked me to take over, sir," Colin added.

"Were you not meant to be off, Sergeant?" Mackay asked.

"Yes, Sir, but DC Chan, DC Anderson and I were all around. We had work to catch up on."

"Well put the overtime in. But don't do it again. No unauthorised overtime. Budgets are tight," Mackay muttered.

"Thank you, sir."

"Was the girl found?" Mackay asked Tim.

"Yes, Bear and I found her hiding in the middle of a bonfire."

"Oh my God! I cannot imagine what would have happened if you had not found her. Is she going to be alright?" Mackay asked.

"I believe so, sir. Her mother went with her to the Sick Kids. There are questions about historic bruising, but the medics and social workers will advise us if we need to get involved," Tim said.

"However, I did make another discovery when I was searching for the child," Bear said.

"So did I," Mel added.

Mackay nodded at Bear who went on to say, "I was searching the caravan of the girl's aunt and uncle and found this bag of white powder." He produced the offending parcel all neatly double wrapped in cling-film and a carrier bag. "It weighs just under a kilo and looks suspiciously like an illegal substance to me. It was above the kitchen in the area that contains the ceiling lights."

"What was the reaction?" Mackay asked.

"The uncle tried to claim it was flour for his wife's baking, kept there because there was no other place to put it."

"And the wife?"

"She was having none of it," Bear laughed. "She told him it had nothing to do with her and if he'd got himself back into trouble that was his lookout."

"Good woman," Rachael said. "Taking no nonsense."

"Please tell me you've given them a receipt for this and kept a chain of evidence," Mackay groaned.

"Absolutely, Sir. I'll get it to the labs as soon as we are finished here."

"Fine. And you, DC Grant?" Mackay looked over to Mel.

"When Dr Pearson and I were looking in the freezer of the farmhouse for some home-made bread, we found this." She held up a bag that looked much the same as Bear's. "The farmer's brother got very angry and told me to put it back and look again for the bread."

"And?" Mackay prompted.

"I did that at the time to avoid an argument. But as we were leaving I asked the farmer if I could take it for testing and he agreed. He says it's probably some baking of his mother's, but I followed procedure, gave him a receipt and here it is. I think it looks very much like Bear's find," Mel said.

"Fine. Give that to DC Zewedu. There's no point in both of you being lost to science taking stuff to the labs. Just hand them in, fill in the necessary paperwork and get back here, Zewedu."

"Yes, sir."

"There'll need to be an autopsy for DI Wilson's aunt and the other woman who passed away on the same ward," Mackay said. "As she was a witness for us recently, we need to investigate whether that connection with our station is relevant or a coincidence."

"The boss doesn't believe in coincidences, Sir," Nadia said.

"Neither do I, DC Chan. Now, I know it's Sunday, but Dr Sharma and her colleague Dr David Murray have agreed to go in to work at the mortuary to carry out these postmortems today. I need two officers to attend," Mackay said.

Mackay looked around the room and found most of the detectives looking at their shoes. Then he noticed Nadia Chan sitting with her hand up.

"DC Chan?" he asked.

"Sir, I understand from DI Wilson that few of my colleagues can cope with one postmortem, let alone two. But I find them most interesting. I am willing to volunteer."

"Thank you, DC Chan," Mackay said. "Anybody else, or shall I pick a victim?"

"Not sure that's the right turn of phrase, sir, but I'll accompany DC Chan. At least I don't faint," Tim said as he nudged Bear.

"All right, we're done, thank you everybody," Mackay turned to go back to his office and nearly walked straight into Sergeant Charlie Middleton. "Sergeant?"

"Sir, we've just had a call from a Staff Nurse Sarah Anderson, Ward fifty-two at the Western General Hospital," Charlie said.

"That's my sister!" Rachael said.

"Well, she says another old lady, a Mrs Martha Land, came in to them yesterday, and was found unconscious with similar wounds to those endured by Sandra Button and Florence Roberts," Charlie said.

"Not another death?" Mackay asked.

"No, but she's in a critical condition and receiving treatment in intensive care."

"Martha Land? That's the owner of the farm we were staying at," Mel said.

"Oh God, No," Tim moaned. He sat down and looked up at Bear. "Poor Simon and Robin."

"At least she's alive, Tim," Bear said.

Chapter Thirty-Eight

Nadia agreed to drive as she had been to the mortuary far more often than Tim. Nevertheless, the approach to the Edinburgh City Mortuary still made her shudder.

The building was situated in the area of Edinburgh known as the Cowgate. The area derived its name from the historic practice of herding cattle down the street on market days. The day was grey and cloudy, and the street seemed even darker than usual. Nadia looked into the Cowgate and thought what a canyon of a road it was, narrow and only one lane wide in each direction. She stared at the steep gradients leading off to either side. Nadia glanced at Tim and noticed he was frowning. There was nowhere obvious to park, so she lurched the car around and Tim gripped on to the handle of the car door as she swung the car into the morgue car park and drew up at the rear beside the anonymous black 'private ambulances' outside the morgue.

Tim's silence throughout the journey had done nothing to make it more pleasant for Nadia but she understood that Tim was attending the postmortems out of a sense of duty to Hunter. She entered the building in front of him.

***

Meera scrubbed up and disinfected her hands then she made her way over to the examination room where David Murray was already waiting for her. He had wheeled in the body of Sandra Button and had already transferred it to a stainless-steel table that occupied the middle of the spotlessly clean white floor. Sandra was lying on her back with her arms loosely resting by her sides.

Meera glanced at David and shook her head. "This is so sad," she said.

"Yes, and so very difficult for Hunter and his family."

"I don't expect him to come today, someone else will surely attend in his stead."

"Nadia Chan?" David suggested. "The others in the team don't have the stomach for a postmortem, from what we've seen."

Meera nodded. She turned her attention to the body on the table. She noted the livor mortis on the woman's body caused by the settling of the blood. "She was definitely killed in the location where she was found."

David frowned. "Yes indeed. Oh, it sounds like the boys in blue are arriving."

As Tim and Nadia walked towards the examination room, Nadia was amazed, as always, how much it resembled an operating theatre.

The door opened. Meera looked up. She smiled at Tim. "DC Myerscough, DC Chan, thank you for coming. It seems we guessed correctly, David, when we thought someone else would be here instead of Hunter."

"I wouldn't expect him to attend the postmortem of someone in his own family," Tim said quietly. "His aunt is his blood. He was very fond of her, apparently. It would be too gruesome for him to attend."

"True, of course, Tim. Thank you for being here. Always good to see you again, Nadia. You are becoming Edinburgh's go-to girl for postmortems," David smiled at the young detective constable.

"It is always interesting, but I would happily never come here again if it meant that people stopped getting hurt," Nadia looked at the floor then up at Tim. "We should get gowned up," she said.

"Lead the way, Nadia. There really is a distinctive smell in here, isn't there?"

"Yes, a bit like a combination of formaldehyde, antiseptic and industrial soap, isn't it? It's also a bit chilly, just those few degrees below what would be considered comfortable makes all the difference," Nadia said.

When Tim and Nadia returned to witness the postmortem, Tim commented, "It's quite a big room."

"Yes, well by the time I've got my large double sinks along the wall, a metal counter to hold all the tools and the channel leading to the drain, I suppose it has to be big," Meera said. "It also looks a lot bigger without you filling up my space, DC Myerscough," Meera smiled.

"Thanks, Doctor Sharma," Tim replied with a grin.

"When you two are finished sparring with each other, can we get on?" David asked.

The two DCs moved so that they could see the body on the stainless-steel examination table below the powerful circular halogen lights which were suspended from the ceiling. Meera positioned herself on the other side of the table from the two detectives.

They watched in silence as Meera freed the body from its old-fashioned slippers. There were old cuts and grazes on Sandra's feet from the night she had escaped from hospital in her bare feet. Meera also noticed the tiny abrasions and colour changes to Sandra's ankles.

"David, look at this," Meera said.

"Her ankles were bound, held or restrained in some way, by the looks of things." David pulled a face as he watched Meera remove the old woman's dressing gown. "There's bits of grass and dirt stuck to that," he said.

"Probably from her 'escape' from hospital the night before she died," Meera said.

"Yes, DI Wilson told me about that. Poor old soul," Nadia said.

After the pieces of clothing were taken from the body, Meera carefully gave them to David. He put each item carefully into plastic evidence bags which would be handed over to the forensics experts for further examination. Meera then took blood, urine and hair samples as well as oral, vaginal and anal swabs. Meera then removed the victim's nightgown – the first thing she noticed were the ligature marks on Sandra's wrists.

"Look at this, David," she said.

"Nasty!" David Murray frowned.

"I don't suppose it's that surprising when you found the marks around her ankles," Tim grimaced.

"True, but these look like they were even tighter. Who would do this to an old lady, and why?" Nadia asked.

Meera used a pair of safety scissors to cut open Sandra's underpants. As she pulled them off, her eyes slowly ran up and down the old lady's torso.

"Oh God!" Meera muttered.

Nadia gasped.

Tim closed his eyes.

"Monster!" David whispered. "Who would cut off an old woman's nipples?"

David reached for the digital camera and documented everything as Meera finished undressing the body. She sprayed it with fungicide and used a hose with a powerful water jet to methodically wash and disinfect the corpse fully. When she was finished she turned on her voice recorder and dictated the official examination. She began by stating the date and time, followed by the case number then she described the general state of the body, before she moved on to describe the grisly details.

Meera checked that the directional light in her headset was switched on. It gave her a couple of seconds to compose herself discreetly before she began checking the skin around Sandra's neck.

"No other suspicious bruises," David commented.

A touch check of Sandra's neck revealed that neither her larynx nor her trachea had collapsed. "Her thyroid bone in her neck isn't fractured, so there is nothing to suggest that she was strangled, either," Meera said, glancing at David.

She then turned her attention back to Sandra's body and began to check for signs of sexual molestation or any other kind of aggression. She began with the mouth, pulling it open and checking for any trauma or skin and teeth colour alteration in case a poison had been used that discoloured the teeth or tongue or perhaps burned the skin inside her mouth. Meera

147

found no primary indications of poisoning, but the results of the toxicology report would be crucial.

"Look, David, is that a little nick on the inside of her cheek. Do you think she bit herself? It looks too small for that to me," Meera said.

"It is too small. My guess is she was scratched or injected by someone inexpert and either subdued or died as a result of whatever she was given," David said. "The toxicology report should tell us more."

"Yes, it will," Meera said.

Then she moved to the breasts. "The nipples have been severed carefully to try to avoid nicks or tears. Who would do that? Who could do that?"

**

In the car on the way back to the station Nadia and Tim were exhausted having attended not only the postmortem of Hunter's Aunt Sandra but also that of Mrs Florence Roberts.

"You realise we may be back here tomorrow for your friend's mother, if she dies?" Nadia turned to Tim.

"Please don't even think that, Nadia," Tim whispered.

"Did you notice how neatly their nipples had been detached?" Nadia asked.

"I tried not to look. It's disgusting and I don't look forward to discussing this with the boss. But it makes me think we're looking for someone meticulous, well-organised and with attention to detail. It's as if he takes pride in his work, even if that is mutilating his victims. On top of all that, Ailsa and I have a visit with our father this evening."

"Another little slice of heaven," Nadia smiled.

Chapter Thirty-Nine

Colin and Mel arrived at the Accident and Emergency Department of the Edinburgh Royal Infirmary to interview Linda. They went up to the reception desk only to be informed that Linda Maguire had been taken to a ward.

"She's had her leg plastered up, so she's been taken along to a ward until she's ready to go home," the receptionist said. She gave them directions to the ward and the detectives set off to find their witness.

"I hope she's going to be well enough for us to question her," Colin said.

"So do I," Mel agreed. "I hate hospitals and I'll be glad to get her statement and get back to the station."

"Or back to the ranch, as the boss says." Colin smiled.

"I feel so sorry for him. It's bad enough losing a loved one, but in such strange circumstances, it's horrible," Mel said.

They walked the rest of the way to the ward in silence. Colin thought about the two previous occasions he had visited the Royal Infirmary with his wife, Maggie. First, when she gave birth to their daughter Rosie and more recently for the scans showing their new baby. They had chosen not to be told the gender of the baby. It made no difference to them. When the baby came, he or she would be much loved.

"Here we are," Mel said, interrupting Colin's reverie. "Why do all hospital corridors look exactly the same?" she asked, pushing open the door to the ward.

"Thank goodness for signs," Colin smiled.

They found the staff nurse and were given permission to question Linda. However she did tell them that Linda was still traumatised after the accident and her partner's death. Colin and Mel said they would be as quick as possible and promised to withdraw and tell the nursing staff if Linda became distressed.

They got to the private room that Linda inhabited. Colin could not help thinking of the poem *Visiting Hour* by Norman Maccaig he had studied for his exams so many years ago. He began to think aloud: "*She lies in a white cave of forgetfulness.*"

"What are you muttering about?" Mel asked sharply.

"I don't really like hospitals," Colin said.

"Me neither. Just pull yourself together and let's get this done."

Mel entered the room first and introduced herself and Colin to Linda. She looked around the hygienic little room and saw two straight backed blue plastic chairs in the corner. She went to get them and separated them so that she and Colin could both sit down. She noticed that there were no personal items in Linda's room. No cards or books, not even any flowers or supplies of juice or sweets. Mel was kicking herself that she had not thought to bring in a magazine or a bottle of diluting juice for Linda. As she thought about this, Mel listened quietly to Colin as he chatted quietly to Linda and tried to put her at ease.

"I've lost my baby," she blurted out.

"It must be very distressing for you," he said. "I didn't realise you were expecting."

"Not even Bob knew," Linda said softly. "I was waiting for the right time to tell him and it just never came. And now the baby's gone."

Mel watched as Linda's face crumpled and tears poured down her face. The worst part was there was no sound. The woman wept silently, her shoulders heaved and her whole body shook, but she made no noise at all. Mel reached out her hand to hold Linda's. She was trying to be comforting, but she soon realised how stressed Linda still was when she jumped at Mel's touch. Mel felt terrible. The last thing she had wanted to do was to cause Linda more grief.

"Have they said how long you'll be in hospital?" Colin asked.

"I don't know," Linda said. "Now that Bob is gone, I suppose I live alone. They say I can't go home until I can take care of myself. I can't do that with my leg in plaster and my nerves shot to pieces, can I? And I'm anaemic and bruised all over. Oh God, I want my Mum!" Linda burst into tears again.

Mel pulled a tissue out of the box of hospital tissues on Linda's bedside cabinet and poured her a glass of water.

"Drink this, Linda," she said. "Things will get better."

"Well they can't be much worse. I've lost my boyfriend, my baby and I can't even go to the loo on my own!"

A nurse popped her head into the room, "Are you all right, Linda? Shall I ask the detectives to come back another time?"

"No, they're the only company I've got. Anyway, if I'm going to get into trouble, I might as well know about it," Linda said in a dejected tone of voice.

"Alright, but press your buzzer if you need me," the nurse smiled at Linda. "Don't be too long," she said to Colin and Mel.

"Linda, we are not here to cause you trouble, we just need your help to find out what it was on Friday evening to make your van leave the road so suddenly," Colin said. "Can you tell me what happened?"

Mel took out her notebook and wrote down the salient points from Linda's answers. She watched Linda as she looked straight at Colin and mentioned first about being a bit late leaving home. Linda explained why she had offered Bob a lift to work, although she wasn't supposed to carry any passengers. She had tears in her eyes as she told Colin about Bob trying to stop her running over a rabbit and how the van shot off the road and rolled over. Mel believed Linda. Her eyes never left Colin's.

"Can you explain how you and Bob suffered such sharp cuts?" Colin asked softly.

"Oh, that bloody paring knife." Linda glanced at Mel and then turned back to Colin. "Bob forgot his piece box. He needs a bite to eat when he's on a nightshift. The canteen is shut. He had ham sandwiches and an apple. I got those nice crisp Granny Smith apples, but he thought they were awfy hard. So, he picked up my wee paring knife to cut slices from it. I told him to put the knife in his piece box because it's so sharp. But he didn't. Did he?"

"No, I don't think he did," Colin said softly.

"I know he bloody didn't. It sliced open his neck and ruined my jeans and cut the parcel left in the back of the van because I couldn't deliver it, and now he's dead. It's not my fault," Linda wailed. She looked at Colin and, without pausing for breath, spilled out her recollection of the fatal night and the long uncomfortable wait that followed.

Colin and Mel listened in silence.

"I understand," Colin said. "Thank you for talking to us, Linda. We'll leave you to rest now."

"Did he suffer?" Linda whispered.

"I think it would have been a very quick end," Colin said.

"Good. And what happened to the lads who found me? They called the ambulance?"

"I don't know. I don't even know who they are. They had scarpered by the time I got there," Colin said.

"I just wanted to thank them because I know they didn't want the police to see them, but they did save me. If they hadn't stopped by I'd probably be dead too. Oh well, thank you anyway, Jamie and Frankie, whoever you are. And I do like your designer stubble, Jamie."

"Jamie and Frankie?" Mel reacted. "What the hell do they have to do with all this?"

"Nothing but coming to my rescue," Linda said. "Who are they?"

"Double trouble, that's who. Does nothing happen in this city that they're not right in the middle of?" Mel asked.

"But how did they know you were there?" Colin asked.

"Why did they go looking? Those two never do anything but with an eye to the main chance," Mel said.

"I think a visit to Thomson Top Cars is called for, Mel. Let's go."

They took their leave of Linda and, as they walked down the corridor, Mel said, "I believe her. But where do Jamie Thomson and Frankie Hope fit in?"

"Yes, I believe her too. Her answers were straightforward, and she looked right at me," Colin said. "But God knows what those lads have to do with this."

"Now to Thomson's Top Cars?" Mel asked.

"Thomson's Top Cars," Colin agreed.

Chapter Forty

Sir Peter sat alone to eat his meal. He was quite pleased about that. Eating alone was not something that had ever really bothered him, and it bothered him even less since his incarceration. He had often had to do it in the past, when he travelled for business, attended official visits to other police forces or government policy meetings, but those days were long gone. The only remnant of his former life as Chief Constable of the old Lothian and Borders Police Force and then as Justice Minister in the devolved Scottish Parliament in Edinburgh, was his title. Of course it was that title that made him stand out from most of those around him now that he resided at her majesty's pleasure.

Someone slipped into a chair at the far end of Sir Peter's table. He looked up and saw Ian Thomson sit down and nod an acknowledgment towards him. Sir Peter noticed that Ian looked solemn, maybe even worried. It could only mean that something was up with his son, Jamie. He knew Ian so well by now that, when the hard man's mask slipped, he was aware that it was only ever caused by concern about his family. Sir Peter slowed his eating. He would wait for Ian to speak first, if he wanted to. He was very conscious that being seen socialising with him could cause Ian more problems amongst the general population. Then he saw Arjun Mansoor come up behind Ian. The man whispered into Ian's ear, too quietly for Sir Peter to hear his comment.

Sir Peter watched as Ian gripped his cutlery until his knuckles went white and his face flushed red. He glanced back at Mansoor.

"Fuck off you bastard. And tell your friend O'Grady to watch his step. If he messes with my family, he'll be sorry,"

Ian said.

"But you're here and we've lost two kilos of coke. Someone is going to have to pay for it, and your boys are in the frame," Mansoor growled.

"Bugger off!" Ian said.

Sir Peter kept his head down, pretending to be deaf and blind but, as Mansoor passed him, he heard clearly enough.

"And your fucking copper son better watch out too."

"I'm sure he will. His eyesight is excellent," Sir Peter said in an even tone.

Sir Peter watched Mansoor walk away towards the table at the back of the dining hall. He glanced over at Ian and saw the gangster nod at him. Sir Peter ate the last mouthful of his food and got up to put his tray away. He walked back to his cell and sat down on the hard, blue, plastic chair and waited for Ian to arrive.

***

Ian walked along to Sir Peter's cell, making sure that none of the other lags on their corridor witnessed his journey. When he got to the cell, he entered swiftly and sat behind the door so that he would not immediately be seen if anybody walked in. He needed to talk to Sir Peter in private, run a few things by him, secure safety for his boy.

"Ian," Sir Peter said. "Want a coffee?"

"I brought my mug," Ian smiled.

"The coffee's only instant I'm afraid," Sir Peter said.

"The mug's only plastic, Sir Pete."

The door flew open and Irish Mick stood at the door. He was far too high on some illegal substance to notice Ian. He looked at Sir Peter. "Shit, wrong place. You don't got any gear," he said and stormed back out again.

Sir Peter raised his eyebrows and sighed.

"Mick looking for Arjun again," Ian said.

Sir Peter nodded and handed Ian the plastic mug full of instant coffee. He opened his window to retrieve the carton of milk from between the window and the bars outside of it, then poured some into both of their mugs. He unlocked his private drawer and took out an unopened packet of chocolate digestives.

"Lucky Mick didn't know you have these. He'd have had those away with him," Ian said, taking the top three biscuits from the packet.

"I thought I had my bodyguard present. It doesn't inspire confidence in him." Sir Peter smiled and claimed the next biscuit as his own. "So, to what do I owe this pleasure? Are you here because you've run out of milk or because you want to sound off about Mansoor?"

"You're quite the comedian, Sir Pete. But don't give up the day job."

"Indexing the prison library? No, I think I've got a few years before I finish with that. Anyway, what's up?"

Ian thought while he began to drink his coffee, then he took another biscuit and frowned. "Well, it's like this," he said. "I told Jamie that he had to avoid any contact with the dodgy side of Mansoor and O'Grady's business. He and Frankie have to keep away from the cocaine."

"Very sensible."

"Aye, but sensible and Jamie are not words you often hear in the same sentence. The bold boy and his daft cousin, Frankie, decide to go looking for a lost DayGo van."

"And it's got a consignment of cocaine in it?" Sir Peter asked.

"No, Sir Pete, it's got a corpse as well as a block of snow," Ian reached for another biscuit and dunked it in his coffee. "I couldn't make it up, could I?"

"Good Lord! A corpse, as well as cocaine? That's a heady combination. What is the whole story? I doubt Jamie or Frankie have taken up killing," Sir Peter said.

"No that's true. The boys saw a bright red van veering off the road on Friday when they were driving home after visiting me. They reported it, but on Saturday Frankie caught a glimpse of a vehicle in the same shade of red in about the same place," Ian said.

"The boys go and check it out?"

"Aye, because O'Grady's told them he's had vans going missing, so he'll pay a reward for any that are returned to him."

"Of course, his vans go missing – they're stuffed with cocaine, aren't they? The drivers don't have to be Einstein to work that out. Your boys think they'll make a quick buck, but find this van has been involved in a genuine accident?" Sir Peter asked.

"Exactly. Not that the lads are interested in drugs. You know that," Ian said. "But having seen the van go off the road days ago, they thought it would have been towed. They couldn't believe their luck that it was still there and then they find the driver half deed and the passenger completely kyboshed. Jamie tried to phone your lad for advice. But he didn't pick up."

"He and Ailsa were away, but they're coming in this evening," Sir Peter said.

"Ask him why he didnae pick up will you, Sir Pete? And why nobody went out to those poor souls when Frankie called? He could find out. And can he no see to sorting O'Grady?" Ian said.

"He's only a detective constable, Ian. Tim doesn't run Police Scotland, you know," Sir Peter laughed.

"I'd better go. There'll be searching before visits," Ian said.

Sir Peter smiled. "I'll ask Tim what he can find out and tell him about O'Grady's vans distributing cocaine around the country under cover of the legitimate deliveries, but I can't promise anything. You know that."

Ian nodded and swiped another three chocolate digestives. "I know, Sir Pete. But if nothing else the police and ambulance should have answered Frankie's call."

"That's got to be right, Ian. I'll ask for you. Now, get a move on. I want to get washed and put on a clean shirt before you finish my biscuits."

"I'm going," Ian said, and, unnoticed he slipped back along the corridor, to his own cell.

Chapter Forty-One

Cameron picked Hunter up the following day so that they could go back to his parent's house. Hunter agreed that Cameron would collect him in the afternoon so that they arrived after his parents had been to church. They had decided that this would give Cameron time to collect Lucky and Sophie from the farm and take them back to Lucky's estate. It would also mean that Hunter was not obliged to attend church with his parents or make an excuse as to why he would not be doing so. Hunter sat in a large room with his son and his parents. He tried to think of something comforting to say, but how could he when such a beloved member of the family had been murdered? He looked at his father, the old man seemed to have aged even more since the previous day. His mother just looked so sad. Why hadn't he listened to Sandra? If he'd paid attention to her claims and fears, maybe he could have saved both his aunt's and old Mrs Roberts' lives. He should have saved them.

Hunter sat and listened in silence as his mother kept repeating how she wished she had done more for Sandra, how she wished she had been there for Sandra. Poor Sandra.

"Darling, regrets will help neither you nor my dear sister," the old man said. "You have nothing to reproach yourself for. You loved her like one of your own family from the day we met and, for over fifty years, she loved you too. Sandra is at peace now, in the glory of God, with her own beloved Ross. Give yourself the joy of peace in that knowledge."

Hunter caught Cameron's eye. It was clear from his son's expression that he did not believe a word of what his grandfather had just said. Hunter frowned and made a quick sign for Cameron to say nothing. He was relieved when he nodded his assent.

Only when he could bear it no longer did Hunter look at his phone as if he had received a message. He stood up. "Mum, Dad, Cameron and I will need to take our leave of you. I have had a message from Meera, and she has finished the emergency postmortems that were scheduled for today. She's heading home."

"The girl will be tired. How good of her to make extra time to carry out Sandra's operation so quickly," his father said.

"I'm sure she will be tired because she has completed two postmortems today and, I understand, another woman has recently also been found with similar injuries."

"Another death?" his father asked. "God in heaven preserve us from the violence of others troubled by a darkened soul."

"No, the third woman is still alive, but is in a bad way," Hunter said. "My team must investigate how she came by her injuries."

"Of course they must. Of course," his father muttered.

"It's Martha Land, Grandad. Lord Buchanan phoned to tell me because a group of us were out at her farm for the weekend. This is going to keep you busy too, Dad," Cameron said. "You need to find out who's doing this and why. The Lands lost their father not so long ago. This is grim."

"Yes, it is grim all right. As if the Lands hadn't suffered enough already. Mrs Land's son helped me out a while back too," Hunter said. "My team is meeting for a briefing tomorrow morning. I couldn't face the station this morning, but I'll be back at my desk tomorrow. The team is going to get this bastard, whoever he is."

"Language, Christian, please," his mother said.

"Sorry Mum," Hunter said.

"Can you give me a lift back to my flat, please Cameron?" Hunter asked. "I'll meet Meera there."

"Do you need to take some food with you? We have plenty to spare," his mother said.

"No, thank you, Mum," Hunter said. "I think we'll just go down and have a bite to eat at the Persevere Bar along my street. I might even relax by throwing a few darts and getting some practice in."

"Come on then, I'll give you a ride. I'm staying at my flat in Frederick Street tonight," Cameron said.

"We must come and see your flat soon. I hear it's very fancy," Hunter's mother said.

"Anytime, Gran. But there are quite a lot of stairs. I'm on the second floor," Cameron said as he kissed his grandmother on the cheek. "I can come and visit you too. It's only a few blocks. When I'm not working, I could eat well here!"

"Any time," smiled his grandmother.

"You've got a cheek, boy!" Hunter said. "And do remember, it's not his, Mum. He gets to live there because of his job. Working for Lord Lucky Buchanan has its perks."

"Do you want this ride or not, Dad?" Cameron grinned and led the way to his car.

***

"I'm really not hungry, Hunter," Meera said. "I am just so tired, I'm going to have a long, hot shower and then get into bed. You go down to the pub if you want to and get something to eat, unwind a bit. It would be good for you."

"Yes, but I feel bad leaving you here alone when you have had such a tiring day. Would you like me to run you a bath?"

"No, Hunter, I'm even too tired for that. You go. I'll be sound asleep long before you get back, believe me," Meera smiled wearily at him and shooed him out of the flat.

Hunter went down to the Persevere Bar and ordered a pint of McEwan's extra and a burger with fries. He was pleased to see his darts teammates Tom and Jim in the pub and the three enjoyed a couple of hands of darts until Hunter's meal was ready. When it arrived he bought another round of drinks for himself and his two friends and then ate quickly before heading back to Meera.

He let himself into the flat quietly and found Meera fast asleep, sprawled across his side of the bed.

160

Chapter Forty-Two

Tim and Ailsa chose the quietest table in the visiting hall. Tim could not help but notice that the hall always smelled stale but with strong undertones of disinfectant, bleach, floor cleaner and furniture polish. It was a heady mix, particularly as none of the windows opened. They saw the door at the back of the room open and the convicted prisoners who had visitors that day walked into the hall wearing their brightly coloured tabards so the prison officers could easily identify prisoner from visitor.

Sir Peter kissed Ailsa on the cheek and shook Tim by the hand.

"No bruises today, Dad. You're looking good," Ailsa said.

"Ian has been taking good care of me," her father smiled. "Could you get us each a coffee and a KitKat, darling? There's something I just want to ask your brother."

As Ailsa walked to the vending machines, she endured a number of wolf whistles and catcalls. "I should have got the drinks," Tim said. "It's horrible for Ailsa having to put up with that."

"I'm sorry, son. I wasn't thinking," Sir Peter said.

"What's so important anyway?" Tim asked.

Sir Peter explained Ian's worries to Tim. He told his son about the contract the boys had made with Connor O'Grady to respray his DayGo company's vans and get them through the test required by the Ministry of Transport.

"Sounds like good business to me," Tim said. "It's a big courier firm. Even though O'Grady is bad news, Jamie and Frankie should be able to manage that deal without getting into too much trouble."

"If that was all, it would be true," his father said. "But, you see, O'Grady has got into bed with Arjun Mansoor, so he not only supplies cocaine in Dublin now, but in Edinburgh too. The vans do ordinary courier deliveries, of course, but they also have cocaine drops with the drugs hidden in the vans. The drivers don't know, but the drug dealer does. So he'll have to be in and sign for the drug supplies mixed with the regular deliveries while the courier waits."

Tim nodded. "Do Jamie and Frankie know about the drugs? It's not their style."

"They didn't when they signed the contract, but they do now," Sir Peter said. He thanked Ailsa who had just returned to the table with coffees and biscuits. Sir Peter accepted all three of the KitKats. "Ian Thomson ate half my chocolate digestives yesterday, greedy sod. Anyway, Tim, the problem is, some of the vans have been going missing."

"Quelle surprise," said Tim sarcastically. "Jamie and Frankie are helping DayGo distribute cocaine to dealers around the city? Are you sure, Dad?"

"No, not at all. Ian warned the boys about Connor O'Grady and told them to make sure they searched every van that came into them to make sure it was clean. He didn't want the boys or their mechanics returning the vans to a designated drop-off only to find they were transporting cocaine when the police stopped them for running a red light or something."

Tim took a sip of his coffee and let his father go on.

"O'Grady mentioned to Jamie and Frankie that he was offering a reward for return of any of his missing vans. Apparently it's mostly his casual drivers that cause a problem. He has a few illegals and travellers that drive for him when he's busy, cash in hand."

"And he's surprised the junk or vans go missing? Is he daft?"

"No. He's dangerous but he doesn't want to punish anybody without proof"

"How very moral of him."

"That's what I thought. Anyway, he told Jamie and Frankie about this reward and Jamie and Frankie went out to look for one of the missing vans yesterday."

"And it had drugs in it?" Tim asked.

"Yes, it also had a corpse in it," Sir Peter said. "Jamie and Frankie had seen this van career off the road on Friday. They reported it, but none of the emergency services attended and the passenger died."

"We were talking about that in the briefing this morning. It's under investigation," Tim said. "I wonder if that's why Jamie was trying to get hold of me yesterday."

"I don't know, but it must be the same van we saw," Ailsa said. "Gillian reported it when we witnessed it leaving off the road."

"Yes, she did. I wonder how many times it was reported and not acted upon," Tim said thoughtfully.

"And wasn't there an old black DayGo van in one of the barns at Landsmuir?" Ailsa asked. "I remember Gillian and Mel talking about it when we were packing up this morning. Mel said they found a strange looking piece of baking in the freezer, but Robin was sharp with them and told them to put it back."

"Hmm, but luckily Simon allowed them to take it for examination when we left this morning," Tim said, sweeping the room with an observant stare. "And Mansoor has a visitor, Dad."

"How interesting. Yes, he does. It's Connor O'Grady. As I live and breathe, I'd recognise the bastard anywhere."

Chapter Forty-Three

As Mel and Colin walked into the showroom at Thomson's Top Cars, they saw Jamie was on the phone at the reception desk. He waved and signaled for them to go into his office. As they crossed the showroom, Colin noticed the top of the range Bentley that had taken its place nobly beside the sporty red Ferrari. He sighed and thought how nice it would be to drive something flash, something other than his sensible Skoda Octavia although he knew it was the right car for his young family at this time. He saw Mel shaking her head at him and smiling, so he followed her across to the office.

As Jamie walked into the room he smiled at Mel. "DC Grant, my darlin' girl, it's been too long. Have you ditched that big black copper of yours to allow our true love to blossom?"

Frankie walked in behind him. "Shut up Jamie. Do youse two want a coffee or a tea?" He asked the detectives.

"No thanks, Frankie," Mel said. "You're looking well. How are the twins?"

Frankie grinned. "Aye they're doing good, thanks. But Jamie and I found my girlfriend's pop dead and she's really lost the plot."

"She's a right nice girl, but she just can't stop crying," Jamie added. "She should be at the reception desk today, but we can't have that in the shop here."

"That doesn't sound very sympathetic, Jamie," Mel said.

"The reason we're here may relate to that," Colin said.

"Oh aye?" Jamie asked.

Colin explained that they had just come from the hospital where they had interviewed Linda Maguire, the driver of a DayGo van who had left the road on Friday evening. He looked at Frankie who jumped in with a comment.

"We saw that! The van was speeding, eh, Jamie?"

Jamie nodded.

"It went off the road just in front of us. We were on the way back from the big house visiting Jamie's pop. Eh, Jamie?"

"Did you not think to stop and help, or even just report it?" Colin asked.

"Aye, we did!" Jamie said. "Or rather Frankie did. Report it, that is. We told them coppers and ambulance, didn't we Frankie?"

"Aye. There was no point in us stopping. I mean, what do we know about car crashes and cuts? And the twins needed their tea," Frankie said.

"That's a pathetic excuse, Frankie," Colin said. "But are you sure you called it in? Did you get through?"

"Aye! I did. I got through to some lass at Police Scotland and gave her the details. Mind, I withheld my number. I don't want every cop in the country having my phone number," Frankie said.

Colin took notes from the boys about their recollection of the evening, the time and place at which they made their call. He was aware that the details they were giving him matched the comments made by Mel about the call made by Gillian. He glanced at her, but neither of them said anything to the boys. Colin just could not fathom why neither of the notifications had initiated a response from officers on duty that evening. He wondered what DC Angus McKenzie would discover.

Now he needed to find out why Jamie and Frankie went back to the van. Colin drew a deep breath and asked the boys what they were up to when they eventually found Linda.

"What makes you think it was us?"

"The driver identified you, Jamie," Mel said sourly.

"We dinnae ken Linda," Frankie said.

"Maybe not. But she heard you talking and mentioned the names Frankie and Jamie. She also mentioned your new look, Jamie. She likes that designer stubble," Mel said.

"Who could blame her for that? Do you like it, Mel?" Jamie swaggered a bit.

"It's DC Grant to you, Jamie," Colin said. "So why did you

go back to look for the van, lads?"

"We've got a contract to re-spray and MOT DayGo's vans. Connor O'Grady, the new owner, contacted us special," Jamie said.

"Uncle Ian wasnae that chuffed. He reckons O'Grady's a wide boy," Frankie said.

"Not so much a wide boy as a very dangerous gangster, Frankie. He's a well-known drug dealer in Ireland," Mel said.

"Aye, we heard," Jamie said. "A bit late, but we heard. Anyway, Mr O'Grady told us that he had a problem with some of his vans going missing, especially when he has some of his occasional drivers. Do you think it's got anything to do with his drug deliveries, Mel?"

"I couldn't possibly comment. Not all of his vans will carry drugs. Most of them will do ordinary deliveries of mail ordered goods. That way the chance of O'Grady losing a shipment of cocaine or getting caught transporting it is very small."

"I suppose," Jamie said.

"Did you think there was a shipment of cocaine in that van?" Colin asked.

"Oh, give me a break, man. Did we heck as like, that's not our style at all. Is it, Frankie?" Jamie looked at his cousin.

"No, it's not for us. We thought enough time had passed that the folk in the van would have been taken away, probably to the hospital."

"Aye, you get that, Mel?" Jamie raised his voice.

"Yes, lads. I get it," Mel agreed.

"Did you see anything that might be a consignment of cocaine in the van?" Colin asked.

"Not at all! I was looking at the deed guy. I saw it was Donna's pop. And the smell was bauffin'. I didn't go too close," Frankie said.

"I saw the driver was still alive, so Frankie called 999, *again.*"

"So, why were you there at all, really?" Colin asked again.

"We thought the van would be empty and we could take it back to Mr O'Grady and get a reward from him for his missing van," Jamie said. "Also, Pop told us to check all his vans for coke when he put them into us for work and to refuse to do any work on those that have packages of cocaine hidden in them. I hoped, if he thought we were alert and straight, he might not put any dodgy vans to us."

"You never told me that, Jamie," Frankie complained.

"No, but I thought it."

"I see what you mean," Mel said. "But I think you were being a bit optimistic. O'Grady doesn't think like the rest of the world."

"When you found the van wasn't empty, what did you do?" Colin asked.

"Phoned it in again," Frankie said. "But when we saw the cops coming, we ran."

"Why? You had done nothing wrong," Colin said.

"Aye, but how many cops would believe that if they saw us there? Honestly?" Jamie said.

"I get that too, lads," Mel said.

"The worst of it was looking into the van and seeing Donna's pop and then having to tell her. That was bad, so bad," Frankie sighed. "I have to be strong for her. Could her pop have been saved if you'd come the first time I called?"

"I don't know the answer to that. But I'm so sorry for Donna," Mel said.

"She needs to know," Frankie said softly.

Chapter Forty-Four

DCI Allan Mackay walked into the room, immediately aware of the tense atmosphere. There was a pervasive, hushed quiet, broken only by the occasional murmur of comments rumbling around. Bear wasn't even eating his habitual bacon roll, by way of a breakfast, nor was Colin Reid chomping on an apple. His gaze finally rested on DI Hunter Wilson. Mackay thought Hunter looked drawn, as if he had had no sleep at all. Mackay doubted Hunter should be working today, but he knew the DI well enough to know that he could not stay away when one of his own had died in such suspicious circumstances. Bloody awful about his aunt. Apparently, Hunter had been very fond of her and, as she had turned to him complaining of her treatment at the hospital just the evening before she died, Mackay knew that must be especially difficult for Hunter. He called the room to order and the murmuring ceased quickly.

"I know you will all join me in welcoming DI Hunter Wilson back to us after his regrettable family loss. Hunter, I'm sure I do not need to say that, if at any time you are required to support your family, you are free to leave," Mackay said.

"Thank you, sir. I believe DC Myerscough and DC Chan attended my aunt's postmortem yesterday?"

"Yes, that's right. The report is in from Doctor Sharma this morning. She's on her way to join us to speak to that report. Do you want to stay for this part of the briefing, or would you find it too difficult?" Mackay asked.

"I'd rather stay, sir. Meera gave me some of the headlines at home yesterday, but she didn't have the toxicology report through until this morning."

"They must have shot that to the front of the queue," Bear muttered. "I won't get the results of my tests that quickly."

Tim frowned at Bear and signaled to him to be quiet. "I'm sorry you had to lose your aunt in this way, boss. Nadia and I considered it a great privilege to be present at the postmortem for you, but it was an unpleasant experience."

"Your aunt and the other victim, Mrs Florence Roberts, died in similar circumstances. I don't know whether you've heard, but Martha Land, Simon's mother, has taken ill in the same ward with similar external injuries," Nadia said.

"I didn't know about the injuries, but I knew she had been found unconscious," Hunter said. "Will you keep me up to date with any news you get from Simon please, Tim?"

"No problem, boss," Tim said. "Of course, I will."

Meera walked into the room and, again the room fell quiet. Mackay introduced her formally, although it really wasn't necessary.

"Let me make this as brief as possible to minimise any gruesome details but make you all aware of what you need to know," she said.

"Yes, please do that, Doctor Sharma," said Mackay.

"The injuries and method of death were the same for both Mrs Button and Mrs Roberts, so I will not repeat the injuries for both ladies, just take it as read they are nearly identical," she said.

"That's fine," Hunter said. "I'm sure once will be enough."

The team listened quietly while Meera explained that both ladies has been restrained by their wrists and ankles. She could not tell exactly what had been used but it was something narrow like a slimline belt or a cord or a tieback of some kind. She clarified that the wrists had been tied more tightly than the ankles, which made her think that the wrists had been restrained first. She explained that the injuries visible on the bodies were not those that killed the women.

"The toxicology results showed a remarkably high level of cocaine in the bloodstreams of both victims. I had not noticed any puncture marks, except for those made by the canula used to provide fluids and medication to both women," Meera said. "It was unlikely those had been tampered with, because that would have shown up in the ward records. I had another look

169

for injection marks. They are usually in one of the various orifices, in the scalp or under the arms so they're hidden by the hair, and the injections in our women were indeed in a hidden place."

"Where on earth were the marks?" Nadia asked.

"In the mouth," Meera said.

"How did you find them?" Hunter asked.

"To be honest, I found slight scratches, but I didn't realise they were the method of inserting the poison. When my colleague Dr Aiden Fraser was checking that the dental plates we had been sent were the correct ones and he noticed scratch marks on the inside of each woman's right cheek. He thought to do a swab and traces of the drug were found there. That is how we became aware of the way the drug was administered."

"Fuck! This is really calculated," Tim said.

"It looks that way," DCI Mackay said,

"There is only one other injury that you should be aware of," Meera said. "The nipples of the victims were very carefully removed. My guess is they are trophies or proof of a task completed."

"That is really disgusting," Colin said. "We are dealing with a nasty piece of work."

"I completely agree," Meera said. "Now, as I think that's all the information I have at present, I'll leave you to your meeting and get back to the mortuary."

"Thank you, Dr Sharma," Mackay said.

Hunter lifted his eyes from gazing at the floor and made to walk with her to the exit from the station.

"Now, DC McKenzie" Mackay said, "have you been able to divine who had access to each of the three women at the relevant periods prior to death?"

"Yes, Sir. There are actually only four who are relevant for our purposes, Staff Nurse Sarah Anderson."

"Well, that's my sister, so you can discount her straight away," Rachael said.

"No, we really can't," Hunter said walking back into the room. "I'm sorry, Rachael, but it's my aunt we're talking about. We cannot discount anybody without evidence."

"It's my fucking sister! You know Sarah, boss. You know she wouldn't do that. She couldn't do that."

"DC Anderson, she could," Mackay said, "and we will discover whether she did. Now, may we proceed? We are simply getting a list of those whom DC McKenzie has discovered *could* have committed the crimes, nobody is accusing your sister, nor anybody else, of anything."

"There's another nurse, a Staff Nurse Derek Turnbull," Angus McKenzie said.

"Well, I can't see it being Derek," Mel said. "We met him at Landsmuir Farm, and he is devoted to Mrs Land. His partner is her younger son."

Mackay glowered at Mel. She bit her lip so hard that it bled.

"DC McKenzie, please continue," Mackay said.

Angus raised his head from his chest and said softly, "I just did what you asked, Sir. There may be others of course, it's a hospital, not every patient contact was available to me. There were visitors and so on, but the only other two I came across who definitely attended both victims were a student nurse, Angela Bain and a porter, Andy Roberts."

"Well, Student Nurse Bain took very good care of my parents and me when we went to see Aunt Sandra for the last time and I met Andy Roberts and he seems as unlikely as any of the others," Hunter said. "He may have unusual taste in head gear but he's Florence Roberts' grandson and was dedicated to her."

"I would appreciate it very much if everybody would stop telling me how impossible it is for any of our suspects to be guilty," Mackay said. "Let's have some professional detective work, people. DC Grant and DC McKenzie, I want you to arrange bringing in these four suspects for interview. All four of them, do you hear me? Now, what do we know about the van and the victims from that accident, DC McKenzie?"

***

Angus stood up awkwardly, his cheeks got progressively redder as he tried to clear his throat of phlegm and the tension that made it so hard to swallow. He was a quiet man from the islands of the Outer Hebrides in the north-west of Scotland and he still found his new home in Edinburgh too fast and too noisy for his liking. He certainly did not like the limelight. Moving from foot to foot, he looked again at DCI Mackay for encouragement.

"Go on, son," Mackay said. "What did you find out?"

"It seems the van left the road just after half past five on Friday afternoon. It has been recovered and is being examined to see if there was a mechanical fault. I'll report back when those results are through."

"Do we know why the original call reporting the accident wasn't acted upon?" Mackay asked.

"Sort of, Sir," Angus McKenzie said.

"Go ahead, DC McKenzie," Mackay said.

Angus wriggled in his shoes. "There were two calls in total about the van going off the road," he began. "One was made by Dr Gillian Pearson. She identified herself to the call handler and accurately indicated the site of the accident. Unfortunately the call handler was a new operator employed by Police Scotland. They failed to record the call in such a way that it would be actioned. In fact, it took a long time to trace the call. It was only because Tim and Bear mentioned that Dr Pearson had definitely made it that I kept looking."

"Failure to act on that call was ours?" Mackay asked.

"It would appear so. Yes, sir," Angus said.

"Don't comment, lad. It's way above your pay grade," Hunter said as he glanced at Mackay. "That will need to be escalated from this station, unless you have better news on the other call."

"Not really, boss," Angus looked at his shoes.

"It's not your fault, son. What happened?" Mackay asked.

"There was another call almost immediately after Dr Pearson's. They withheld their number. It was a male voice with a local accent," Angus said.

"Why can I hear a 'but' coming?" Hunter said.

"Well, the call handler left the note of the call on a post-it note and went to the toilet," Angus said. "He intended to action it on his return, but lines got busy. Friday evening, see. He forgot all about the notes he had lying on his desk to be dealt with. It was only recorded by the call handler who took over his desk at the end of his shift. Unfortunately she assumed it had been actioned without being written up."

"Assumed? Oh God! What bloody fool assumes in this day and age? You couldn't make it up, could you, sir?" Hunter sighed.

"So whichever way you look at it, the delay lies at our door," Mackay looked at Hunter. "I'll contact the Professional Standards Department today."

"Police Scotland is such a new entity, I think you are right not to try to deal with this from the station, sir," Hunter agreed.

"And what do we know about the people in the van?" Mackay asked.

Angus swallowed hard and took a deep breath, but before he could say anything, Colin spoke up.

"Sir, I think Mel and I may be able to contribute details about those people who were in the van. We went to the hospital and were able to interview the driver: the passenger died in the crash."

"What did you find out, DS Reid?" Mackay asked.

"The driver was a young woman named Linda Maguire. She's a delivery driver for DayGo," Colin said.

"I remember that name. She was a witness for us in a murder a few months ago," Tim said. "Do you remember her, boss?" He asked Hunter.

Hunter shook his head. "No Tim, I don't remember. But I'll be honest, I can't see past the bastard that killed my aunt."

"Linda Maguire was driving a works van back to DayGo's depot, but she was going to drop her partner off at work on her way. His name was Bob Findlay," Colin said. "He died more or less on impact."

"Linda told us the Bob had taken a sharp little knife from their kitchen to slice an apple he had taken in to work to eat on his night shift," Mel said.

"She seemed so sad, but also quite cross because she told

him how sharp the knife was and told him to put it in his box with his sandwiches to keep it safe. But he didn't," Colin said. "She did say she was going quite fast because they were late leaving the house and Bob pulled the steering wheel while she was driving to try to avoid them hitting a rabbit and the van rolled."

"That would make sense as to why I couldn't work out why the van went off the road. I wouldn't necessarily see a wee rabbit across the street," Bear said.

Colin nodded. "That backs up what Linda said. Because she said Bob lost his grip on the knife during the accident and the knife flew around the cab. She seemed to think Bob's neck got cut and that's what caused a lot of the gushing blood. It was probably an arterial bleed from the amount of dried blood that we saw all over the inside of the cab when Nadia and I got there on the Saturday. The knife also sliced through the cover of a parcel still in the van. She had been unable to deliver it: nobody home and it was a signed-for only package. Linda told us was full of powder and the dust covered her and Bob. When she licked it off her lips, they felt different and, although she is not a regular drug user, she wondered if it were cocaine."

"Why would she come to that conclusion?" Hunter asked.

"Apparently, she tried it once as a youngster, boss," Colin said. "We've sent the item to forensics to find out what's inside and if there are any useful identifiers on the packaging."

"There probably aren't," Mackay said. "But I agree we need to go through the motions, DS Reid. Get the examination of that package fast tracked, will you? If it contains a Class A drug, I want to know about it,"

"Anything else?" Hunter asked.

"Just one thing. The other interesting thing she said was that when, eventually, someone came near the van on the Saturday after the accident. She heard them mention their names, Jamie and Frankie," Mel said.

"Jamie Thomson and Frankie Hope?" Tim asked.

"That might explain why Jamie was looking for you that evening, Tim," Bear said.

"It probably does, but I didn't call him back."

"Well just to make sure, Mel and I went around to Thomson's Top Cars to interview the bold boys," Colin said.

"And was it them, Colin?" Hunter asked.

"Yes, boss, it was. They went looking for the van on the basis that they might get a reward from the new owner of the company for returning the vehicle to him. They hadn't expected the van still to be occupied because they saw it leave the road and called it in. And they did phone the emergency services again when they found Linda still alive." "That must have been the second call where the number was withheld," Angus said.

"I agree, Angus," Mel said. "They say they didn't see the parcel and they probably didn't. It would be dark by then."

"Yes, it would," Colin agreed.

"But when they saw a police car attending the scene they scarpered in typical Jamie Thomson fashion," Mel said.

"Why?" Mackay asked. "They had done nothing wrong this time."

"I don't think they wanted to stay around and have to explain themselves, sir. You know we're not exactly Jamie's favourite emergency service, sir," Colin said.

"Speak for yourself!" Mel joked.

Chapter Forty-Five

Tim asked Hunter for permission to take time out to travel over to Landsmuir farm to speak to Simon and Robin, in case either of them actually knew what was in the package in their fridge. He wasn't at all surprised when Hunter agreed that this was a good use of his time. He was, however, a little taken aback when Hunter indicated that he wanted to come with him.

"I think it's appropriate for a senior officer to attend, young Myerscough," Hunter said. "And Simon Land was most helpful to me when I ended up in his field unexpectedly. I don't want him to find himself in hot water."

"I remember the assistance he gave you, boss. To be honest I would expect no less of Simon. He's a thoroughly decent bloke. Always has been."

"I don't doubt that, but I also want to meet his brother and look around the farm. I want to see where Bear and Mel found those plastic packages of powder and where that DayGo van is hidden. Sometimes things seem to make more sense when I see a site."

"Do you want to take my car or a pool car, boss?"

"Don't ask silly questions, young Myerscough. It doesn't become you."

Tim grinned and led the way to the car park to unlock his comfortable BMW.

***

"Good afternoon, Tim, DI Wilson," Simon said. He shook both men firmly by the hand and purposefully led the way into the farmhouse. He closed the door and turned to them. "We've

176

just had a call from the hospital. Mother has passed away. Really, since Robin's accident it's been one bloody thing after another here. What the fuck do we do now?"

"I'm extremely sorry to hear about your mother's death," Hunter said.

"Yes, that is dreadful news," Tim said. "I am so very sorry. If there's anything I can do to help, please let me know. A friend to go for a pint with, shout at or help with the immediate financial issues. Just tell me, Simon. I don't want to intrude, but I'm here."

"Thank you, Tim. I appreciate the thought. The arrangement I have with Lucky causes me some disquiet. But he seems to cheer Robin up and he did offer immediate financial assistance when we needed him. As it is, first, we need to find out what happened with Mum. It's horrendous. You know, she never really got over Dad's death. She could be quite confused at times, but Robin and I certainly didn't expect her to die any time soon," Simon said.

"Of course. It must be a terrible shock," Tim said.

"You know your mother was the third person to pass in suspicious circumstances in that same ward?" Hunter said.

"I saw something in the paper," Simon said.

"One of the other old dears was my aunt. So I know what you're going through. "

"Thanks for telling me that. I'm sorry for your loss, DI Wilson. Come on in. Do you have time for a cup of tea? Robin make one of his fruit cakes yesterday."

"We'll always make time for Robin's baking," Tim smiled.

When Simon showed Hunter and Tim in, he was surprised that neither Derek nor Robin were there. Simon was aware that his brother had been suffering dreadful pain and that his mood had been very low over the last few days. Simon worried that now both their parents had passed, his brother would give up his struggle entirely. He knew how difficult it had been for Robin to make the transition from being an active sportsman to his life in a wheelchair. He also knew that, in his darkest days, Robin had contemplated suicide. Simon was conscious of the effort his brother made to be useful around the farm for their parents' sake. While Simon valued that, he worried that Robin's last motivator, their mother, had gone. He had lost his father and now his mother. The last thing Simon wanted was to lose his brother.

"I thought Robin and Derek were here," Simon said to Hunter and Tim.

"I'll have a look through in the living room and see if they are there," Tim said.

"Would it be all right with you if I wandered over to the barn where the DayGo van is parked and have a look?" Hunter said.

"Yes, of course. Go out of the kitchen door and the barns are to your left. You can't really miss them. They're the size of barns," Simon joked. "I think the van is in the second or third one along. I'll have the tea ready by the time you get back."

Tim found Robin and Derek in the living room. He saw Robin lying on the couch with Derek hunched over him. Tim felt very uncomfortable. Derek held a syringe and appeared to be administering a drug to Robin, that Tim understood, but would have preferred not to have seen.

"Don't tell anybody, Tim," Robin begged.

"Please, Tim, it will cause me such a lot of trouble," Derek said. "I shouldn't give him this, but Robin was desperate. He is in so much pain."

"It's true. At least the drugs Derek can get for me give me some relief," Robin said.

"What do you give him?" Tim asked Derek.

"I think in the movies they plead the Fifth." Derek smiled. "What you don't know can't hurt you, Tim, and I would never hurt Robin."

Tim turned and walked back into the kitchen. He was troubled by what he had witnessed. He looked around the room for Hunter, but he had gone.

"Your boss has gone to have a look at the barns. I think he wants to see the DayGo van. I wish I knew what Lucky was up to having that van here," Simon said as he chatted quietly in the kitchen with Tim as they drank tea and ate cake.

"Is it always the same van?" Tim asked, helping himself to

a second slice of the fruitcake.

"Evidently not," Hunter said as he came back into the house. "The bloody thing's gone, hasn't it?"

"Oh God, so we can't get it forensically checked for traces of cocaine?" Tim said.

"No we can't," Hunter said flatly.

"Do you want to see where we found the packages, boss?"

"Good idea," Hunter said.

Tim showed Hunter the freezer in the kitchen and then led the way down to the caravans. On the way he explained to Hunter what he had seen Derek doing to Robin. He told his boss that he had been asked to keep their secret but had declined to do so. Tim was all too aware that a member of Police Scotland who agreed to keep a secret like that was an open book for blackmail further down the line.

When they got to the caravans, Tim knocked on the door of the one he remembered that Jonny occupied. His wife came to the door.

"He's run off. He left the day after you went home. Some bastard called O'Grady has promised him his freedom and a job in Ireland, so he says. He wanted me to go too, but what's there for me and the weans in bloody Ireland?"

The woman hadn't paused for breath, so Tim waited until she had finished before he introduced Hunter and asked if they might see where the package had been that her husband had hidden in the caravan.

"You're as big as that black lad who found it. You don't half clutter up the place. It's quite roomy when you're not here. Anyway, Jonny hid it above the kitchen, in amongst the lights, tried to say it was my baking flour. Is it heck as like? I keep me flour here – see? All in jars and labeled, plain, self-raising and bread flour. Why the hell would I put flour up there with the lights? I couldn't even reach it, see?"

"Could we take a swab from the space?" Hunter asked.

"Swab away, but whatever you find has nought to do with me," the woman said firmly.

Tim took the kit from Hunter and reached up to remove the panel, swab the underside and return the swab stick to its container. As he put the panel back, Tim saw Hunter nod his head. He knew his boss had seen all he needed to see. Tim and Hunter thanked the woman and left. Just then Tim saw Nicky and smiled at her. She waved to him and pointed to her hat. He gave her a thumbs up.

"I don't know about you, but if I'd been married to her, I'd have taken O'Grady's job in Ireland too! My God, that woman can talk," Hunter said. "I think I need the tea and cake from Simon now."

"Yes, I left you a small piece of cake," Tim smiled. "Shall I contact the station and tell them we'll pick Derek Turnbull up for questioning while we're here?"

"Yes. Are you insured for business?" Hunter asked.

"Of course, boss. You know me, belt and braces. When we get back to the station, I'll need to meet up with Nadia to attend Mrs Land's postmortem."

"I'll call the team together for a briefing at five o'clock. That should give you and Nadia time enough to get back to the ranch," Hunter said.

"The way Nadia drives, I'm sure you're right. And Bear and I should get to rugby training for seven o'clock."

"You certainly will. I'll be finished long before that. I've got a darts match starting at seven too."

Chapter Forty-Six

As Hunter was about to call the briefing to order, he saw Bear pick up another slice of pizza from a box on the desk. Hunter realised that he hadn't eaten anything apart from a slice of fruit cake since breakfast. He signaled to Bear to pass him a slice of the Hawaiian pizza. What was wrong with pineapple on pizza anyway? Hunter ate quickly and washed it down with some of the strong black coffee he had left in his mug, then thumped the desk with his fist to get the attention of the team.

"You all know DCI Mackay has left for the day," he began.

There was a rumble of cheering all round.

"You are all left in my tender care," he finished

The team grinned as they booed loudly.

"All right, all right you lot. Let's get a sense of where we are. With the case, don't say 'the station', Bear."

Bear grinned and held up his palms in supplication. "You got me, Boss. However, I do have news on my white powder and the mystery package in the back of the van."

"That's fast," Hunter said. "Tell us all about it."

"Well, it's not baking powder. All three bags are high quality cocaine – the same type of stuff we found coming out of Peru a few months back."

"That makes sense if Arjun Mansoor is in the mix for both. I want to nail O'Grady for this."

"Yes, Boss. As the packet in Linda Maguire's van was the same source, and Jamie and Frankie were nosing around there, I wondered if we might speak to them about helping us out," Tim said.

"Needless to say, the cocaine we found at the farm was not as pure. It had been cut with both caffeine and boric acid. The drug was less than fifty percent cocaine. But the package in

Linda's van didn't seem to have been processed yet," Bear said.

"Even at fifty percent, it's stronger than usual," Hunter said. "Have we picked up the intended recipient?"

"Not yet, Boss. We thought O'Grady might get wind of that," Mel said.

Hunter nodded. "Good thinking."

"My guess is that is because Lucky Buchanan is back on the snow, he doesn't want it cut too far," Bear said. "I saw him with Robin while we were at Landsmuir Farm and he was so confident he had just snorted it off a table."

"Oh God, I don't want Cameron to be led down that path again," Hunter said. "Angus, you and Rachael go and get Lucky Buchanan tomorrow morning. If he's back on the drugs he's getting it from somewhere."

"And if he's stealing it from Connor O'Grady, he'll be safer with us," Tim said.

"The lab guys thought this was a first cut, so we found two kilo-sized bags, the original uncut snow was probably a kilo, like the one in the van," Bear said.

"I wonder if it came from that van you found in the barn, Mel."

"It might have, I didn't look. I didn't know to look for that kind of evidence," she said. "I was just looking for the wee girl."

"And now the van is gone," Hunter said.

"Fuck!" Mel said. "But I was thinking, Boss, whatever happened to the wee girl?"

"Tim and I saw her yesterday. She has been returned to her family and the uncle who beat her has left and is, apparently, plans to go to work in Ireland for O'Grady, so she should be safe. But I don't doubt there will be plenty of social work involvement," Hunter said.

"Poor wee sod," Rachael said. "Janey was in the care system and she says the social workers were only slightly less scary than the child catcher in the old film *Chitty Chitty Bang Bang*."

"Poor old Uncle Jonny when he finds O'Grady isn't going

anywhere near Ireland," Tim said with a laugh.

"I couldn't possibly comment," Hunter smiled. "Now, Tim, Nadia, what did you find out at the postmortem today?"

"It was very difficult watching Dr Sharma and Dr Murray slice into a woman I had known since I was a young boy," Tim said.

"God, Tim, I forgot. I should have relieved you," Hunter said.

"No, Boss, it was probably better the team was the same for all three postmortems," Tim said.

"We really don't have anything new to say. The injuries and cause of death were determined to be the same as for Mrs Button and Mrs Roberts except her nipples hadn't been removed," Nadia said.

"The murderer probably didn't have time as Mrs Land was found and removed to the high dependency unit," Hunter said.

"The only other difference that Dr Sharma noticed was that there were several scratches on the inside of Mrs Land's cheek, not just one as Dr Fraser noticed on the other ladies."

"Now that is interesting. Tim tell the team what else you witnessed when we were at Landsmuir Farm."

"I went into the living room from the kitchen. Simon wanted to know where Robin and Derek were," Tim said. "They were in the living room. But I saw Derek injecting Robin with pain killers."

"Into his mouth?" Nadia asked.

"No," Tim shook his head. "But he indicated they were strong medication that he shouldn't be giving Robin at home."

"Fuck, you have got to be joking!" Bear said.

"That's too sick a joke even for you two," Colin said. "What happened? What excuse could he give?"

"He's one of our four suspects too," Angus said. "You brought him in, didn't you?"

"Yes, because of the actions that Tim witnessed, we couldn't let it go," Hunter said. "He's in a cell and we'll question him later. Let him stew for a bit. Are the other suspects here?"

"Yes, Boss," Mel said. "While you were at the farm with Tim, Bear and I interviewed Andy Roberts and Angela Bain."

"I remember where I've heard the name Bain before," Colin said. "I've been wracking my brains since she was identified as a person of interest at the last briefing."

"Is this something we *really* need to know, Colin?" Mel asked sarcastically.

"I thought you might be interested. It's our former colleague John Hamilton's middle name. He said it was his mother's maiden name."

"That is interesting, Nadia. Can you find out if she is related to Hamilton?" Hunter said.

"Yes, Boss. I'll do it before I go home. It shouldn't take long," Nadia said.

Mel handed her a note stating Angela's full name and date of birth.

"What did you two learn from Andy and Angela today?" Hunter asked Bear and Mel.

"If I were a gambling girl, I'd rule out Andy Roberts, Boss," Mel said.

"Why?" Hunter asked.

"To be honest, his skill set is wrong. He doesn't have the expertise to carry out the attacks these women suffered," Mel said. "Andy is working as a porter in the hospital to fund his way through a creative writing degree. His interest is to become an author and playwright. He has no interest in science or which chemicals do what."

"He was also extremely fond of his grandmother and went to visit her whenever his schedule allowed. I liked wee Mrs Roberts too when I met her as a witness," Bear said.

"Does he inherit anything from his grandmother?" Hunter asked.

"No. The old lady didn't leave a will so his father and his aunt will inherit. Andy might be given something by his father, but he certainly doesn't inherit directly from Mrs Roberts," Mel said.

"Yes, I remember at the hospital he asked if his dad and his aunt would be able to visit Mrs Roberts before Meera carried out the postmortem. They sounded like quite a close family," Hunter commented.

"I just don't think he had either the skill or the will to carry out these crimes," Mel said. "He's a decent guy, working hard to achieve his ambition. He had no axe to grind with any of the women."

"He did push each of them around the hospital in wheelchairs, so he knew who they all were," Bear added.

"I don't think he's the one. It doesn't make sense," Mel said.

"What about Angela then?" Hunter asked.

"My God, she's a big woman!" Bear said. "She must be about five feet nine inches tall and easily the same weight as me. I wouldn't want to get on the wrong side of her."

"It seemed like she has been very upset by the deaths," Mel said. "In fact, she has taken a break from her training. She told us her tutor suggested she take a year out to 'grow up a bit' and decide whether she still wants to be a nurse."

"What *is* she doing now?" Hunter asked.

"Moping about her house, eating pizza, drinking too much and taking her dog for an occasional walk," Mel said. "Anyway, Boss, I'm not sure she had the knowledge to carry out these murders. She is only a student nurse, after all."

"She might, though, and she would certainly have had the strength to restrain the old women. She would have had no problem tying them up either. She is a big woman," Bear said.

"They've both been released on bail?" Hunter asked.

"Yes Boss.".

"I want to us interview Angie tomorrow. We'll pop round to her home and bring her in. Mel, maybe you and Bear could do that. I'm interested in what you all found out today, though. And what were your thoughts about O'Grady, Tim?" Hunter asked.

"I know that Jamie and Frankie have a contract with O'Grady to service repaint the DayGo vans and O'Grady has complained that a some of his vans have gone missing."

"Okay, go on, Tim."

"How about we ask Jamie to phone O'Grady and tell him he and Frankie found one of his vans with an undelivered parcel in the back? It's true, after all," Tim paused. "They could explain to O'Grady where they found it and when he goes to retrieve it there won't be any parcel."

"That could place Jamie and Frankie in a great deal of danger. I don't like it," Hunter said.

"I would deal with the danger, Boss," Tim smiled.

"Let me run it past DCI Mackay tomorrow," Hunter replied.

"Boss, if there is nothing else, can Bear and I get off? If we're late, coach will have us lapping the pitch and doing burpees until morning," Tim exaggerated.

"Go on with you. It's been a long day for all of us. Let's start early tomorrow and get the remaining questions answered," Hunter said. "I'm off to play darts."

***

"Clouseau!" Tom shouted from the bar. "What's wrong with you? You're almost not late."

"Ha, ha." Hunter smiled at the team captain and picked up the pint he was pointing at. "And this pint is almost not flat. Are we all here?"

Tom laughed. "Aye, Jim's just in the bog. And we're going to win today, I can feel it in my waters."

Chapter Forty-Seven

Connor O'Grady was not a morning person, but today he'd got up with the larks and arrived at the Edinburgh DayGo depot office before it opened at six o'clock. He stood with his feet apart and his hands on his hips and glared at Jonny. Somehow, somebody was aware of which of his vans transferred his shipments of cocaine around Edinburgh and he was damned if he could work out how. He was fairly sure he knew who his weak link was. What he didn't know was if Jonny was connected to the problem and whether he had been betrayed. How had it taken him, the top man, Connor O'Grady, so long to work it all out? He was cross with himself for not noticing the problem sooner.

Jonny looked at the ground. "You've got that van back, Mr O'Grady," he said.

"Yes, but where are the contents?" O'Grady shouted. "My valuable merchandise is missing from the van and my sources tell me that it is in the hands of her majesty's finest. How did my snow get from my van into police hands, I ask you, Jonny? I want my money. You said you had a buyer, didn't you Jonny? I don't just give the stuff away."

"Yes, but he only bought one packet, Mr O'Grady. You're telling me two have gone missing," Jonny whined.

Jonny kicked a pebble that he conveniently noticed in front of him. It had suddenly become the most interesting thing he could find to keep his eyes away from O'Grady. He winced as O'Grady pulled his face up to look at him. Jonny could see the fury in the man's eyes. How could he explain without dropping the others in it? Of course, if push came to shove, he would sing like a canary. Jonny knew that much about himself. O'Grady had offered him a new job and a new life in Ireland.

It didn't take a genius to work out which side his bread was buttered on and, admittedly, Jonny was no genius.

O'Grady squeezed Jonny's cheeks.

"That hurts, Mr O'Grady," Jonny said.

"Good. Do you think better when you're in pain?"

Jonny tried to shake his head, but O'Grady held his face firm and that just caused more pain.

"What I want to know is who found out which of my vans is more valuable than the others, Jonny. As one of my drivers, did you know?"

"I was only ever a casual driver, Mr O'Grady. The manager only called me when he had more deliveries than drivers," Jonny said.

"True enough. Yet yours was one of the first vans to go missing and when you 'found' it and returned it, my merchandise is gone. Worse than that, the fucking boys in blue have it? Do you think that pleases me, Jonny? Do you think I want the fucking police knowing my business?"

"No, Mr O'Grady, but my customer paid up. Now that girl's van went missing too and she was on the books, she was a regular driver. What about her?" Jonny struggled desperately to say something that would free his face from O'Grady's tight grip.

"There is one big difference, Jonny. The only thing lost in the girl's van was a life. I've had a call from those lads at Thomson's Top Cars that are doing my resprays and servicing, they've come across the van and we can go and collect it, complete with an undelivered parcel in the back. I can insure against death, but in your van, I lost uninsurable goods. Do you see the difference? I didn't lose any money from the girl's van, but the loss from your van has cost me two hundred thousand pounds. Your customer paid fifty. Do you see the difference? Do you understand why that would make me angry?"

Jonny tried to nod. "Yes, Mr O'Grady, I can see that," he said.

"Who's got my gear, Jonny? Who found out when the coke left here and in which vans? Who do you know who has that kind of money, Jonny? Because you certainly don't," O'Grady whispered.

"We could ask the boys at Thomson's Top Cars. They must have heard something," Jonny offered.

"You think that's where we should start? Then you come with me. We'll take my car and pick up the lost van on the way. And if they say they don't know anything you can beat the fucking shit out of them until they tell us the truth. Come on, Jonny," O'Grady led the way to his car and drove off immediately Jonny had fastened his seat belt.

"What if they don't know anything, Mr O'Grady?"

"Then you'll have blood on your hands, Jonny."

***

Jamie and Frankie were standing at the reception desk of Thomson's Top Cars staring solemnly at Donna.

"Well why did you agree to it if you didn't want to do it?" she asked.

"At the time it felt like we could get rid of O'Grady and his contract for the price of a phone call and all our problems would be solved," Jamie said.

"And now?" Donna asked,

"Nothing's ever that simple," Frankie groaned.

"No, it's not cuz. And I have this feeling that O'Grady won't be too pleased when he finds that parcel from the back of his van is gone."

The phone at the reception desk rang and they all jumped. Donna answered it.

"Yes, of course, Jamie and Frankie are both here today, DC Myerscough. Now? That's early but you are welcome to stop by any time. Yes, Jamie called Mr O'Grady and told him where the van was found. He just told Mr O'Grady that there was a parcel in the back. We'll see you soon, then." She turned to the boys. "DC Myerscough said the police have been watching Mr O'Grady and just saw him arrive at the van. O'Grady had a look in the back and left immediately. He seemed angry about something."

"I bet he was," Jamie said.

"He has left in his car. There's another man driving the van. DC Myerscough believes they're on their way here, so he'll arrive shortly."

"If he's right. Blondie better be here pronto," Jamie said.

Just then Donna saw Connor O'Grady pull up on the forecourt of their showroom. It was all happening this morning. She pointed him out to the boys.

"Mr O'Grady, good to see you," Jamie said as he held out his hand to shake hands with his most important customer.

He was taken aback by the ferocity with which O'Grady swept his hand out of the way and he strode passed him into the showroom. Jamie thought that O'Grady had a face like fizz and if even half of what Pop had said about him was true, things were about to get very uncomfortable. Then he noticed Jonny. Fuck, Blondie was right. O'Grady had not come alone. This wasn't a good sign.

"Never mind the fucking 'good to see you' routine," O'Grady said loudly. "I am reliably informed that you two found some merchandise that my van was carrying and you stole it when you went scouting around my van. I want my merchandise back, in full, no questions asked."

"What?" Jamie said. "Do you know what he's talking about, Frankie?"

"Not a scoobie. What are we meant to have done wrong?"

"Theft, Frankie. Theft," O'Grady growled.

"We haven't stolen bloody nothing," Frankie said. "We went to get your van back for you cos you said there'd be something in it for us if any of your missing vans got returned to you."

"Aye, but the parcel you said was in the back of it is gone. That is not okay, unless you got it here for safekeeping lads. You're clever boys. Just hand it over," O'Grady said.

"The van had one of your drivers in it. We saved her," Jamie said.

"Nothing I couldn't replace," O'Grady moved menacingly close to Jamie. "But it should have had a parcel in it, valuable merchandise, irreplaceable and uninsurable, but it's not there."

"Goodness, what could it be that is irreplaceable and

190

uninsurable? Can you think of anything, Frankie?" Jamie turned to his cousin.

"Oh, the only thing I can think of is cocaine," Frankie said.

"How did you know about that?" O'Grady said.

Jamie stood firmly on his cousin's foot to remind him not to say anything more.

Jamie smiled. "A lucky guess."

"I don't think so, but maybe my friend Jonny here can help your memory along." O'Grady took a step back and signaled to Jonny to take over.

Immediately the man took his belt off and, with the buckle end, whipped it so fast and so hard at Jamie's face that his cheek was gashed.

***

Jonny watched as the blood poured down Jamie's face. He was used to beating the kids and his wife when things didn't go his way, so he found this quite exciting. He followed the boys as Jamie and Frankie ran back amongst the cars, trying to get away from the belt. He watched Jamie hold his cheek and so this time flicked the belt hard towards Jamie's chest. Jonny knew a shirt didn't offer much protection. He saw Jamie turn his back, but the strike still got home. He was getting more of a thrill out of this than he'd expected, but the next time Jonny rolled back the belt to whip it at Frankie, he felt a strong tug to the extended leather.

Jonny turned around and saw the tall, broad, blond man who had found Nicky at the farm. He had caught the belt in mid-air and wound it around his hand. He was dragging Jonny towards him. Jonny was so horrified that he froze and forgot he could just let go of his end of the belt. Who had the kind of reflexes that allowed them to catch a belt in mid-flight? The man remained silent. He just glowered at Jonny. And then Mel spoke.

"Connor O'Grady, you are arrested on grounds of assault," Mel began as she secured her hand cuffs around O'Grady's wrists and made sure his hands were firmly behind his back.

"And Jonny, I think we've met before," Tim whispered menacingly into Jonny's ear as he finally threw Jonny's belt onto the ground. "I'm interested to see that you've graduated from beating little girls to taking on grown men, but it's still not nice, is it Jonny?" Tim stated the charge against Jonny was also assault and advised him of his rights.

"But I didn't do anything," O'Grady said. "It was him."

"You told me I had to," Jonny whined.

"Don't you just love honour among thieves, Mel?" Tim smiled.

"Mel, darlin', I'm so pleased to see you. You and Blondie here saved our bacon, but aren't you going to do him for the snow?"

"Not yet, Jamie. We have to make that case," Mel said quietly. "In the meantime we can arrest them for what we have witnessed."

"Admit it, DC Grant, you can't bear to stay away. There's a chemistry between us that cannot be denied," Jamie said.

"Aye, dream on, Jamie," Mel smiled.

He removed his hand from his face, revealing the gaping wound.

"Jamie, that looks awful," Tim pulled a face at the sight of the open gash. "And he's got your back too. We'll take you to the hospital on our way back to the station."

"Aye? That's right good of you, Blondie," Jamie said.

"Let's get your face seen to," Tim said.

"Can you and Donna manage here, Frankie?"

"As long as those two don't escape and come back we'll be fine," Frankie said.

"You go and sit in the office, Frankie, and I'll make you a cuppa. You need a hot sweet tea after a shock like that," Donna said.

"What do you mean *he* got a shock?" Jamie shouted. Jamie raised his eyebrows to heaven and followed Mel out to the car.

***

192

"Where is Jamie, then, Frankie?" Ian Thomson asked his nephew. He tried to call Jamie several times a week to see how the business was going. "Got a new bird has he?" Ian went on. Then he listened while Frankie explained the agreement they made with Tim and what had happened when O'Grady arrived at the showroom mob-handed before Tim got there.

Frankie couldn't see him, but he knew, just by the sound of Ian's voice that he was furious. "Will he be okay, Frankie? Will he have a scar on his face? Fuck, I wish I could get to see him." Ian listened to the rest of the tale. "You take no more work from O'Grady, you hear me. There's no fucking contract! He beat up my boy." Ian slammed the phone down and immediately regretted doing that to Frankie. The lad didn't deserve it.

Ian smiled at the prisoner behind him in line for the public phone and sauntered down the hallway to Arjun Mansoor's cell. He knew as well as anybody that there were cameras all over the prison, but none in the cells. He wasn't in there for long and washed his hands before he came out.

Mansoor would later claim that he had lost teeth by chewing a very hard toffee and the gash on his head happened when he hit his head on the metal frame of the bed. That part, at least, was true. He just couldn't remember how many times Ian Thomson had hit his head off the bed frame before Mansoor passed out and Thomson draped his flaccid body onto his bunk. No, he hadn't passed out, he claimed that he often enjoyed a nap – it helped to pass the long days of incarceration.

Mansoor might be many things but he wasn't a grass. That was the worst thing of all. Ian Thomson would get his comeuppance. Mansoor would make sure of that. He was a time-millionaire and would take his time and get it right.

Chapter Forty-Eight

Mel glanced at Tim as they pulled up outside of the Accident and Emergency Department of the Edinburgh Royal Infirmary. She had heard Jamie say that he was well enough to go in himself, but Mel had insisted in taking him to the reception. She went with Jamie as a nurse guided him towards a cubicle so that no other patients would be upset by the sight of his wounds.

"Thanks Mel," Jamie said. "You and Blondie arrived at just the right time. I thought he was goin' to kill me,"

"Don't worry, Jamie. O'Grady and his sidekick are in for a most uncomfortable morning," Mel said. She smiled at Jamie and turned to go back to the car.

***

"Good morning one and all!" DCI Mackay shouted as he rapped the desk with a folder. "I see some of us didn't have time for breakfast at home, DC Zewedu?"

"Well this is a bit early, Sir, and I'm not the only one who's eating," Bear said. He watched while Rachael stuffed the rest of her bacon roll into her mouth and Colin threw his apple core into the bin.

"No you're not, Zewedu, and at least you're here. Where are Myerscough and Grant?"

"Right here, Sir," Tim said. "Mel and I went over to Thomson's Top Cars to make sure Jamie and Frankie stayed safe. Unfortunately we were just a little later than we would have liked."

"Why was that?" DCI Mackay asked.

"When we arrived we found Connor O'Grady and his heavy

attacking Jamie and Frankie. Jamie had a slash across his face and the back of his shirt had been ripped too. Mel took care of O'Grady and I arrested his mate. We had to take Jamie to the A&E Department at the Infirmary before bringing O'Grady here. And you'll never guess who the heavy was," Tim looked at Hunter.

"Jonny, the fellow whose caravan we visited, I'd guess," Hunter said.

"Exactly so," Tim smiled and reached for one of the bacon rolls still in front of Bear.

"What are they saying?" Mackay asked. "You've interviewed them?"

"Not yet, Sir. O'Grady wants them both to have a lawyer. The offices don't open until nine, so we'll interview them after the briefing," Tim said.

"Before we go any further, can I just voice something that has been troubling me?" Hunter said.

"Of course, DI Wilson. Go ahead," DCI Mackay said. "What's worrying you?"

"Well, each of the three women that were killed recently has a connection to me. Now, I don't believe in coincidences and this makes me feel like I have their blood on my hands."

"Well, that is ridiculous," DCI Mackay said. "You didn't kill these women, Hunter."

"No, I didn't kill them. Of course not, but look at it this way, Sir. One of the women was my aunt, a very dear and much-loved woman. She didn't have her own children and was extremely fond of me and my brother, and we were fond of her. She was very important in my life, especially when I was growing up. The second victim was Mrs Florence Roberts. She was a critical witness in a big case last year and important to me. The most recent victim who finally lost her battle for life yesterday was Mrs Martha Land. I found myself on her farm and her son helped me greatly at a time when I was vulnerable. Her family didn't have to help me, but they did. Mrs Land was important to me."

"Do you see what I mean, Sir? I feel guilty by association," Hunter said.

"I understand your feelings, Boss. But this is not your fault," Tim said.

"I know this doesn't happen often, but Tim is right this time, Boss. It might help if you hear what Sarah Anderson had to say during her interview," Bear said.

"You've interviewed her already?" Mackay asked.

"My sister's a nurse. She starts work at seven in the morning. Of course, they have already met with her," Rachael said flatly.

"Alright, let's hear what Staff Nurse Anderson had to say," Hunter said.

"Sarah arrived promptly and declined the advice of a lawyer. She explained that as she was a senior staff nurse, she would generally see every patient on her ward during most of her shifts. She agreed that, as such, she should be interviewed," Mel said.

"Well, forgive me if I disagree! You all know my sister and you know she wouldn't hurt any of her patients. You know it!" Rachael thumped the desk.

"Do you want to be excused from this part of the meeting, DC Anderson?" Mackay asked.

"No, Sir," she said in a huffy tone of voice.

"Then you will be quiet."

"Sarah went on to tell us that, if the patients had been in such pain that they needed a strong painkiller, she would have administered the drug, if appropriate through the canula that each patient had in their hand. Sarah was quite clear that to inject the patients inside their mouths was unusual. She explained to us how frightening it would be for vulnerable patients, especially if they had to be restrained with such force that they would be marked or bruised." Mel glanced at Rachael. Her long dark curls bounced up and down as she spoke.

"Sarah did say that the elderly patients sometimes bruised when a drip or a canula were inserted but she looked genuinely upset when she was talking about the injuries she had seen on her patients when their deaths were discovered. There wasn't bruising in places she would normally expect," Mel said.

"Naturally she would be upset," Rachael barked.

Mackay glowered at her.

Rachael crossed her arms and her face sunk further down towards her chest.

"Sarah seemed particularly fond of your aunt, Boss. She did comment that Mrs Button was always a bit reserved around male staff. Did you ever notice your aunt's reticence around men, Boss?" Bear asked.

"No, not at all," Hunter said with a laugh.

"But what was really interesting was what Sarah said, almost as an afterthought as she was leaving the room," Bear said.

"Really? What did she say?" Rachael asked, looking livelier.

"Sarah reminded us that, although there are no CCTV cameras in the rooms of the wards, there are lots of CCTV cameras in the public areas of the hospital. She suggested there might be something on those recordings that might help us," Bear said.

"That is a great idea. DC Chan, DS Reid, take a look at the CCTV from the day before the first death until the day after the last death. I want to know everything that is relevant to the victims or our four suspects," Mackay said.

"How exciting, a little slice of heaven, Sir," Colin said.

"You and Nadia are meticulous, you are the obvious choices," Tim said.

"Thank God," Bear said.

"Tim, you get on to the CSIs. I want them to find the detached nipples," Hunter said.

"I may have to be careful how I put that request, Boss," Tim grinned.

"Oh Boss, Derek Turnbull is also still here, waiting to be interviewed. He wants to be seen as soon as possible," Bear said. "However, as Mel and I met him socially so recently at Landsmuir Farm, we thought you and Rachael might interview him."

"Yes, that makes sense. How come he wants to be seen so early?" Hunter asked.

"My guess is he's going on shift and doesn't want to be any later than necessary," Rachael said.

"I see. So has he had anything to say for himself already?" Mackay asked.

"Colin and I spoke to him briefly after you and Tim brought him in, Boss. He just commented that as a senior staff nurse, he would see each patient in the ward during every shift, as Sarah said."

"What did he say about the bruises on the victims?" Hunter asked.

"He didn't say anything about that. But he did mention that painkillers injected intravenously work more quickly than those taken orally. When we asked him about injecting patients in the mouth, he said that would work as well as putting the drugs into a patient's canula," Nadia said.

"Well that's just a truism," Mel said. "Did he say anything about the victims?"

"Nothing we didn't know," Colin said. "He talked about your aunt's 'escape' the day before she died and said she had been very confused because she had a urine infection. He told us about speaking to you, when you took her back to the ward, Boss."

"Yes, you're right Colin, but we knew all that and I gave him a bit of a roasting when I returned her to his care. Auntie Sandra kept telling me that she was being mistreated, how I wish I had listened," Hunter said.

"Derek did also comment that he wasn't on duty when Mrs Land went into hospital, but accepted that he had gone in to see her. However, he was not alone with Mrs Land because, although Simon took the opportunity of his visit to answer a call of nature, the student nurse Angela Bain came in to take her blood pressure and check her temperature. It probably rules him out," Nadia said.

Mackay drew the meeting to a close, making sure each of the team knew what he expected of them: Nadia and Colin left to get the CCTV footage; Mel and Bear went to collect Andy Roberts and Angela Bain; Angus and Rachael were charged with picking up Lucky Buchanan. Tim and Hunter went to fetch Jonny and Robin with a view to having them available for interview.

"I want to lead the interviews, people," Hunter said.

"Fine. But today is going to be a long day for all of us, team, and I want us all to meet back here at five this evening for an update. No excuses," Mackay said.

Chapter Forty-Nine

"Is naebody comin'? Fuck's sake, I've been here ages and I'm in right agony. Does naebody care?" Jamie said. He clutched a bloody gauze bandage to his face and poked his head out of the cubicle. Then he shouted, "Come on folks, let's get a bit of action here!"

Doctor Ailsa Myerscough entered the cubicle. "I thought I recognised that voice. Jamie, what are you doing here? Good Lord! What happened to your face?"

"Hiya, Doc. This must be my lucky day."

"Not from where I'm standing, Jamie," Ailsa said.

"How's your wee green car that I sold you doing?" Jamie said with a wink.

"Better than your face, I think. What happened to you?"

"I got onto the wrong side of a leather belt, but your bro and Mel arrived. You should have seen the other guy," Jamie said.

"I'm sure," Ailsa said.

"So, Doc. I'm still single if you are?"

Ailsa began examining the wound on Jamie face. She couldn't help smiling at his impudence. "Don't you think that would break Mel's heart," she teased.

"Aye well, if you're no fast you're last, Doc. I cannae wait for her forever. You could get lucky, Doc," Jamie said as he tried to grin. Then he grimaced and grabbed his face. The pain of the movement was etched across his eyes.

"Come on, Jamie, let me take a proper look," Ailsa said. "Lean this way for me." She touched his back to indicate what she needed him to do.

Jamie gasped. "That's awfy sore, Doc."

"Wow, what happened to your back too?"

"I took a beating with the clasp end of the same heavy

leather belt. I've not seen it, but it hurts like fuck," Jamie said.

"I'm not surprised, these are deep cuts. Look, Jamie, these are not wounds that I can deal with here in A&E. You're going to need a specialist surgeon to stitch you up. I'll give them a call to get them to come down and talk to you about what needs to be done. Let me get a nurse to give you some pain relief now," Ailsa said.

Ailsa left Jamie and asked a nurse to insert a canula into Jamie's hand while she went to speak to one of the surgeons. She explained to the surgeon that the gash in Jamie's cheek was wide and needed to be expertly stitched to minimise any scarring. She also told the surgeon about the wounds to his back. After listening carefully to what she was told, Ailsa put the phone down and went back to speak to Jamie.

***

Jamie's phone rang. He took it out of his pocket and stared at the unknown number. He moved the phone to the ear away from his open wound. "Hello Pop," he said.

"How did you know it was me, son? I don't usually call at this time," Ian said.

"Who else phones me at odd times of the day and night from random unknown numbers? Where did you get this one from, Pop?"

"Irish Mick lost his phone to me in a card game," Ian laughed.

"What would he get in the unlikely event that he won? Poor sod," Jamie said.

"Well, that was never going to happen, but I promised him a half of a packet of fags, a Mars Bar and a KitKat," Ian said.

"In exchange for a phone? Is he mad?"

"No, not mad. He's just addled by drugs and the demon drink, and he does love chocolate," Ian said. "How's life with you? I tried the house and Frankie said I'd need to catch you on your mobile."

"Did he say why?"

"Aye, sort of. Exactly what happened?"

Jamie took a deep breath and told his Dad about the attack that Connor O'Grady had orchestrated against him. "To be honest Pop, I'm just glad Blondie turned up when he did. He stopped the attack and took O'Grady and his henchman to the station. He and DC Mel Grant even brought me to the hospital. Not all coppers are rotten. But I'm going to need stitches. I saw Blondie's sister at A&E but she's going to have to get a proper surgeon to sew me up and then I'll have to stay here overnight at least."

"O'Grady and his crew are going to fucking suffer for mangling my boy. I've already beat the shit out of Mansoor," Ian said.

"Won't that get you a longer sentence?" Jamie asked.

"Mansoor'll no talk," Ian growled.

The phone cut off suddenly. Jamie couldn't work out whether the charge had run out or whether his Pop had hung up in temper.

***

"How come you and I always seem to get landed with the job of watching CCTV, Colin?" Nadia asked.

"Because we're good at it?" Colin suggested.

"I think it's because DCI Mackay hates us," Nadia sulked.

"I honestly think it's because we're observant, Nadia," Colin said. "We need to get to the bottom of these deaths and find the murderer. If this is how Mackay thinks we can best help, let's get on with it."

"You're right. Maybe we're the favourites," Nadia winked. "Shall I get us some tea and we can get going?"

"A glass of water is fine for me," Colin smiled.

"Then I'll get me a tea. I'll be right back," Nadia said as she got up and wandered towards the kettle.

Chapter Fifty

Hunter stormed into Mackay's office. The door rattled on its hinges and the glass shuddered in its frame.

"Who the hell let O'Grady go, *Sir*?" he growled. "Which genius sanctioned that, huh? Charlie Middleton just told me that scum bag been bailed. How the fuck did that happen?"

Mackay raised his eyes from the statement on his desk.

"And a good afternoon to you too, Hunter," the DCI said in a slow, measured voice. "May I offer you a seat? I understand that you do not approve of my decision to bail Mr O'Grady." He watched as Hunter strode across his room and then hovered by a chair.

"No, Sir, I do not. He is a drug trafficker and a flight risk," Hunter inhaled deeply.

Mackay said nothing, but waited for Hunter to calm down from boiling point to a steady simmer. Eventually Hunter sat and Mackay realised he had been holding his breath. Mackay breathed out slowly and then spoke quietly. "Now, first, don't you ever speak to me like that again and do not behave like that in my station. Second, what's the matter and how can I help you, Hunter?"

Hunter sighed. "Charlie Middleton just told me that the turd who is Connor O'Grady has been released from the cells on bail."

"Yes, that's true. He and his sidekick were here charged with assault. They've been questioned, charged and released on bail," Mackay said. "Hunter, we had no grounds to hold him, you know that. We have yet to prove the drugs charge."

"He is a flight risk, Sir. He will be off to Ireland at the drop of a hat and God knows where to after that."

"He and his accomplice, Jonny Baird, have agreed to

203

surrender their passports," Mackay countered flatly.

"I don't see O'Grady having too much trouble getting a false document, Sir. I also know that he has been ferrying cocaine around the city in his bright red vans. I want to stop that supply," Hunter spoke through clenched teeth.

"Then go and get your proof. I've called a briefing at five o'clock this evening, so you have time. Come back with something meaningful to tell the team this afternoon."

"Could you at least authorise investigation into Lord Lachlan Buchanan's bank accounts," Hunter asked. He saw Mackay raise his eyebrows. "We have evidence that he is using cocaine again and has bought a batch from O'Grady and Baird. If we're right, there has been a large payment made recently."

"Consider it done. Now get out of here, you're cluttering up my office," Mackay dismissed Hunter with a wave of his hand.

***

"Why do you think you and I were chosen to pick up Lord Buchanan and bring him in for questioning?" Angus asked Rachael. "It's a long drive. Wouldn't it have been better to get Tim to call him and invite him to come in for questioning?"

"I don't think we can avoid our job on the basis that it's a long drive, Angus! Anyway, my guess is the boss wanted to keep Tim, Bear and Mel out of it as they had been socialising with Lucky Buchanan at Landsmuir Farm recently," Rachael said.

"That would make sense, I suppose," Angus said. He turned and looked out of the window. He sat in silence until Rachael pulled up outside Lucky's home. Angus gazed at the impressive stately manor. "How long was that driveway from the gates?" he asked. "And how long would it take to wash all those windows?"

Rachael laughed. "We are both so prosaic. I was thinking how long it would take to vacuum this place. I wonder how many staff he has."

"I never thought of staff," Angus said.

"Well I can't see Lady Sophie and Lord Lucky doing their own dusting, can you? Come on, let's get this over with."

Rachael led the way to the entrance and pulled the handle that rang a loud, sonorous bell. A man in a smart black three-piece suit answered the door. He looked the detectives up and down. Rachael could not help feeling they had been judged and found wanting.

She showed her warrant card and asked to speak to Lord Lachlan Buchanan.

"His Lordship cannot have been expecting you. He is out riding in the grounds of the estate with Lady Sophie," the man said.

"That's all right, we'll wait," Rachael stepped forward, but the man did not move.

"His Lordship may be some time."

"That's all right, we'll wait," Angus also took a step forward and this time the man had no choice but to step back, unless he wanted his feet under the islander's heavy brogues.

"Harris?" he asked Angus when he heard his accent.

Angus smiled. "I spent time there, but also on Lewis before I moved South to the big smoke."

"My mother was a native Gael from Harris. I don't get much chance to speak the mother tongue nowadays," he said.

Rachael listened in wonder as the men reverted to their native Gaelic language and followed them into a large room lined with books. How she wished she and Jane had a home big enough to indulge in a library. Some of the books looked old and dusty, but Rachael noticed that modern authors, including Michael Jecks and Sophie Hannah, were well represented. Then she noticed both men were looking at her.

"Callum is asking if you would prefer tea or coffee," Angus said.

"Tea please. That would be lovely," Rachael said.

After the man had left the room she turned to Angus, "So how did we get from being in the man's face to 'Callum' in such a short space of time?"

"His gran lives along the street from my auntie. I used to deliver her papers. Small world isn't it?"

"I suppose it is. Did you find out anything else?"

"Lord Buchanan has his mobile with him. Callum will call him and tell him we're here. But he'll give us time to enjoy a couple of Flora's scones before he does that," Angus grinned.

"And who the hell is 'Flora?" Rachael asked impatiently.

A little woman in a striped blue skirt and crisp white blouse backed into the room carrying an enormous tray. "That would be me, madam."

"Let me help you with that, Flora," Angus said as he rushed to relieve her of the burden. He asked her a question in Gaelic, and she pointed to a coffee table between two large chairs. Rachael watched Angus put the tray down and then gave her a hug. They exchanged a few more words and Angus shook his head as Flora left them alone again.

"Wasn't that a bit forward, hugging the cook just because she brought you a scone?" Rachael asked.

"Not really. Flora is my godmother. She only took up the position of housekeeper a couple of weeks ago. I had no idea she was here. It's lovely to see her. Now, shall I be mother?" Angus reached for the teapot and poured for both of them.

Rachael and Angus had finished their third cup of tea and eaten all the scones before Lucky made an appearance. Rachael watched as Lucky walked over to Angus and shook his hand.

"DC McKenzie, good to see you again," Lucky said. "But I don't think I've had the pleasure of meeting your colleague."

"DC Anderson, my Lord," Angus said formally. Had Rachael noticed him give a little bow?

"I'm sorry I wasn't here, I didn't know to expect you, but I see Callum and Flora have taken care of you."

"They have indeed, Lord Buchanan, but I'm afraid this is not a social visit. We must ask you to accompany us to Fettes Police station in Edinburgh," Rachael said.

"How may I be of help?" Lucky asked.

"We will discuss that at the station," Rachael said as she led the way to the door.

"Can't you give me a clue?"

"We think you may be able to help us with inquiries we're

making relating to dealing with and use of class A drugs," Angus said.

"I doubt that very much indeed," Lucky spluttered.

"Thank you, Angus, that will be enough. This way, Lord Buchanan," Rachael strode out of the mansion and stood holding the rear car door open. Angus could sit in the back with his lordship, in silence, she decided.

***

When Nadia came back with her tea, Colin looked up and smiled.

"There are a lot of cameras," he said. "This was a good tip from Sarah."

"Is it just going to confuse us?" Nadia asked.

"No, I don't think so. Let's check all the cameras for each hour and see what we can learn," Colin said. He started peeling a satsuma and switched on the first film.

"I've had better movie dates," Nadia commented and then settled down to jot down anything that might be of interest.

The room was quiet as neither of them was speaking and then Hunter stuck his head around the door, swearing. He left almost immediately, leaving Nadia and Colin, somewhat nonplussed.

"Fuck, fuck, fuck, fuck, fuck," Hunter shouted increasingly loudly as he marched into Mackay's room. Hunter slammed the door. "He's only made it out of the country to Ireland, hasn't he? I fucking told you he would. Straight from here to Cairnryan across to Belfast and over the border as quick as you like."

"O'Grady?" Mackay asked.

"Yes, fucking O'Grady and his bloody henchman. A local bobby recognised him and remembered. When I called the port, I got the news. Tell me, Sir, just why did we let them go, again? I can't believe we had that rat here and let him go," Hunter grumbled.

"We had no choice! We couldn't hold him any longer. He was only charged with the assault on Jamie Thomson. There

207

was no reason to keep him here. You know that, Hunter, so hold your temper," Mackay said. "I've got us a warrant to search DayGo's depot and offices as well as one to allow investigation of Buchanan's accounts. That should provide us with the evidence we need relating to cocaine distribution in the city, if, indeed that's what he's been up to. We'll get him back from Ireland. He's as loathed there as he is here."

"Good as it gets, I suppose," Hunter's voice calmed down.

"I'll get the uniforms and CSIs to take care of that inspection at DayGo. In the meantime, I think you have some interviews to attend to," Mackay said.

Hunter nodded and left to find Rachael, slamming the door again on his way out.

***

"Thank you for attending today, Lord Buchanan," Hunter said as he entered the interview room.

The room was small and dark. The only window had bars across it and was almost at the height of the ceiling. Hunter couldn't see out of it. The smell in interview rooms was never fresh. It didn't matter how much disinfectant the cleaners used or how much air-freshener the officers sprayed around after the rooms were used. They always smelled of dirt, body odour and farts. This room was no different.

"Your colleague here didn't suggest there was any alternative. So how may I assist your enquiries, DI Wilson? And may I just say what a fine employee your son, Cameron is? An excellent worker."

"This interview has nothing to do with Cameron but, for the benefit of the tape, I'll confirm that my son is employed by you as a driver," Hunter said.

"Do you want to have your lawyer present?" Rachael asked.

"Do I need her?" Lucky asked.

"Now that I cannot answer," Rachael said.

"Well, I think it's unlikely. Ask your questions. If I can help, I will. I certainly have nothing to hide."

Hunter nodded and began to question Lucky about his

financial relationship with Simon Land and the vans he had parked in the barns at Landsmuir. He watched as Lucky explained that occasionally if a vehicle broke down near the farm he might offer the owner that he would store it there until a repair could be arranged or a buyer found.

"I have a paying hobby dealing in classic and vintage cars," Lucky explained.

Hunter offered no comment, but could not help thinking this explanation sounded weak. It bordered on ridiculous.

"You paid Landsmuir a monthly fee to enable you to keep things at the farm, occasionally?" Hunter asked.

"Yes. I collect classic and vintage cars and sometimes need a place to store them," Lucky said.

"You may deal in or collect old cars, but the only vehicle you had stored at Landsmuir Farm recently was a tatty van belonging to the DayGo delivery company. A van we believe was carrying a consignment of cocaine," Hunter said.

"Oh, goodness me, DI Wilson. Did you find cocaine?" Lucky asked.

"No, the vehicle was removed after my officers found packages of cocaine hidden on the premises within the farm."

"My goodness, that's worrying. As you know, I went to rehab to get over a cocaine addiction. I am best to avoid users, you know. You would need to ask Simon or Robin Land about any cocaine found, or perhaps, Derek. He and Robin are very close. Robin does nothing without Derek knowing, believe me."

"I believe your bank accounts will tell a different story, Lord Buchanan,"

"Can we believe a word you say, Lord Buchanan?" Rachael asked.

"Of course, you can, and you must. I do keep parcels on the farm, but they only contain parts for cars, that I may need for my cars. The vehicles on Landsmuir Farm vary from time to time. Ask your son. He often drives them to their final destination for me," Lucky smiled. He offered a long, rambling explanation as to why he preferred to keep some vehicles at Landsmuir than on his estate. Then Hunter watched as Lucky drew a gold, monogrammed cigarette case out of his pocket and asked. "Can I smoke in here?" he asked.

"I'm sorry, no. Health and safety or something," Rachael said.

"Then let's get this done. I'm gasping for a fag."

"We may be just a while longer," Hunter said. "This might be a natural point to take a break if you would like. Rachael could accompany you outside the station where you could smoke."

"That would be good, thank you," Lucky said.

"You go, Rachael. I'm going to grab a coffee," Hunter said.

***

As Rachael and Lucky stood in the car park, Bear wandered over towards them carrying a large mug of coffee.

"Winston," Lucky hailed the big man by his given name.

"Lucky. How's life for you?" Bear asked cordially.

"Not too bad. Just helping your boss with a few enquiries about DayGo and Landsmuir Farm," Lucky said.

"That's good of you. Simon told Tim and I that you have been helpful to him since his father died," Bear said.

Lucky took a long drag on his cigarette. "He had a little cash flow problem and I had a problem about where to keep some of my stuff, so it worked for both of us."

"What sort of stuff? Isn't there enough room at your own estate?" Bear asked.

"Sometimes it's better to keep things nearer the city, you know?"

"No, not really. But if it works for you and Simon, I suppose that's all that matters. And are you managing to keep away from the snow, then?" Bear asked.

"Oh, yes, unless I'm skiing," Lucky stubbed out his cigarette and smiled.

"Good. That's good. But strange. What did I see you snorting when you and Robin left the singsong at Landsmuir on Friday night? Was that something you were keeping nearer the city? Something you shared with Robin, perhaps?" Bear

210

asked. "He certainly looked much happier after."

"Me? I think you're mistaken, Winston. I'm clean now. Been to rehab and all that," Lucky said. He lit another cigarette and stared at Bear.

"You may think I'm mistaken, but I know I'm not," Bear said. "I suppose I can't prove that, can I?"

"No, you can't prove what didn't happen," Lucky said.

"But I saw you and so did Robin. So that would be two witnesses. And Robin hid some coke in his freezer for you. Your stash. His evidence could reduce any sentence he had imposed by the courts, if it got that far. I believe the stuff you were drawing from was in Jonny's ceiling until I spotted it. That's what Robin was arguing about with Jonny Baird when wee Nicky went missing. Am I right? Is that the kind of stuff you were talking about keeping at Landsmuir Farm?" Bear asked.

"You've talked a lot of nonsense in your life, but today you are spouting even more rubbish than usual, Winston. I am not the one you are looking for here. Come on, DC Anderson, let's get back inside and get this over with. I'm a busy man and I need to get home," Lucky said and marched back into the station ahead of Rachael.

Bear smiled at Rachael. "The Boss came into the briefing room and bribed me with a decent coffee me to come down and soften Lucky up. Have fun," he winked.

***

Hunter rejoined Rachael and Lucky and took a seat next to the DC. It was obvious that the dynamics had altered since they had been in the room previously. Lucky's demeanour had changed. He seemed unsettled, angry. Hunter hoped his idea of sending Bear out to talk to Lucky and make him aware of what he had seen might allow the continuing interview to make some progress. He noticed Lucky just staring around the bare, smelly little interview room. Hunter switched on the recording devices and re-introduced the three people present.

"I understand that, when my officers were looking for a

missing child at Landsmuir Farm, they found two kilos of cocaine. We've checked and it's cut, but it's still an unusually strong mix. Have you any idea how that came to be hidden there?" Hunter asked.

"Now how the hell would I know that?" Lucky challenged. "It's not my farm. They're not my drugs. What on earth makes you think that I know anything about this at all, DI Wilson?"

Hunter nodded. He looked solemnly at Lucky and sat so quietly for so long that he was aware even Rachael turned to look at him quizzically. And still he sat. Silence had never made Hunter uncomfortable, but he was well aware that it had an unnerving effect on other people.

"Well if you've nothing else to say I'll go. I'm free to go, aren't I?" Lucky asked.

"You may leave at any time, but I'm not quite finished," Hunter said.

"Well ask away then. Let's get this over with soon," Lucky said.

"Two kilos of coke are very valuable to find on a farm with cash flow problems. And it did have cash flow problems after old Mr Land died suddenly didn't it?"

"Yes, I helped the boys out. They let me leave some stuff there and I helped get them out of the financial mire. A win, win situation. Not one I should be vilified for, surely."

"Well, yes and no," Hunter said. "What exactly did you leave on the farm?"

"I collect and renovate and sell vehicles. When it was easier for a client to drop off or pick up a vehicle nearer the city than from my estate I'd leave it at the farm. Or sometimes Cameron or one of the old gypsies would deliver them for me and it was sensible to do it from there not from home. It's just too far away," Lucky said. He threw a winning smile at Rachael, unaware that he had hit rocky ground.

Hunter noticed that the young man was back to his chatty charming self. There was no doubt in Hunter's mind that Lucky thought he was much cleverer than either himself or Rachael.

"Does your collection of vehicles extend to modern

delivery vans?" Hunter asked.

"I shouldn't think so. The classic and vintage cars are more my line. Good profit in them, you know? But we seem to be going around in circles. I told you all this before."

"I just like to get things straight in my mind before I make an arrest. Can you think of anybody else connected to Landsmuir Farm who would have the ready cash to buy an uncut kilo of cocaine from Connor O'Grady and arrange to have it cut for use? Because I can't." Hunter said.

"So while you were out having a smoke I called DayGo. The manager recognised the registration number of the van that had been at the farm and it had been driven by one of their casual drivers, Jonny Baird, before it went missing. Jonny found the cocaine and set up a deal between you and O'Grady, didn't he? He knew he'd be a dead man if he cut O'Grady out. It was days before he got the van back to them and O'Grady was furious. Can you think why he was furious, Lucky?"

"Search me," Lucky shrugged.

"Not yet," Hunter said. "He was furious because something valuable belonging to him had been removed from the van. The manager said he didn't know what it was, and I believe the manager. Do you know what it was, Lucky?"

Lucky shook his head. "Would you just stop?" He shouted. "You go on and on. Just stop!"

"It was cocaine. A kilo of cocaine. And O'Grady didn't like sharing the value of that with Jonny, did he? Jonny found the cocaine in the van and cut it to double its weight so it wouldn't be too strong for regular users and then he sold the cut cocaine to you. Half of it was hidden in the farm freezer. A few baggies were released for use and the rest was stashed above the lights in Jonny's caravan. Robin took it down to him. That's what he and Jonny were arguing about when the wee girl ran away. What do you say to that, Lucky?" Hunter smiled a thin, tight smile and waited for Lucky's reply.

"That's all guess work, DI Wilson."

"Maybe, but it won't be when I check your bank records and have a sample of your blood examined."

The young man finally looked up from the table. "Even if

you're right, DI Hunter, the van had nothing to do with me. Jonny found the coke and cut it. He couldn't hide all of it in his ceiling, it was too heavy by then. He went up to the farmhouse and spoke to Robin and Derek about where to hide it. Robin is so depressed and in such agony all the time, everybody knows he is a weak link."

"Is that how you think of Robin, a weak link?" Rachael asked. "Then you should worry he'll crack and tell us what he knows."

"All I'm saying is that getting the snow had nothing to do with me. I'm clean. Or I was. I did yield to temptation when Robin offered me some at the farm. But use is all you've got on me. Jonny, Derek and Robin are the ones you need to be after. And Robin can't inject himself – he hasn't got the dexterity now. Derek gives him all his injections."

"He could snort," Rachael said.

"Only if someone set it up for him."

"That doesn't matter. None of them had the money to buy it in bulk. That lies at your door, Lucky. You may have shared, or sold individual baggies on, but only you could afford the bulk buy."

Hunter stood up and walked to the interview room door. "Thank you for your time, Lord Buchanan. That has been very helpful," Hunter said. "Rachael, book Lord Buchanan for use of a class A drug then bail him and arrange to have one of the uniforms take him home, will you?"

"Yes, Boss. Of course," Rachael said.

"Do you happen to know the owner of DayGo, Lucky?" Hunter asked.

"Connor O'Grady? Yes, I do. Fenian bastard. You don't want to get on the wrong side of him. He's one nasty piece of work."

"I believe he's using his delivery vans to get cocaine around the city," Hunter said.

"I heard that too," Lucky said as he put on his jacket and tied a silk scarf around his neck.

"I wonder how anybody would know which vans have the coke in them."

"My guess is that a lot of them do. It is a most efficient way to deliver to dealers. The twenty or more honest deliveries pay for the van and driver, the one delivery to a dealer is just a hidden bonus. It's when the dealer doesn't get his delivery, like when Jonny brought the van to the farm, that the fun kicks off," Lucky said.

"But nothing kicked off about that delivery not reaching the dealer, because you bought it," Hunter said. "And Jonny certainly doesn't have the cash to buy all that cocaine. Neither does Derek. He's getting by on a nurse's wages. And you've told me the boys at the farm had cash flow problems so Robin couldn't buy the goods. Now that only leaves you who knew anything about them, doesn't it, Lucky? I think we better go through this all again before Lord Buchanan leaves, don't you, Rachael?"

"Yes, Boss. I think we should. Take a seat, Lucky,"

"I think I should call my lawyer now," Lucky said.

***

Hunter walked into the murder room and smiled. He saw that Rachael was huddled over a chamomile tea talking with Bear and Tim about the interview with Lucky.

"Rachael, when you've written that up, just get off. You've had a heavy day," Hunter smiled.

"If you're sure, Boss, that would be great. Janey and I are going to go for a run tonight," Rachael said. "It was really funny when, as we were getting ready to take Lucky home, he just threw Jonny, Derek and Robin under the bus."

"Lucky was never going home, Rachael. But I'm glad I'm a good enough actor that you thought he might."

"What did you book him for, Boss?" Bear asked.

"Possession with intent to supply."

Tim whistled. "He could get seven years for that."

"He could, but I'll bet he bloody doesn't," Bear said. "That man has a charmed life."

Chapter Fifty-One

Frankie held the door as Donna pushed the double buggy towards Jamie. He smiled at his cousin who was still sleeping after the operation. He held his finger up to his mouth to signal to the twins that they should be quiet, and they copied him but blew raspberries instead of going 'Ssssh'. He laughed with Donna and felt that he had rarely been as happy since he had met her. It was good to see her laugh. She hadn't done much of that since her pop died.

Frankie picked up chairs from the side of the ward and carried them towards Jamie's bed, walking slowly behind her so that neither of them tripped up. He took the box of Jaffa Cakes and cans of beer out of the bag and slipped the cans into the cupboard beside Jamie's bed. He didn't look at Donna because he knew that she wouldn't approve of the contraband. However, he wasn't quick enough with the Jaffa Cakes and the twins both pointed at the brightly coloured box expectantly.

"Right enough, your only chance of getting one of these is to have it before Uncle Jamie wakes up," he said.

"Then they've got nay bloody chance. Give me my Jaffa Cakes. I don't have to share with snotty nosed small girls like Kylie-Ann and Dannii-Ann," Jamie said with a yawn.

"Hello cuz. How are you feeling?" Frankie asked.

"Sleepy and sore," Jamie said.

"Of course. You'll be sore from batting away the attention of all those love-struck nurses," Donna said.

"You know me so well, Donna," Jamie tried to smile and then grabbed the bandage on his face. "Fuck, that was sore. Hang on while I ring for some painkillers, will you? And give the girls a Jaffa Cake. I can't bear to look at those wee faces staring hopelessly at the box."

216

Frankie laughed and handed a treat to each of the girls, patting their heads. He watched a petite young nurse walk towards them and heard Jamie ask for some pain relief. She looked at her watch and Frankie saw Jamie's face fall when she told him, in her lilting Irish accent, that he'd have to wait another half an hour.

"Norah!" Jamie said. "For the love of God darling, babe, can you no' give me something to take this ache in my face away? If not paracetamol then maybe a long, lingering kiss. You know you want one." Jamie made little kissing noises and pointed to his mouth, but the action caused him pain and he grabbed his face again.

Frankie watched the nurse smile and shake her head as she walked across to tend to another patient.

"Did you bring me some cans?" Jamie asked hopefully.

"Of course," Frankie smiled.

"Is the Pope Catholic?" Donna said sourly.

"Come on, let's go into the dayroom. I'll get into trouble if they catch me drinking one in the ward," Jamie said.

"You'll get into trouble if they catch you drinking it in the dayroom," Donna argued.

"Aye, but they rarely go there," Jamie said.

He led the way towards the dayroom in the corner of the ward, as Frankie bent down and released two cans of beer from their plastic holder. Frankie could see no reason for him to miss out. He saw Donna stop in the doorway of the small room and she bent over the back of the buggy. He could see her shoulders shaking. What had Jamie done this time? He hurried towards her and put his arm around her. Donna fell backwards into his arms and he juggled the beer as he used his arms to support her towards a chair.

"What's up darlin'?" Frankie asked. "What has that numpty of a cousin of mine said this time? Honestly, Jamie, you know Donna's just lost her pop and she's been doing so well, holding it together an' all."

"Thanks for the vote of confidence, but it's nought to do wi' me," Jamie said, grabbing a can out of Frankie's hand. He nodded to the other occupied chair in the room.

Frankie stared at the other woman blankly. She had one leg plastered all the way to the thigh and a rigid ankle boot on the other leg. Her left arm was bandaged and part of her head had been shaved and stitches applied. But he couldn't work out why seeing her had caused Donna to collapse. He sat beside Donna and snapped open the can; absentmindedly, he offered her a drink and she accepted without thinking.

"Yugh! I don't like that beer, Frankie," she said, screwing up her face.

"Now who's the numpty?" a triumphant Jamie asked.

Frankie kept stroking Donna and holding her close. The twins nibbled at their biscuits and their fingers became more and more chocolatey. They began to rub their hands on each other – almost like face painting. Frankie saw the fun was only going to get wilder, so he took the messy treats away and wiped their hands and faces, then gave them each a stick of carrot. When Frankie returned his attention to Donna he found she was calmer.

"Frankie, I'm not sure if you've met Dad's girlfriend, Linda Maguire," Donna nodded at the other woman in the dayroom.

"Fuck, no! I mean, sort of," Frankie said.

"You must be Frankie and Jamie," Linda said. "Thanks for getting help for me."

Frankie stared at her, open mouthed. He took long gulps of beer while processing the information and then crushed the can when the drink was finished. He turned his gaze to Jamie. His cousin was sitting triumphantly sipping his beer.

"Did you know who she was?" Frankie asked Jamie.

Jamie nodded. "Recognised her from that van. You said the guy was Donna's pop, so I put two and two together," he tapped his head. "Not just a pretty face, me."

Frankie watched as Donna got up and crossed the room to sit next to Linda. She took Linda's hand in hers.

"Please, tell me what happened to my dad," she said gently.

Chapter Fifty-Two

Hunter and Rachael waited in the interview room for Derek to arrive. Hunter looked around the bleak little space and noticed that the fixing for the camera on the wall needed a good clean. It was caked in grease, grime and dust. He stared at the picked paint on the walls and the graffiti inked onto the table and shook his head. He looked up when Angus opened the door and entered with Derek. He signalled to Derek that he should sit in one of the chairs opposite Rachael and himself. Angus stood at the door.

"You aren't allowed to hold me this long. I've been waiting ages," Derek said.

"I think I'll be the judge of that," Hunter said. He sat back, crossed his legs and let Rachael lead the questioning.

Hunter liked her questions, they were sharp, succinct and pointed. She covered the ground that she knew Derek knew they knew quickly and then moved on to the information Lucky had given them.

"A witness has told us that Robin Land suffered from dark bouts of depression since his accident. Would you agree?"

"Anyone who knows him could tell you that," Derek said. "It's hardly surprising, is it? The transition from teenage rugby player to being paraplegic and wheelchair bound isn't a life choice anybody would make."

"Robin had not come out as gay before his accident, but you are his partner now. Can you explain that?" Rachael asked.

Derek smiled. "Not sure I have to. I doubt it's relevant, but I am gay, and Robin is bi. So what? The one good thing that came from Robin's accident is that he could express his true feelings without having to play the rough tough rugby player.

He always said that only after his accident was it possible, and then he felt able to be his true self. We love each other very deeply."

"And yet, you would help him die?" Hunter asked. "A witness told us that you administer cocaine to Robin on a regular basis. Is that true?"

"Goodness me, no! I'm a registered nurse, a medical professional. I couldn't give cocaine to anybody. I would lose my job. Anyway, I wouldn't know where to get cocaine even if Robin asked me to help him take it. He wouldn't know where to get it either. He rarely leaves the farm except to go to hospital," Derek said.

"Well we've been told more than that," Hunter interrupted. "Our witness informs us that you were involved in giving Robin doses of cocaine from a stash found in a DayGo van owned by Connor O'Grady."

"And that is possession with intent to supply. More accurately supplying a Class A drug in your case," Rachael added.

Derek spluttered. "Who? What? I don't even know who that man is! I would not do that. It would be stealing, and I've never stolen anything in my life. Robin is so physically fragile that I could not give him a regular dose of any drug without killing him. And I would never want to do that."

"No, the cocaine wasn't stolen, but it was too pure to use so it was cut and re-sold. In fact I believe you were planning to assist Robin to take his own life. You planned to help him die didn't you, Derek?" Hunter shouted.

He watched as Derek burst into tears. Hunter thought that the nurse was either an excellent actor or a damned liar. He asked Angus to get teas and coffees for them and waited until Derek had calmed down and drunk his tea before he indicated to Rachael that she should continue her questioning.

"Derek, you seem to want us to believe that the information that we have been given about you is inaccurate. What would you like us to believe?" Rachael said.

"I have never stolen a single thing in my life," he repeated. "Except for a Mars Bar when I was eight and when my mother discovered about that. She made me take the money to the store and give it to the shop-keeper with an apology. I have never been so embarrassed in my life. I never did that again."

"I can understand that would be a reasonable reaction," Hunter said. "I don't think you stole the cocaine. But I know you knew it was being used."

"How can you know that? Let me tell you about me and Robin. I met Robin Land when he was in hospital after his accident. I worked with trauma patients then, but I found it too emotional, so I retrained in care for the elderly. But I kept in touch with Robin. I liked him. We got along. You might say I fancied him. Then, when his father died and Simon was often out on the farm, I was looking for a place to stay and I moved in with the Lands to help care for Robin and Martha. It seemed to be a good solution for everybody. Martha never recovered emotionally from her husband's death. She needed to be there at Landsmuir rather than being on her own," Derek said.

"But you work long shifts. You can't always be there. Anyway, I want to know about the cocaine, I don't need a history lesson," Hunter said.

"Both Robin and Martha became increasingly depressed. I wanted to cheer them up."

"You gave them cocaine?" Rachael said in disbelief.

"No! You stupid woman," Derek said.

"You're the one under suspicion of killing three people, and you think I'm the stupid one?" Rachael said sarcastically.

"Killing? Bloody hell no!" Derek stood up. He was shaking.

"Sit down, Mr Turnbull," Hunter said. He shook his head at Angus who had moved away from the wall towards Derek. "Explain to us your version of what happened,"

Derek sat down. Hunter noticed he looked nervous. He saw Derek's eyes dart from left to right as he thought about what to say.

"I noticed Lucky Buchanan used to come by a lot after old Mr Land's death and Robin seemed more cheerful when he was there. He looked forward to Lucky's visits, especially when he came on his own and not with his girlfriend," Derek said.

"Lady Sophie Dalmore is his girlfriend, right?" Rachael asked.

"Yes, Sophie. One day I came in and Lucky was holding a plate up for Robin. He was breathing in deeply through a rolled ten-pound note. Then when Lucky saw me he blew some powder off the table and said something about dropping sherbet onto the furniture. He and Robin burst out laughing. I think I knew then, but I didn't want to believe it," Derek sighed.

"I love Robin," Derek said. He hung his head and looked at the table. "I explained to him the dangers of cocaine, especially as his immune system was weakened after his accident. I said taking it could kill him. He's so frail but he didn't seem to care. I told him I'd need to know how strong the mix was so that the drug wouldn't kill him. He said Lucky had that all sorted, and I needn't worry. How could I not worry? Of course, Robin never really adjusted to the limitations of his life after his accident. I tried to take him to play wheelchair rugby and, out of the rugby season, wheelchair tennis. He liked it well enough at the time he was there, but then we'd get home and quickly the 'black dog', as he called his depression, would return. It was getting worse and worse, except when Lucky came by. He always seemed able to cheer Robin up."

"How did all that make you feel, Derek?" Hunter asked.

"Honestly? Jealous. Really envious that Lucky could make Robin laugh when all he did with me was cry," Derek paused. "Have you ever seen someone you love with all your heart in such pain that they weep? Big tears pour down their cheeks and you just want to hold them and take that pain away, but you can't. You can't take the pain away and both of you know it will still be there tomorrow and the day after and the day after that. Do you know what that feels like, DI Hunter?" Derek challenged Hunter.

"No, I don't," Hunter said.

"Then you're a lucky man," Derek said softly. "And do you know how it feels when a person you love more than anybody else in the world is so miserable, low and depressed that

222

almost every day they beg you to help them to die? How would you cope with that, DI Hunter?" Derek shouted.

Then, softly, barely in a whisper, he said, "I wanted Robin to be as happy as possible. I wanted him to be as safe as possible, so I ignored what went on between him and Lucky. I acted friendly with Lucky and let them have their fun together. I didn't tell anyone about it. I told Lucky that I knew he was supplying cocaine to Robin and how dangerous that was to him in his weakened state. Lucky said he would stop, if Robin asked him to. And then he laughed and said, if the withdrawals didn't kill Robin, the misery would."

"What happened then?" Hunter asked.

"I knew he was serious. Lucky wanted Robin's company when he took his cocaine. It was more fun doing it with a friend, more empowering giving it to Robin. Lucky is evil. I don't trust him."

"You're not the first person I've heard say that," Hunter said.

"So?" Rachael prompted.

"I gave in. I asked him to continue to give Robin the coke. He laughed at me and said he might. If the price was right," Derek sighed.

"What did he ask for in return?" Hunter asked.

"Silence. He got me to pick up baggies of cocaine from the caravans sometimes so that I was implicated in the deals. But most of all, Lucky wanted my silence so that I would never betray the fact that he, too, was a user."

"Fuck," said Rachael. She looked at Hunter. "I thought he had beaten that demon."

Hunter nodded and stared at the camera near the ceiling and sighed. "So did I," he said quietly.

"It was overdoses of cocaine that killed the three patients on your ward and you must have known that an overdose of the cocaine could kill Robin," Hunter said.

"That's true, it could. Lucky and I made sure that would never happen. And I know nothing about cocaine on the ward." Derek smiled. "As I said, I'm a medical professional, I couldn't use cocaine on the elderly patients in my ward although I suppose they'd hardly be missed. Other nurses may have done so, but the patients on the ward are so frail, their immune systems are often compromised to the extent that we could not give them a regular dose of any strong drug like that without risking their lives."

Chapter Fifty-Three

Donna sat beside me and listened carefully. She held my hand while staring at the floor. It meant I couldn't see the expression on her face, but whenever I told Donna something that upset her, she squeezed my hand. I could feel her tears dripping onto my skin.

I realised that she needed to know how her dad had died, what had caused his death, why the crash had happened. She gasped when she heard how her dad had held us back.

"He was always late for everything," she said.

Donna covered her mouth when I told her how her dad had grabbed the wheel to save the rabbit.

"To save a rabbit. Oh, Dad! I know you love animals, but really."

She cried when I told her about the knife, how it sliced Bob's neck deep and true, right into the artery, and there was nothing either of us could do. She left the room to throw up when I spoke softly about being sprayed with Bob's warm blood and tasting it on my lips. Then Donna came back and asked me to finish the story. She sobbed when I described watching the life ebb out of her dad's eyes.

Then when I had told her all there was to tell, Donna begged to hear it again, as if the ending would change in the re-telling.

***

Colin and Nadia strode down the stairs to the interview room where Angela was waiting.

"Good to escape from the CCTV, isn't it?" Colin said to Nadia.

"Yes, it'll be interesting to see if what we noticed matches up with what Angie tells us."

"Is she related to John Hamilton?" Colin asked.

"Yes, cousins. Mothers are sisters," Nadia said. "I'd like her to confirm that for us, though. And are we playing good cop, bad cop as usual?" Nadia asked as they reached the door.

"Of course. We do it so well," Colin said.

"Okay, but can you be bad cop today? I'm feeling too mellow after all we learned from the CCTV," Nadia smiled.

"I'm not surprised, that was a great tip of Sarah's. I wonder how the boss and Rachael are getting on with Derek?"

"I wouldn't like to be Derek right now," Nadia smiled.

"Right, here we go," Colin opened the door and walked into the interview room just behind Nadia.

"Hello, Angela. Thank you for helping us with our investigations today. I'm DC Chan and this is my colleague DS Reid," Nadia said as she sat down.

"Mind you, if you hadn't come in voluntarily we'd just have come and got you," Colin snarled.

"Ha bloody ha," Angela looked at Colin. "My big cousin told me you were a shit."

"Your big cousin, who would that be?" Colin asked.

"The one you and that smart-arse Hunter Wilson forced out of the police. He was even your partner and you were quite happy to see the back of him. You're a right bastard you are. My big cousin is John Hamilton and he told me to mind how I go with you," Angela sneered.

Colin tried to look surprised. "John Hamilton is your cousin, is he? Well there's no doubting he's a big cousin. Is he as fat as he ever was?"

"That's just rude," Angela said, pulling her tight top straight across her ample bosom.

"If John Hamilton is your cousin, you'll know how these interviews work, Angela," Nadia smiled.

"Aye, he told me you ask a whole lot of bloody stupid questions and try to trip me up."

"Not at all," Nadia said. "And if you want a lawyer with you, you can have one. It's no problem at all."

"I don't need that. John told me I don't have to say anything," Angela said.

"John will have told you we record the interviews. There'll be a tape recording taken and you'll get one copy and we get the other. We also take a video copy of the interview with that little camera up there." Nadia pointed up to the ceiling.

Nadia watched as Angela touched her hair to make it tidier for the video. Then she switched on the recording equipment and introduced those in the room for the benefit of the tape.

"John is right that you do not have to answer our questions, but three women have been killed on your ward. Surely you would want us to track down the killer and punish them," Colin asked.

"I'm sure she'll help us," Nadia said. "We're interested in those that had most contact with Mrs Button, Mrs Roberts and Mrs Land, Angie. Can you help us with that?"

"Well the consultant is in charge. Maybe you should ask her. I'm only a student nurse. In fact, I'm not even that now. Witnessing all this death and misery, three deaths one after the other, it's too stressful. I've taken time off from my course. Don't know if I'll even go back, to be honest."

"That would be a shame. Good nurses are hard to come by. Do you think the nurses on the ward are good at their job?" Nadia asked.

"I suppose," Angela said. "Sarah and Derek were the head nurses. Why don't you ask them? They'd know more than me."

"We'll ask them, but right now we're asking you," Colin said. "Were you in the team which dealt with the three murdered women?"

"I suppose, but I never did much. I'm a *student* nurse, but," Angela emphasised.

"But what, Angela," Colin said. "Did you ever attach medication to a canula for any of the murdered patients, take their blood pressure, take their temperature or take blood samples?" Colin raised his voice. "Come on, Angela. Help us find the killer."

"Which of the senior nurses did you work with most closely?" Nadia asked.

"It depended who was on shift. But I liked working with Derek better than Sarah. She was a bitch to me. Kept telling me off and correcting at me. Derek was more understanding if I made a mistake," Angela said.

"Did you make a lot of mistakes, Angela?" Nadia asked.

"No more than anybody else, but," Angela said defensively.

Nadia noticed Angela's body position. She sat forward with her arms tightly crossed. Nadia's gaze fell to Angela's chest. She felt strangely jealous of Angela's large breasts. She had always wished for more, but her husband told her that more than a mouthful was wasted.

"Sorry, what did you say, Angela?" Nadia asked, bringing herself back to the present.

"She says Derek was more considerate of the patients' pain," Colin said. "She said he would give them painkillers and taught her how to do that so the pain relief would get to the blood stream faster. Did anybody else ever take time to explain that to you?"

"Not that I remember, but," Angela shrugged. "Derek only showed me how it was done. It was good to see how quickly they felt better. Nice that. His friend said it was awfy important that they didn't suffer when they didn't have to."

"Which friend?" Nadia asked.

"Robin I think his name is. He joined us for lunch in the canteen once or twice. In a wheelchair, still fit."

"Derek's friend witnessed the procedure? Isn't that a bit strange? Did you know that the women that died were tightly restrained during the administration of the overdose of cocaine that killed them? And they were mutilated, their nipples removed," Colin said.

"Cocaine? Nipples? You're mad!" Angela sniggered.

"Do you think murder and mutilation are funny, Angela?"

He saw Nadia move her hand as if she wanted him to drop that line of questioning.

"Why did Derek's friend think this treatment for the old ladies was important? Was he a medical man? How could he form a view?" Nadia asked Angela.

"Stop it!" Angela cried out. "You're asking me everything

228

at once. I'm all confused. Leave me alone!"

"Why don't we take a break, Angela," Nadia said. "Let's get you a cup of tea and a biscuit and give you a break."

"I'd like a ciggie," Angela said.

"You can't smoke in here, but I'll take you to the car park," Nadia said, leading her out of the interview room.

"I'll have another look at that CCTV," Colin whispered to Nadia. "Back here in fifteen."

As they stood in the car park, Nadia watched Angela. The big woman looked thoroughly miserable. Her hair was badly beached and revealed her dark roots, her nails bitten right down to the quick. Nadia doubted Angela's track suit bottoms had ever been near a track. She watched as Angela blew confident smoke rings after each drag. Then noticed Angela return her gaze.

"D'you like being a cop?" Angela asked.

"Yes, very much. I like being useful and helping people," Nadia replied. "I suppose it's the same feeling if you're a nurse?"

"Doubt it. Everybody loves us. They all think you're just pigs in uniform."

"Let's go back inside shall we?" Nadia ignored the jibe and led the way back to the station.

Sitting back in the smelly little interview room, Colin stared at Angela as Nadia re-introduced the group for the benefit of the recordings. He noticed that the young woman did not meet his gaze but bit her nails and picked at the cuticles. It struck Colin that she was neither as fastidious as he would like a nurse to be nor as self-confident.

"You would often take lunch in the canteen with a colleague?" he asked Angela.

"Yeh, I s'pose a classmate or someone else from the ward. Whoever I was on the same lunch break with. Sometimes I'd sit with friends from University too. Even if they were on different wards we could catch up. So what?"

"You said earlier that Derek's friend, Robin, joined you for lunch in the canteen once or twice. But it was more often than that wasn't it? When you had lunch with Derek his friend would often join you."

"That's not unusual," Angela said.

"But this friend is not a member of staff here. Not the member of a team," Colin said flatly.

"Oh, you mean Robin? Well, yeh, he's Derek's boyfriend, Robin. He's funny."

"What would you and Derek and Robin talk about?"

"The grotty food, high prices and lack of vodka in the canteen," Angela sneered.

"And what else?" Colin asked flatly.

"Did Robin ever talk about his accident? His pain? Problems?"

"No. Why would he? He teased Derek about his bad choice of films, getting drunk and living in the middle of nowhere. He didn't like living on the farm. Said it was isolating, extra isolated since he had to use a wheelchair."

"Anything else?"

"He said he wanted to see how we gave injections so that he could inject himself when Derek was on shift and he was at home."

"Did you ever see Robin give an injection to a patient?" Colin asked.

"What?" Nadia asked in an alarmed tone of voice.

"Don't be soft. Of course not!" Angela said. "I helped."

"Why did you agree to help administer the cocaine?" Colin asked.

"No bloody coke! Pain relief. You're not pinning fucking cocaine on me, or Derek. He's a good man. We take pain away from patients when we can, to help them feel better, not be in such pain. You know?" Angela stared at Colin defiantly. "Some of the old women in the ward knew your boss. Goodie two shoes, Hunter Wilson. Did you know that? But there was no bloody coke as far as I know. Too expensive for the NHS hospitals," she laughed sourly.

"When did you learn that DI Hunter Wilson knew the Lands?" Colin asked.

"My big cousin John told me after the accident with Wilson. He discovered the name of the farm. He's got contacts you know, so it wasn't difficult for him," Angela smirked.

"Does Derek know John?" Nadia asked.

"Dunno, ask him yourself. Are we about finished here? I'm getting tired and hungry?"

"You had a break a few minutes ago!" Nadia said.

"Just one more thing, Angela," Colin said. "How do you think those elderly women got cocaine into their bloodstreams in your ward?"

"Dunno, do I? I'm only a student nurse. Anyway, they're just old women. Nobody will miss them, even if they did die of a shot of coke."

"Nobody will miss them?" Colin exclaimed.

***

As Colin watched the hefty young woman waddle along the corridor towards the exit, he couldn't help but think about the chocolate wrappers that littered the floor of the car when he and John Hamilton had been partners. John did hold a grudge, he thought.

Chapter Fifty-Four

Jamie watched as a nurse walked briskly towards his bed. He smiled his most ingratiating smile and stuck another Jaffa Cake in his mouth. He fervently believed that the world would be a much sadder place without Jaffa Cakes.

"Nurse Norah, how happy I am to see you. Shall we pull the curtain around to give ourselves a little more privacy?" Jamie said.

"I have deeply upsetting news, Jamie," the nurse grinned. "Our relationship is at an end. The doctor says you're well enough to go home."

"Oh no! Don't let this come between us," Jamie smiled. "After all, I haven't finished me Jaffa Cakes yet."

"Doctor says you can leave the rest of the box for me and the other nurses," Norah said.

"Look, Nurse, this may be love of the very deepest kind, but I don't love anyone enough to give them my last Jaffa Cakes," Jamie tucked the box into a plastic bag with his unopened cans of beer and the painkillers that had been issued to him.

"The district nurse will come and check on your wounds until they heal, just to make sure there's no infection," Norah said.

"Is she as pretty as you, Nurse Norah?" Jamie asked with a wink.

"Never!" Norah winked. "There's a fellow called Mark waiting for you in reception to take you home."

"Aye, the chief mechanic at my garage. My useless cousin cannae drive," Jamie said.

As Jamie wandered down the corridor towards the elevators, he passed the door of Linda's room.

"That's me away now, Linda. It was nice meeting you. And thanks for being so patient with Donna. It must have been really hard going over everything again and again with her."

"Nice to meet you too, Jamie. Thanks for calling the ambulance and that," she said. "I can't go home yet. Now that Bob's gone I'm on my own and I can't manage with my leg until they get a care package in place."

"Aye, I've to get the district nurse to come in and sort this out," he said, pointing to his face. "Look if you need any help or that, give me a call." Jamie wrote his number on the plain cardboard on the inside of the Jaffa Cakes box. He was about the tear it off and hand her just the number, but he stopped and smiled. He gave her a wee kiss on the cheek. "You can even have my last Jaffa Cakes."

"Thanks Jamie. Thanks very much."

***

Jamie's phone was ringing as he walked into the semi-detached house in West Mains Road. He waved to Mark from the door and took the call.

"Hello Pop. Where did you get this phone from?" Jamie asked. He listened to his father's reply and then laughed. "Poor old Irish Mick. You'd think he'd know better than to play cards with you."

He sat down on the large black leather sofa and listened to his pop's voice. Should he tell him about Linda?

"The girl me and Frankie rescued was in my ward at the hospital, Pop. She's decent. Maybe O'Grady did me a favour getting me beat up, cos I got to meet her properly. See her man who died, Pop. He's Donna's dad. Aye, Frankie's Donna."

He smiled as his father said he was about to get to the end of the money left on Mick's phone. "No Pop, I'm home now. But I did leave the rest of my box of Jaffa Cakes with her."

"Ooh, and they said romance was dead," Ian teased his son.

"Shut it, Pop!" Jamie said. "What? Oh, Mark drove me home and Frankie and Donna'll be back with the twins in a couple of hours. So I'm getting the tea tonight. I'll get us a

chippy supper delivered. You enjoy your porridge then, Pop."
Jamie laughed as he ended the call and turned on the Bang &
Olufsen sound system to listen to Drake before he phoned to
order the meal.

Chapter Fifty-Five

Colin Reid was sitting eating an apple and reading his notes as DCI Mackay walked in and slammed a file on the desk. Colin looked up and glanced at Nadia. He saw her shrug and Rachael Anderson looked up from her mug of chamomile tea with a frown. Even Tim, Bear and Mel stopped talking. Colin watched Hunter follow Mackay into the room and sit on the front desk.

"Now, your attention and information, that's all I ask. I need these killings solved because now that we have three corpses on our patch, our new Major Incident Team is looking to take over the hospital investigation," Mackay said. "I have already spoken to Superintendent Miller. He's furious that we hadn't brought in MIT to work the killings sooner. I've tried to smooth things over by explaining that the deaths have only recently been identified as murders."

"Was he impressed by that argument, Sir?" Hunter asked.

"What do you think?" Mackay grumbled. "What do we know? Who is my murderer?" Mackay thumped the desk angrily.

"We interviewed Sarah and she pointed us to the CCTV in the hospital," Nadia said. "Colin and I reviewed it carefully. From that it seemed that there were combinations of people in and out of the hospital that you would not have thought about."

"DC Chan, I am not interested in thoughts," Hunter said. "I want to know who killed my aunt and why? Is that unreasonable?"

"No of course not, Boss," Nadia blushed.

"And have we found my nipples?" Hunter asked.

Tim couldn't help grinning when he explained that the CSIs

had indicated there might be a problem finding body parts so small and delicate, when nobody had told them where to start looking. However, they had taken the initiative and were searching the hospital lockers of the four main suspects.

"I should bloody hope so," grumbled Hunter.

Tim was grateful to Colin when he steered the discussion away in another direction.

"One thing we do know is that Angela lied to us during our interview with her," Colin said.

"Surprise, surprise. Derek lied to us during his," Rachael said.

"You go first. How did you notice Angela give herself away?" Hunter asked.

"It wasn't that difficult," Colin said. "Nadia and I went to study the hospital CCTV, and we found that Angela often had lunch with either Sarah or Derek."

"Why did that make you think she was lying?" Rachael asked.

"Well, Boss, she said she hated Sarah and that Sarah picked on her. If that were true, why spend any more time with her than you have to?" Colin said.

Hunter nodded. "Did she confirm that she's related to John Hamilton?"

"Yes, Boss. With pride. You and I are bullies and devils," Colin replied.

"And she lied again when it came to Derek," Nadia said. "Angela said Robin had only joined them once or twice for lunch. But on the CCTV we could clearly see the three of them going along the corridor to the canteen, frequently," Nadia said.

"Yes, at first she made out like she hardly knew Robin. Later on she could recall social conversations the three of them had," Colin added.

"She also denied any knowledge of cocaine use or the mutilation of the patients' breasts but showed no surprise or shock. In fact she sniggered. She said the women were old and would not be missed," Nadia said.

"Bitch," Hunter said. "Nothing could be further from the

truth."

"She did give a good account of how you came to know Mrs Land, Boss," Colin said. "Big cousin John told her."

"She's a liar. But is she a killer?" Hunter asked.

"How did you and Rachael know that Derek lied, Boss?" Tim asked.

"He lied about knowing there was cocaine around the farm," Hunter said.

"Derek claimed that he loves Robin and doesn't want him to die or commit suicide. I believed that."

"But Derek said when Lucky agreed to continue supplying Robin with cocaine, he required him to keep silent about his own habit. I believe that, but he denied giving cocaine in the hospital, although he described both Robin and the women on the ward as frail and said he made sure that the strong cut of cocaine wouldn't kill Robin.

"I don't understand how he could work with Lucky to ensure Robin never overdosed while still having no knowledge of where Lucky got his supply from or how strong a dose he gave Robin. Derek said it was Lucky that gave the cocaine to Robin, not him. But Lucky was adamant Derek gave Robin all his injections, and that makes more sense. Derek would have the skillset to do that.

"Remember, Boss, he kept going on about being a health care professional, a State Registered Nurse, how he would lose his job if he administered cocaine," Rachael said. "And Derek said Lucky swore him to silence, but he told us about his habit fast enough."

"He knew about the cocaine supply, health professional or no," Hunter said.

"You can't trust anybody these days," Bear said.

"Did you notice how he smiled at the end of his interview? That was unnerving," Rachael said.

"Boss, I've just had a text from the CSIs. They've found your nipples," Tim laughed.

"Where were they?" Hunter asked.

"Between two strips of paper towel in a small box in Derek's locker."

"You were right about the payments from Lucky's account," Mackay said to Hunter. "I've just got a copy of the statement form one of his off-shore accounts. There's one payment of fifty-thousand to O'Grady and another of twenty to Jonny Baird."

"Fucking hell. Jonny sold himself short," Bear smiled.

"That man's never seen twenty-grand in his life before," Tim said softly.

Epilogue

Florence Robert's funeral was well attended. It was clear she was much missed.

The family, led by Andy Roberts's father, was devastated by their loss. The eulogy, read by the priest, told of her keen interest in baking, needlepoint and bird watching.

Police Scotland was represented by Hunter, Bear, Tim, and Rachael. When her grandson, Andy Roberts, came over to shake their hands, he thanked them for coming.

"I didn't realise your grandmother was a twitcher," Rachael smiled. "It's one of my partner's interests too."

"Yes, she was observant and retained her interest in ornithology until the end of her life," Andy said. "Will you come back to the Lady Nairn Hotel for a cup of tea with us?"

"No, Andy. We've got to get back to work," Hunter said. "But thank you."

"How did you find out that that nurse was the killer?" he asked.

"Lies, exaggerations and contradictions often tell us more than the truth," Hunter said. "The nurse, Derek Turnbull, was deeply in love with Robin Land and was willing to allow his friend Lord Lachlan Buchanan to supply him with cocaine provided Derek, in turn, kept quiet about his lordship's addiction."

"Yes, but why did he murder the old folk?" Andy asked. "My grandmother was a sweet old lady who never harmed anybody in her life."

"My aunt and Mrs Land were the same, but all three were slender and frail. Robin had suffered muscle wastage since his accident, so was also slim and frail. Not heavily muscled as he used to be like these fellows." Hunter pointed to Tim and Bear.

"As Lucky was cutting the cocaine himself, Derek wanted to be sure it wasn't too strong for Robin, so he tested it out on his patients of similar weight and build."

"When it was too strong, they died." Andy shook his head. "Why give it to them in the mouth?"

"Who would think to look there for scars if an investigation were carried out?" Bear asked. "If Dr Fraser hadn't been so meticulous in sorting out false teeth, the scratches in the mouths might never have been found."

"Derek was really cynical. He checked the strength of the cocaine on old people, because he thought they wouldn't be missed," Tim said.

"When you see this large turnout for your grandmother, you realise how wrong he was. The final straw was when the CSIs checked the lockers of our four hospital suspects and found the nipples carefully placed between two pieces of blotting paper in Derek's locker," Hunter said.

"Why?" Andy asked.

"Trophies, ghastly, weird, control freak trophies," Hunter said.

"Will he go to jail?" he asked.

"Oh yes, have no fear of that. With a triple murder charge and possession and supply of cocaine, Derek Turnbull will be care of Her Majesty for a long, long time," Hunter said.

"Thank you, DI Wilson," Andy said as he walked away, to rejoin his family.

"I heard O'Grady and Jonny Baird both made it to Ireland hoping to avoid their charges of assault, as well as distribution and supply of cocaine," Tim said.

"Yes, but we'll get them. It'll just take longer," Hunter said.

"I don't fancy Jonny's chances when O'Grady works out that he cut and re-sold that kilo of his cocaine to Lucky!" Bear laughed.

"True, I hadn't thought of that," Hunter smiled. "It angers me that Lucky's brief managed to get him off with a suspended sentence and time in rehab."

"It's amazing what money and a good lawyer can do," Tim said. "Lucky does scrub up well, and you have to admit he talks the talk, Boss."

"That he does, I wonder what his real punishment will be."

"Sophie's dumped him and moved back to her apartment in Gillespie Crescent," Tim said.

"Is that a punishment? I thought it would be a relief," Rachael winked at Tim.

"Tim, thanks for speaking to Simon about giving Cameron a job on the farm. I think that will be good for him."

"It will be good for both of them because Simon won't be alone out there while Robin's in rehab."

"I'm guessing you paid for Robin's rehab,"

Tim shrugged. "That would be between Robin and me."

Rachael smiled. "That's the difference between you and Lucky."

"One of the many differences, Rachael. I'm also much better looking," Tim laughed.

"All right, enough of that, boys and girls. Enough chat. We have work to do. Let's get back to the ranch."

Hunter led the way back to their cars.

Hunter's Secret follows soon

Fantastic Books
Great Authors

darkstroke is
an imprint of
Crooked Cat Books

- Gripping Thrillers
- Cosy Mysteries
- Romantic Chick-Lit
- Fascinating Historicals
- Exciting Fantasy
- Young Adult and Children's Adventures
- Non-Fiction

Discover us online
www.darkstroke.com

Find us on instagram:
www.instagram.com/darkstrokebooks

Printed in Great Britain
by Amazon